'Murder, sadistic sex and black magic – all the ingredients for a really hair-raising thriller here, used very coolly in a police procedural story. What seems at first straightforward rape and killing of a teenager turns out to lead into murky waters of specialist kinky prostitutes, bookshops for Crowleyites, international drug peddling and white slave traffic. All this is sorted out by Chief Inspector Saltfleet, a new fictional copper who combines painstaking investigation with a Maigret-like human sympathy'
Sunday Telegraph

'Satisfactory and suspenseful . . . Kinkiness, the occult, a clairvoyant witch and the ghost of Hitler beckoning palely from the shades – these are the ingredients which Mr Wilson has stirred into an exotic crime curry, which certainly held my attention . . . For sheer readability, THE SCHOOLGIRL MURDER CASE merits high marks'
The Scotsman

Also by Colin Wilson in Panther Books

The Mind Parasites
The Philosopher's Stone
Order of Assassins

Colin Wilson

The Schoolgirl
Murder Case

Panther

Granada Publishing Limited
Published in 1975 by Panther Books Ltd
Frogmore, St Albans, Herts AL2 2NF

First published in Great Britain by Hart-Davis,
MacGibbon Ltd 1974
Copyright © 1974 by Colin Wilson (Publications) Ltd
Made and printed in Great Britain by
Hazell Watson & Viney Ltd
Aylesbury, Bucks
Set in Linotype Times

For
Don Rumbelow

Acknowledgements

This book owes much to the ideas, suggestions and criticisms of many people, especially Donald Rumbelow, former curator of the City Police Museum. The manuscript was completely rewritten in the light of his comments. I have also received helpful suggestions and encouragement from many people at New Scotland Yard, including David Streatfield, the librarian, Mr and Mrs Fred Taylor, Mrs Shirley Becke and Ian Irvine. On medical matters that arise in the text, I owe a great deal to the help of Dr Andrew Crawshaw, Dr Dennis Hocking, the Cornwall County Pathologist, and Professor Keith Simpson. None of these advisers should be blamed for factual inaccuracies in the book, some of which are due to ignorance, some to the desire not to stick too closely to actual Yard procedures – a precedent established by my friend John Creasey in his Gideon books.

COLIN WILSON
GORRAN HAVEN

One

Saltfleet woke up in the middle of the night and thought about the dead girl. That was a mistake – it made it impossible to sleep. He lay there in the moonlit room, listening to his wife's quiet, regular breathing; the moonlight fell on her forearm, raised above her head, and on the silky material of her nightgown. Miranda was forty-five; in the half-light, she looked twenty. He thought: older than that poor girl, even so.

The Scene of Crimes Officer had covered the body with a blanket before he arrived. She lay at the side of the drive, half-concealed by rhododendron bushes. Tall elm trees explained why she had not been seen earlier from the houses on either side. He could see, from the shape under the blanket, that one knee was raised, the other leg flung out, the position typical of rape. A shoe lay about five feet from the body. He stood there for several seconds, looking carefully around, before dropping on to one knee, and carefully removing the blanket.

She had been strangled, and also – probably – struck a blow on the temple. A length of electric flex was deeply embedded in the flesh of the neck; a piece of white cloth protruded from the open mouth. Her face looked swollen and blotchy. She had an underdeveloped figure, with small, flat breasts. The black stockings were held up by broad elastic bands. The open legs looked obscene, like a drawing in a public lavatory.

He had seen many bodies, but they never ceased to produce shock. It seemed a kind of insult that they should look so useless, so discarded.

Detective-Sergeant Crisp stood waiting, his notebook open. Saltfleet began to dictate:

'Body of a young girl, probably between twelve and fourteen years of age. Death apparently due to strangulation with white plastic-covered flex, tied around throat with three knots. A sharp knife has apparently been used to cut through navy blue school tunic and white cotton underslip, both cut from top to bottom. Vertical cut about nine inches long from lower ribs to pubis. Slight bleeding. White blouse and undervest pushed up under armpits. No brassiere. White cotton knickers around left ankle, untorn...'

He stood up, blowing out his breath violently to relieve the oppression; the pity was a swollen lump that contracted his breathing.

Crisp said: 'Been dead for some time from the look of it.'

Under normal circumstances, it took a body about twelve hours to lose its natural heat. It had been a warm day, and although the body had been lying in the shade of the bushes, heat loss should have been normal, about one and a half degrees Fahrenheit per hour. Rigor mortis was complete, indicating that she had probably been dead for more than ten hours.

The Scene of Crimes Officer, a detective-constable from the local station, joined them. He had made a careful examination of the scene before Saltfleet arrived. Saltfleet asked him: 'What do you make of it?'

'No drag marks on the gravel, nor signs of a struggle. So it probably didn't take place here.'

'Find anything over there?' He pointed at the bushes at the far edge of the lawn, where a constable was still searching.

'Nothing so far, sir.'

It was now 7.15 in the evening. Saltfleet would normally have been on his way home by this time, driving to Thames Ditton. He had been in the Information Room when the call came through at 6.32: a dead schoolgirl found in a Hampstead garden.

He looked up at the house, whose shadow now covered them. It looked mid-Victorian; functional and ugly, with small windows and grimy red brick; the gables seemed to have been designed by an architect who wasn't sure whether to make them Tudor or Gothic. The overgrown lawn was still covered with last winter's leaves.

'What about the house? Have you checked it?'

'All doors and windows seemed to be locked.'

'How long has it been empty?'

'Since last February. Lady Edgton asked us to keep an eye on it when she left. She spends a lot of time abroad.'

Taking care not to disturb the body, Saltfleet felt in the pocket of the school tunic. He found a paper handkerchief with a lipstick stain.

'You've had no missing person report of a schoolgirl today?'

'No, sir. But perhaps she's not from this area.'

'Have you got her description?'

The constable read aloud from his notebook:

'Five feet four and a half inches tall. Blue eyes. Dark brown hair. Appendix scar. Weight – around seven stone.'

Crisp was copying the details into his notebook. Saltfleet told him:

'You'd better ring the Yard and check the missing persons file. If she's been missing all day, someone should have reported it by now.'

The photographer and the police surgeon arrived shortly afterwards. The doctor had to wait while the photographer took his pictures; the doctor would want to disturb the body, and the area around it. The body was photographed from a dozen different angles. After that, the doctor carefully extracted the wad of cloth from the girl's mouth. It came out with some difficulty. He said:

'He meant to make sure she didn't scream. It was halfway down her throat.' He held up the gag while the photographer took pictures of it. 'That's odd . . .'

'What?'

'I've come across cases where the girl was choked with her own panties. But I've never found a case where she had them on as well.' He shook out the wad of cloth; it was a pair of white nylon briefs.

Crisp came back. Saltfleet could see from his face that the result was negative.

'Nothing so far, I'm afraid. There's two missing girl reports, but the descriptions don't fit.'

Saltfleet asked the doctor: 'Any idea how long she's been dead?'

'Difficult to say. Twelve hours or more.'

'But if it was more, that'd mean she was killed in the early hours of this morning. So she'd have been missing since last night. She'd certainly have been reported missing.'

'That's my guess. The rectal temperature's 72.5 degrees. For her size, that's consistent with death between twelve and fifteen hours ago.'

The constable who had been making door-to-door inquiries along the road reported that no one had heard or seen anything. 'But they strike me as the type who mind their own business.'

Shortly after seven-thirty, Detective-Inspector Coventry of the Fingerprint Department arrived with his assistant. He fingerprinted the dead girl. This was little more than a formality, it was a thousand to one chance that her prints would be on file.

He peered at the girl's throat.

'No use trying to get a print from that?'

The doctor shook his head. 'He tied flex around her throat when she was half stunned, then pulled it tight.'

Coventry fingered the edges of the cut uniform.

'Any sign of the knife he used to do this?'

'They're still searching. But he probably took it with him.'

Coventry said musingly: 'Like in those other cases of assault.'

It was the first time it had been mentioned that evening, but it had been in Saltfleet's mind since he received the call. Since last November, six months before, there had been eight cases of attacks on schoolchildren in the North London area, two of them near Hampstead. Most of them had taken place in the early morning; the victims had usually been delivering newspapers. The man, who was described as being in his mid-twenties, with receding blond hair, had threatened the children with a knife, forced them to accompany him to some open place – a park or recreation ground – and there committed sexual assault. It seemed to make no difference to him whether they were girls or boys. On three occasions the child had struggled and been injured, although not badly; the others had escaped unhurt. In the last case, which had taken place near the North Circular Road, the girl had received a black eye and lost a tooth.

Saltfleet said: 'It doesn't look like his handiwork. Besides, she looks too old to be delivering newspapers.' He asked the doctor: 'How old would you say, Ian? Fourteen?'

'Sixteen, more like. But it's difficult to tell. The pathologist should be able to give you a better idea. He'll be able to give you a more accurate time of death too.'

'Who will that be?'

'Aspinal, probably. Eric was talking to the coroner when I came out.' He was referring to Eric Lamb, Commander of the C.I.D., who had assigned Saltfleet to the job. The coroner was responsible for the choice of pathologist. Lamb, whenever possible, used Aspinal, of University College Hospital, or Jackson, of the London Hospital Medical College. Both had thoroughly up-to-date mortuaries, an important consideration in murder investigations.

The Scene of Crimes Officer called out; he was standing at the far edge of the lawn, by the bushes. Saltfleet hurried over. Under the bush, so that it only became visible when the constable pulled the branches aside, there was a square of maroon cloth. He picked it up carefully.

Saltfleet said: 'A pocket from a coat.'

'A school jacket. And it's been torn off.'

'Then where's the rest of the jacket?'

This question was still unanswered at eight o'clock, when the pathologist arrived. Aspinal was a tall man, with a head like a skull; his dress was always so neat that he looked as if he had just returned from a diplomatic reception. Even in repose, the corners of his mouth had a sarcastic twist. Many detectives disliked him. Saltfleet had come to respect, and then to like him. Aspinal's enemies said he was a showman, and there was some truth in this. Medical students had been known to rush out of his lectures vomiting, and other doctors pointedly avoided his table in the dining room because he enjoyed describing the more revolting details of the post mortems. He took a kind of theatrical delight in the grue-some aspects of his profession. But his thoroughness was obsessional – Saltfleet owed the solution of at least two mur-der cases to his curious instinct for suspicious detail.

Aspinal had another peculiarity: his assistants were women, and usually attractive. No one knew how he found so many girls with a taste for the macabre, or whether they became his mistresses. At the moment he had with him a slim, blonde girl, whose horn-rimmed glasses and neatly tailored suit gave her the air of an American college professor.

Aspinal apologized for his lateness. 'Had rather a tussle with the coroner about using my own mortuary. He gave way in the end.' The coroner's assistant, who accompanied him, obviously stood in awe of a man who could win arguments with the notoriously short-tempered coroner.

Aspinal spread his handkerchief on the gravel, and knelt beside the body. The light was failing, and he worked quickly, and with economy of movement. He dictated rapidly:

'Petechial haemorrhages on face, bruising of both sterno-hyoid muscles, bruises on left temple – about the size that would be caused by a wooden stake, not more than an inch in diameter.' He twitched back the eyelid and bent close to the face. 'Pinpoint haemorrhages inside eyelids. Blackish discoloration of the back of the tongue . . .' He glanced at Saltfleet. 'Did you take anything out of her mouth?'

'This.' He held up the panties. Aspinal glanced at the girl's left foot. 'Very odd.' His Mephistophelean eyebrows twitched. He paused, lost in thought. Saltfleet waited. Then Aspinal laid his long forefinger on the top of one of the black stockings. 'Has anyone pulled these up?'

The Scene of Crimes Officer shook his head. 'No.'

'I thought not. Then the murderer must have done it. They must have been disturbed in the course of rape.'

'Was she raped?'

'I can't be absolutely certain until I've taken a swab. But it seems probable, unless he was disturbed. And I don't think he was. The whole layout . . .' He wafted his hand over the body. Saltfleet had never reconciled himself to Aspinal's way of treating corpses as mere objects. He still found it hard to look direct at the dead girl.

Aspinal straightened up, brushing his trousers. 'There's a touch of sadism here – a kind of power mania. He carefully pulls up the stockings – as if he's obsessed by tidiness – and stuffs a pair of panties into the mouth, a pair he must have been carrying.'

12

'Why? She could have been wearing two.'

'Just possible. But unlikely.'

'Why?'

'Both pairs have been worn, if you observe. The slight staining. She couldn't have worn both pairs next to her body.'

The ambulance arrived. As Aspinal supervised the removal of the body, Saltfleet and Crisp stood looking at the house; its gables looked almost theatrical against the deepening sky. Aspinal said:

'Are you going to look inside?'

'Do you think I should?' Technically speaking, a warrant was necessary, but it would be easy enough to break in. The phrase used in reports to explain the broken window was 'stone thrown up by passing car'.

Aspinal was not forthcoming.

'You're in charge of this case, my dear Gregory.'

Saltfleet knew him well enough to make a guess at his train of thought. 'Why do you think he wasn't disturbed?'

'Whoever cut off her clothes did it with a sharp knife. When a man cuts or tears a girl's clothes in the course of assault, he's usually in a hurry. But in this case, the cut was straight and neat, almost as if he'd used scissors. I'd say he felt he had plenty of time.'

Saltfleet said: 'I'd like to know why he cut them anyway. He didn't have to.' But Aspinal was already walking toward his car.

Now, as he lay beside his sleeping wife, Saltfleet again tried to reconstruct what had happened. He had checked the missing persons file again at midnight; there was still no report of a missing schoolgirl. But if Dilnot – the police surgeon – was right about time of death, she had been missing now for more than twenty-four hours. Moreover, local inquiries had failed to identify the school uniform: maroon blazer, blue tunic, black stockings. He could think of only one theory to fit all the facts: that the school was outside London, perhaps as much as a hundred miles away; that her killer had picked her up when she left school on Thursday afternoon, and driven her to London; that he had taken her to the garden

13

where she was found because he knew the house to be empty. But why take her there at all? There must be hundreds of remote places that would be less of a risk . . .

Miranda stirred; she seemed to respond to his restlessness. Saltfleet sat up quietly, found his slippers, and padded out of the bedroom. He closed the bathroom door, then switched on the mirror light; it was less glaring than the overhead light. The bathroom always induced in him a pleasant relaxation, particularly since Miranda had had underfloor heating installed. The coverlet of the lavatory pan was decorated with some kind of candlewick mat – he had often meant to ask Miranda what it was supposed to be. But it made a comfortable seat. He reached out to the corner of the window-sill, where he always kept a spare pipe and tobacco pouch. When the pipe was well alight, he leaned back against the cistern, and allowed himself to relax completely. It was this capacity to relax that made him a good detective, and that had brought him the rank of Chief-Superintendent at forty-six. He had never wasted much time worrying about promotion, looking for opportunities to rise in the Yard hierarchy. The job fascinated him; that was all he asked.

After twenty years of murder investigation, he had developed his own approach to cases of deliberate homicide. At the beginning of a case, he never pushed for immediate results; he treated it almost as if it were a chess problem, requiring slow, deliberate assessment. During this period of assessment, his instincts and intuitions began to operate; he started to form a picture of the kind of person he was looking for. This early impression was often crucial. In the Gaffin case of 1963, he had felt instinctively that Nancy Gaffin and her illegitimate child had not been murdered by a man, in spite of the signs of sexual assault. The impression had been so strong that he had ignored the District Collator's list of known sex offenders, and looked for a woman with sufficient motive. He had found Agnes Devlin within three hours of the discovery of the bodies, before she had had time to destroy the bloodstained riding breeches and boots she had worn to commit the murders; her husband proved to be the father of the child, and she had suspected he intended to leave her.

14

But in cases like the present one, his intuition was disturbed by his sense of urgency, almost of panic. Cases involving children always produced a feeling of anger and outrage, and now there was also the fear that it could happen again before they could catch the killer. Aspinal was right: there was a touch of sadism, of ruthlessness, about this murder. In his own mind, he had already eliminated the North Circular rapist as a suspect. Such a man might kill accidentally, by squeezing too hard to silence a frightened girl – but there would be an unpremeditated air about the crime. The killer of the Hampstead girl was more dangerous, certainly more calculating; he had thought it out, like a poacher after game. There had been a similar murder in M Division two weeks before: a schoolgirl, staying at home with a headache while her parents were at work, had been strangled with her own tights and raped on the kitchen floor. Chief-Inspector Branson, who was in charge of the case, had told him that a tradesman was suspected; but, so far, there was no lead.

A tradesman's van . . . that was a possibility. He could have driven into the garden, knowing the house was empty, killed the girl in the back of the van, then pushed the body out . . .

He finished the pipe; it had relieved his feeling of frustration. There was nothing he could do until morning, when he could check with the Divisional Collator on sex offenders in the Hampstead area. Crisp had suggested that she might have been under the influence of drugs when she was killed; if so, the post mortem should reveal it. He knocked out the pipe into the lavatory, and flushed it, then replaced the pouch on the window-sill. He opened the bathroom window to disperse the smoke. The garden looked quiet in the moonlight, with the moon reflected on the panes of the greenhouse. The night was so still that the alders at the end of the drive scarcely rustled. He could even hear the ripple of the Thames, two hundred yards away, around Thames Ditton Island, and the cry of some night bird. A train rattled by in the distance. As he closed the window, he noticed the hockey stick lying in the middle of the lawn; it belonged to his daughter Geraldine. He sighed, and went quietly back to bed.

The Saturday morning was clear and warm. It was supposed to be his day off; he had been intending to get the boat out and revarnish it. But there were no days off on a murder case.

He ate a good breakfast of scrambled egg and rashers of farm bacon – Miranda drove fifty miles every few months to collect a side of it from a downland farmer. He also drank four cups of coffee, knowing that they might be the last until he got home again. The morning papers arrived as he was leaving the house. The late editions of the *Express* and *Guardian* both gave it a paragraph on the front page; both accounts carried descriptions of the clothes.

He drove up the Portsmouth Road, through Kingston, then between Richmond Park and Wimbledon Common. The grey Rover 90 was twelve years old; but since he seldom drove above forty miles an hour, the engine was still excellent. Miranda sometimes asked why he did not get a transfer from his area in North London – covering five divisions – to the south. He made various excuses; but one of the main reasons was that he enjoyed this drive into London. When traffic was bad, he could park at Putney Bridge and go in by train. If he took over C.I.D. supervision in his own area, the drive would cease to be regular. Besides, he liked North London; he knew his stations and his local C.I.D. men – nearly four hundred, including assistants or 'aids' – and he also knew most of the villains. Some odd territorial instinct made him want to keep his home and work completely separate.

He arrived at the Yard just before nine. His office was still in the old Yard building on the Embankment; some time during the next two months he was due to move to the new building in Broadway. In spite of the inconveniences, he preferred to delay the move as long as possible. The old Yard was shabby and poky, but it had its own character; the new Yard was like any office building.

He asked the duty sergeant: 'Is Chief-Inspector Branson in yet?'

'Haven't seen him, sir.'

'Ask him to give me a ring, would you?'

His office was on the second floor, overlooking Cannon Row. If he had wanted, he could have moved into a room with a view of the river; but it hardly seemed worth while. He was out much of the day, checking on his stations; the office was the place where he did all the paperwork – and a large amount of Saltfleet's time was taken up with paperwork, reading reports, writing them, filling in forms. Even with a full-time secretary – shared, at the moment, with the head of the Flying Squad – there was enough paperwork to keep him at his desk for several hours a day. But this morning the office looked pleasantly clean and empty; Miss Larkhill was not expecting him in. He went to her desk and found the reports that had come in after he had left the office. A suicide in X Division, Harrow Road; the man had cut his throat after trying to strangle his wife. Poliakov – the unusual name rang a bell; he'd been in trouble before for beating his children. Saltfleet made a mental note to find out what had happened to the children. A tobacconist in New Southgate – Y Division – tied up and robbed by two teenagers, and a landlord in Highgate – also Y Division – beaten into unconsciousness by a coloured tenant with whom he had a disagreement. Two teenage girls arrested in Muswell Hill for soliciting; one found in possession of cannabis; they were probably trying to get money for drugs. Y Division had had a busy day; it often happened like that, for no discernible reason.

There were also the criminal record sheets, compiled by the Divisional Collator from the Hampstead station. These contained information on criminals known to be in the area – physical description, Criminal Records Office number, short list of convictions and offences. The Collator had marked several entries with red ink for his attention. The top sheet, dated 12 March – five weeks earlier – had mug shots, profile and full-face, of a respectable-looking middle-aged man with a lined face. The entry read: 'the photo on the right is of James Frederick Henry, C.R.O. 78301-69, born 8.5.1909, Cardiff, of 17 Springfield Gardens, N.W.6, now employed as clerk at Garth Trading Company, 876 Finchley Road, N.W.11. Has 5 convictions for indecent assault on minors, and one for unlawful sexual intercourse with a 14-year-old girl (daughter of landlady). Conditional Discharge in 1969 for one year for making indecent phone calls. Failed to complete psychiatric treatment. Seems most attracted to plump girls, 10-12 age group. Usually attempts bribery with sweets, toys, money. Known to prefer inter-crural intercourse from behind, but has never tried to force this. Says he does this only when intensely depressed. Hangs around school playgrounds, parks, other play areas. At present under surveillance.'

Saltfleet pushed this aside. A man who tried bribery with sweets and toys, and made no attempt to force the girls to submit to intercrural intercourse (using thighs pressed to-gether) was basically non-violent. The defeated, weak face looking out of the photograph was not the face of the man who had strangled the unidentified schoolgirl in Hampstead.

Other entries sounded more likely: a Jamaican builder's labourer, who had served three terms for rape; a television repair man with eight convictions, including two for theft of ladies' underwear from clothes lines and one for rape; a window cleaner who had twice attempted rape when drunk, and a cat burglar who had been convicted eight times for offences against children, usually committed in the course of breaking and entry. All these were possibles, although none struck him as obviously likely; he sent Crisp for their files from the C.R.O.

The phone rang; it was Branson.

'Hello, Tony. What's happening on that rape case of yours, the schoolgirl, what's her name . . . ?'

'Jessie Langton. We got him last night.'

'You did! Good! Who was he?'

'Man named Saxby, from Norwich.'

'What the hell was he doing in Kennington?'

'He ran a farm produce business from his van. We checked all the tradesmen who ever called at the flats – he came at the end of the list. Fortunately another woman in the flats had some potatoes she'd bought from him – Norfolk potatoes. So we checked with the Norwich C.I.D. He had a list of convictions as long as your arm – rape, indecent ex-posure, peeping Tom, the lot.'

'Marvellous work, Tony.' Unlike some senior Yard offi-cers, Saltfleet believed in paying compliments where they were deserved – or even, on occasion, when they were not.

Besides, it gave him genuine pleasure to hear that the man had been caught, and to feel that this had been done through the slow working of the routine machinery of detection. He said: 'Tell me, could this man Saxby have been in Hampstead on Thursday night or early Friday morning? We found a dead schoolgirl in a Hampstead garden.'

'Could you be more definite about times?'

'Say, four o'clock Thursday afternoon, to five or six the following morning.'

'It's possible. He didn't come home all night – the Norwich police were waiting for him. Said his van had broken down. I'll check on it.'

'I'd be grateful if you would.'

He felt a momentary surge of pleasure as he hung up, immediately blocked by caution. This sounded possible. Norwich. That would be about the right distance. He reached out and checked in the AA Book: Norwich to London was 111 miles. In a tradesman's van the drive might take four hours or more. And this man had strangled and raped one schoolgirl . . .

The phone rang again. Divisional Detective-Inspector Crampton of N Division had a tip from a 'grass' about a bank raid planned in Poplar. Saltfleet noted the details; and when Crisp came back with the files, he sent the notes across to Superintendent Norland, who was in charge of the C.I.D. for that area. Norland's man on the spot – D.D.I. Leitch – had a reputation for efficiency; he could probably handle it himself, with the help of the Flying Squad. This kind of thing gave Saltfleet deep satisfaction. The informer might have picked up the information in a Soho club; he would pass it on only to a detective he knew and trusted – in this case, Crampton. Crampton passed it back to Saltfleet, Saltfleet to Norland, Norland to Leitch. Nobody but Crampton knew the name of the grass. It was a roundabout way of doing things, but it worked. Even Saltfleet had no idea of the name of the informer.

The next call was to the Hampstead station, to D.D.I. Murchison, Saltfleet's man there. Murchison had been in Hendon the evening before, investigating a case of burglary and arson; normally he would have dealt with the murder

19

investigation, and sent in a report. If the case looked straight-forward, he would take it over from Saltfleet anyway.

Saltfleet asked him: 'What do you know about the woman who owns this house – Lady Edgton?'

'She lives abroad most of the time – Monaco and Ireland. She has a house at a place called Ballyfoyle, near Kilkenny. Our man on the beat checks her place regularly.'

'Do you know how to contact her?'

'Yes, sir. We've got her address and phone number in both places. The sergeant here thinks she's in Ireland at the moment.'

'Good. Find out, then get on to the local constabulary and get someone to go and tell her what's happened. Try and get them to do it during the next hour, because I'd like to talk to her over the phone. Better give me her phone number.' He could have phoned her direct from the Yard and broken the news, but it was better to allow a local policeman to do it. After all, it was conceivable that the dead girl might be related to her.

He opened the first of the four files. The face that looked up at him had wide, vacant eyes and jug-shaped ears; this was the window cleaner who committed assaults when drunk. Saltfleet pushed the file aside; this was almost certainly not their man. The cat burglar was equally unlikely; he was fifty-eight, and criminals of that age seldom change their method. The Jamaican builder's labourer seemed a possibility, until he noticed that he was described as left handed. The bruise on the girl's forehead had been on the left-hand side, which suggested a right-handed man, and the knot in the cord had been pulled slightly to the left. The television repair man seemed the only real possibility of the four; he was heavily built, in his mid-thirties; the trap-like mouth and piercing eyes indicated violence and a strong will; and his case history showed him to be a man who held grudges. Running through his other crimes – walk-in burglary, grievous bodily harm (prostitute), receiving, possession of drugs – was a thread of sexual perverseness – stealing of underwear, rape of a minor, suspected mutilation of animals. He had spent twelve of the last sixteen years in prison for a variety of offences. Such a man could and perhaps would kill a schoolgirl in the course of rape. He would also drive a van, and know about empty houses in his area. Saltfleet decided to ask Murchison to check the man's whereabouts for Thursday evening and Friday morning.

The phone rang. It was Eric Lamb, Commander of the C.I.D.

'What's happening about this Hampstead case, Greg? The *News* and *Standard* both want to carry it in the midday editions. That'd be useful, wouldn't it? Any identification yet?'

'Not yet.'

'So it *would* be useful? I don't want to push you in any way, but if you feel like it, why don't you talk to them? They'd need the story before eleven. O.K.?' That was typical. Lamb was a powerhouse, perhaps the most formidably efficient Commander the C.I.D. had ever had. To work for him was sometimes wearing to the nerves. But where the press was concerned, he would always leave the decision to the officer in charge of the case. Some detectives loved publicity; others hated the press on principle; others – like Saltfleet – were willing to be co-operative, but preferred to take their own time on a case. At the moment, Saltfleet had nothing in particular to say to the press. But Lamb wanted movement, and perhaps, with Sunday coming up, he was right. Saltfleet had intended to wait for Aspinal to ring him; now he asked the switchboard to get him the path. lab. at University College Hospital.

The nurse told him Dr Aspinal was working, but when he gave his name and rank, she asked him to hold on. Five minutes went by, then Aspinal came on the line.

'Gregory. Sorry to keep you.'

'I'm sorry to chase you, but Lamb wants a story for the midday papers. Anything new?'

'Not a lot, I'm afraid. I haven't got around to the radiological examination for age. She'd had sexual intercourse around the time of death. There was no sign of force being used.' He was speaking slowly, no doubt aware that Saltfleet was making notes.

'Was she a virgin?'

'Oh no. Hymen was ruptured a long time ago.'

'How can you be sure of that?' Saltfleet knew enough of pathology to know that, once a wound is healed, it is difficult to tell its age.

'Because she'd been pregnant.'

'Are you sure?'

'Absolutely. There's no mistaking the thickening of the uterus.'

'Any idea what her age might be?'

'At a rough guess, twenty-five or twenty-six.'

'What?' He found himself staring in amazement at the earpiece of the phone. 'Are . . . are you certain?'

'Not until I've got the radiologist's report on the bones. But from the wisdom teeth, I'd guess twenty-five.'

Saltfleet said: 'My God.' For the moment, he could think of nothing else to say.

Aspinal said: 'Couple more points. That cord used to strangle her was telephone cord. Did your Scene of Crimes Officer spot that? It had four strands instead of the usual three. I'd say it was cut by pliers. And the other thing is: she'd got a burn on her right foot. I'd say it was recent – within an hour of death.'

'Was the stocking burned?'

'No. This was underneath the stocking.'

'What do you make of that?'

'I don't know what to make of it.'

'How about her nails?'

'Nothing under them. He may have attacked her from behind. She wasn't a big girl – probably quite easy to overpower.'

'Have you finished with her now – apart from the radiology?'

'Not yet. I'll be able to tell you the stomach contents in half an hour. And . . . hold on just one . . . yes, here's something. Your killer's blood group was Group O. Not very helpful.'

'Did you find blood?'

'No. That's from the seminal fluid inside her. All right?'

'I can't tell you how much I appreciate this, Martin.'

'That's all right. I'll ring you back later.'

Crisp had been listening with interest. Saltfleet said:

'She wasn't a schoolgirl at all. Aspinal said she was in her mid-twenties. What does that suggest to you?'

'Prostitute, sir?'

Saltfleet said gloomily: 'Me too. Can't think why it didn't strike me. I must be slipping.'

'Oh, I don't know. The face was pretty swollen. And I certainly wouldn't have guessed from the size of the nipples.'

'Call Murchison for me – see if he knows of any prostitute in the Hampstead area who specializes in schoolgirl dress.'

While Crisp phoned, Saltfleet stood by the window and stared out. Why hadn't it occurred to him that she was a prostitute? It meant he was allowing his mind to work in terms of preconceived ideas. He had worked on the Vice Squad for eighteen months, and it had been his least satisfactory period in the force. He had no theoretical or moral objections to loose women, but he had always found it difficult to reconcile himself to the sheer hardness of most of the prostitutes in central London. Before he went on the Vice Squad, he had tended to think of them as unfortunates, 'fallen women'. In fact, most of them were hard-headed businesswomen, capable of removing a stiletto-heeled shoe and cracking the skull of any amateur who tried to move in on their pitch. Or calling in a ponce to mark the intruder's face in a way that would put her out of business for some time. The sight of the dead girl had touched his emotions; it had not entered his head that she might be other than she seemed. Consequently, he had wasted valuable time – fifteen hours in which he might have identified her and found some lead to her killer. That was a bad mistake.

He said over his shoulder: 'Ask him if he's done anything about the Kilkenny police.'

Crisp hung up. 'He has. He says they should have told her by now. And he knows a girl in South End Green who specializes in dressing up for clients – nurses' uniforms and all that. He's going to check on her.'

Saltfleet took the London directory from the window-sill, the E to K volume, and looked up Edgton. It was not there. He said to Crisp:

'Get on to the supervisor at Directory Inquiries and see if you can get the number of Lady Edgton, Wildwood Road,

Hampstead. It's probably ex-directory.'

Crisp picked up the phone. 'Do you think there'll be anybody there?'

'No.'

He glanced through the rest of the Crime Information sheets while Crisp talked on the phone. Now he knew the victim was not a schoolgirl, most of the information was irrelevant.

He could hear the out-of-order signal coming from the telephone before Crisp said: 'The line seems to be out of order.'

'That's what I thought. We should have broken in last night.'

'Why?'

'It could be coincidence. But she was strangled with a piece of telephone cable. We'd better get over there.' He stood up. 'On second thoughts, I'll try and get this Lady Edgton . . .' He asked the switchboard to get him the Kilkenny number.

It came through a few moments later, an Irish voice – female – saying 'Lady Edgton's residence.'

'Could I speak to Lady Edgton, please?'

The girl sounded flustered. 'I'm sorry . . . there's somebody with her.'

'Is it a policeman by any chance?'

'Why yes, it is.'

'This is the police, Scotland Yard. Would you ask her if she'll take the call?'

There was a long silence, then a sharp voice said 'Hello?'

'Lady Edgton?'

'Speaking.'

'Chief-Superintendent Saltfleet, Scotland Yard. You've been told about the girl who was found in your garden last night?'

'Yes.' It was incisive, slightly impatient, as if he had told her that her dustbin had been overturned.

'She was in her mid-twenties, slightly built, dressed rather like a schoolgirl. Does that description mean anything to you?'

'I'm afraid not. I'm sure I don't know her.'

24

'Was your telephone out of order when you left?'

'Not as far as I know. Is it now?'

'Yes. Does your house remain empty all the time, or does someone come in?'

'The housekeeper comes in twice a week to light fires and dust. Her husband does the garden.'

'Could you give me her name and address?'

'Mrs Balmont, 120 Morley Road. That's near Highgate cemetery. She's on the telephone if you'd like the number.' He wrote it down.

'Do you know when she was last in?'

'It could have been yesterday?'

'That's not likely – she'd have found the body.'

'Then it must have been Thursday. I don't tie her down to particular days, so long as she goes in twice a week.'

'Does anyone else have a key?'

'Yes, my nephew. He's writing a book, and he likes to use the library sometimes.'

'Could I have his name and address?'

'Of course. But surely there's no need to bother him?'

'We shan't unless we have to.'

She gave him an address in Burnsall Street, Chelsea, and the telephone number.

'I think we'd better take a look inside your house, to make sure everything's in order. Would you mind?'

'Of course not. Get Mrs Balmont to go with you.'

'That shouldn't be necessary.'

'I see . . . You won't break anything, will you?'

'No, we shan't break anything.'

He hung up. 'She seems to think we're going to tear up the floorboards.' He handed Crisp the housekeeper's number. 'Ring her and find out when she last went to the house.' While Crisp was using the other line, Saltfleet rang Criminal Records for a check on Manfred Lytton, the nephew. It was a routine check, and he was not surprised when they told him there was no listing. Crisp had finished his call too.

'She's not been there since early in the week – she's had a bug that knocked her out.'

'Ah well, that simplifies that, anyway. I think we'd better call on Mr Manfred Lytton.'

25

Two

It was a small, quiet street off the King's Road, with expensive-looking mews-type houses. They took Crisp's Mini, which was easier to manoeuvre in traffic. There was only one empty space, outside a garage marked 'No Parking'. He told Crisp to wait in the car, and walked down to the house near the corner. The sun was almost directly overhead. As he stood at the green-painted door, he felt pleasantly warm and relaxed. After his second ring, the upstairs curtain moved, and a woman looked out. She came down and opened the door. He asked : 'Is Mr Lytton in?'

'No.' He had a feeling she spotted him for a policeman immediately. She was good-looking, in a hard-faced way, with straight black hair descending to her shoulders, and a black dress. She had a good figure, although heavily built.

'Any idea when he'll be back?'

'No.' She looked as if she intended to close the door in his face. He reached for his wallet.

'Chief-Superintendent Saltfleet, C.I.D. I want to talk to Mr Lytton about a murder.'

'He's not in.'

'Then I'd better have a word with you.' He indicated the stairs. She hesitated, then turned and led the way in.

He followed her up the well-carpeted stairs, observing that she wore sheer tights and expensive shoes. Through the door at the bottom of the stairs he had caught a glimpse of a well-furnished dining-room. She led him into a book-lined room that seemed to be a combination of study and sitting-room. A cigarette was burning in an ashtray. The drink cupboard in the corner stood open; in front of it there was a gin bottle and a half-filled glass. She reached for a bottle of tonic water, opened it, and poured some into the glass as if challenging him to comment. Saltfleet went over to the window.

'When did Mr Lytton go out?'

She took her time, taking a swallow of the drink before replying.

26

'He hasn't been back since Thursday evening.'

'Any idea where he might be?'

'No.'

'Does he often stay out like that?'

She shrugged. 'It's no business of mine.' The voice was refined, but with an undertone of cockney. He persisted:

'But *does* he?'

'Sometimes.'

'Are you a relative?'

'His housekeeper.' She smiled with a touch of malice, and took another swallow of the drink.

'Mrs . . . ?'

'Beaumont Ames.' She said it as if saying, 'Mind your own business.'

'Does Mr Lytton drive a car?'

'Yes.'

'What kind?'

'A green Aston Martin, sports model.'

'Number?'

'WP forty stroke ninety.'

'That's not English, is it?'

'No. He bought it in Arles.'

She sat on the deep window-sill, and took a cigarette from a metal box. The eyelashes, he observed, were mascaraed, and the lips had a touch of rouge. The long-sleeved black dress, with its high collar, gave her a slightly school-mistressy air. The strong lines of her face, with its high cheek bones, were incongruent with the effect of femininity she aimed at.

He wrote his number on the scratch pad on the desk.

'When he comes back, would you ask him to contact me at this number?'

She said nothing. He went to the door.

'Have you got the key to the Hampstead house?'

'No.' As he started down the stairs she added: 'He's got it.' It was the first sign of co-operation since he had been talking to her.

Crisp was double-parked outside the door. He said cheerfully: 'Bloke got me to move.'

'What was the car?'

Crisp glanced back, worried. 'I dunno. Morris, I think. Why?'

'I'm looking for a green Aston Martin. Cruise round the block, would you?'

They drove slowly along two sides of the square, and back to King's Road; there was no sign of the car.

'Where to now, sir?'

Saltfleet took the London atlas out of the glove compartment. 'Make for Camden Town. I want to call on the house-keeper . . . Morley Road . . . Let's see.'

When he had worked out the route, he relaxed and lit his pipe. Crisp said: 'Any luck there?'

'Not much. He hadn't been back since Thursday.' Crisp glanced at him. 'Tell me, Steve, what would be your first re-action if I said I wanted to ask you questions about a murder?'

'Well . . . I suppose I'd want to know who was murdered.'

'Quite.' He stared sombrely at a girl in a transparent dress, with nothing underneath it. 'Well she didn't.'

'Who didn't?'

'This woman who says she's Lytton's housekeeper. She looks more like an expensive prostitute.'

'Probably his mistress.'

'Probably. She's got something on her mind, I'm certain of that.'

A clock struck eleven, reminding him that the midday papers wanted their story. He had told the Press Information Officer that the dead girl was in her twenties; that would have to serve. He had no time for talking to the press.

It was nearly midday when the Mini pulled up outside the semi-detached house opposite Highgate cemetery. The man in the front garden laid down his hedge clippers and came over to the car.

'Are you the police inspector who called?'

'That's right.'

'What a terrible thing. Have you got anybody yet?'

'Not yet. I'd like the key to the house. Could you get it?'

As the man went off, he told Crisp:

'Go with him and ask to use the phone. Ring the Yard

28

and get Coventry to come up to the house.'

'O.K., Chief.' Crisp was not even surprised.

It was a difficult decision to make; it might mean a wasted journey for Coventry, or whoever the Fingerprint Department sent in his place. But he was now obeying his detective's instinct.

Crisp came out five minutes later.

'Sorry about the delay – real talkative type. He said it was a real blessing his wife didn't find the body – it would have given her a nervous breakdown.'

'Did you get on to Coventry?'

'I talked to Ted Jackson. He says they should be there in about forty minutes.'

As they drove along Hampstead Lane, Crisp said:

'Do you really think she might have been killed in the house?'

He sighed. 'I don't know . . . I think perhaps we should have broken in last night.'

'But how could he have got in or out without forcing one of the doors or windows?'

'Perhaps he had a key.'

'You mean it might have been this bloke – what's his name?'

'Lytton. It's possible.'

A few curious children were hanging around the gate of the house. A policeman was standing guard at the door. Salt-fleet had contacted the Hampstead station before he left the Yard and asked for two men to keep watch.

In the bright sunshine the place looked different; even the lawns looked less overgrown.

The policeman said: 'Message from Inspector Murchison, sir. He's over in Hendon, but he'll be back by half past twelve if you need him.'

'Thank you, Constable.'

The key-ring contained two Yale keys and an ordinary key. The front door, heavy and black, had two locks. The ordinary key turned easily and smoothly but neither of the Yales would turn in the lock. Crisp and Saltfleet tried for several minutes.

'Someone's slipped the locking catch inside.'

Saltfleet led the way round to the back of the house. There was a pleasant garden with a summer house and apple trees; through the trees at the end a golf course was visible. The constable was sitting on a garden chair, enjoying the sun; when he saw Saltfleet, he jumped to his feet. Saltfleet nodded briefly, and tried the door of the porch. It opened easily. A dead bird, which had evidently become trapped, lay on the floor. Saltfleet inserted a Yale key in the back door and turned it. It refused to move. He tried the other key, but it was impossible to force it completely into the keyhole. He looked at Crisp.

'Somebody's locked both doors from the inside.'

'Well, unless he got out of a window, he must still be in there.'

They walked round the house, trying every ground-floor window. Some had shutters; all seemed to be securely fastened. As they approached the gate that led into the front garden, Crisp said: 'Look.'

The flowerbed contained wallflowers and clumps of lupins, which were beginning to put out new leaves. Some of the lupins were lying on the ground; they looked as if they might have succumbed to a storm. Saltfleet knelt, and carefully raised them. Several were snapped off at the base of the stem. Underneath, on the damp earth, there were shapeless marks.

Crisp said: 'Footprints?'

'They were. Someone's taken the trouble to obliterate them.' He stood back, and looked up at the bedroom window above. A ledge ran underneath it. The window seemed to be tightly closed, although at its edge there was a flicker of white, as if something flapped in the wind.

'Ladder,' Crisp said. 'There's got to be a ladder somewhere around here.'

They found one in the gardening shed, and carried it to under the window. Together they raised it until it rested against the window-ledge.

Saltfleet told the constable at the front door: 'Get to a telephone and ask Inspector Murchison to get up here as soon as he can.' He told Crisp: 'You wait here and hold the ladder.'

Saltfleet stamped on the lower rung, to anchor the ladder in the damp soil, then climbed slowly. He paused at the ledge and examined it carefully, aware of the gaze of the children watching from the gate. There was no sign of footmarks on the ledge. He mounted the remaining steps until his face was level with the middle pane of the window. There was an alcove, and the curtains were drawn inside. He could now see that the flicker of white was string, which disappeared around the edge of the window. He took out his handkerchief, laid it carefully against the window-pane, and pushed. The window swung open. Saltfleet went up two more steps, and climbed over the sill into the room, through the curtains.

It was a very large bedroom, with two single beds: well furnished, but anonymous; probably a guest bedroom. He drew the curtains back, and looked at the window. The string had been tied to its catch, so that the window could be closed from outside. It was tight-fitting, so the string had the effect of wedging it securely, although the catch remained open. With a little more ingenuity, the catch itself could have been closed.

He looked carefully at the window-sill; it had been wiped clean of dust, and there were no marks on it. He went to the other window of the room. Its curtains were also drawn, but the window-sill of the alcove was thick with dust. The window was firmly fastened.

He went to the door and opened it. In the corridor beyond, he was struck by the faint but distinctive smell; for a moment it brought memories of harvest festivals in church in his childhood. But the smell was not flowers; it was more like incense.

He walked slowly along the corridor, opening doors and glancing into rooms. There was no sign of disorder. The floors had been recently polished, and the carpets hoovered. He was walking quietly, listening, although commonsense told him that there was no one there.

On the stair, he noticed the woman's black glove. It was almost invisible against the dark polished wood; if he had been scanning the ground less carefully he would have missed it. It was a thin cotton glove, of a small size; the seam of the index finger was starting to come undone.

The incense smell was no longer noticeable in the hall. The front door had been bolted at the top and bottom, and the locking catch on the Yale lock pushed into position. He unlocked it, and opened the door. Crisp was still at the bottom of the ladder. Saltfleet beckoned to him.

He opened the door at the other side of the hall; there was a corridor and, beyond that, the kitchen. This had the same appearance of neatness, with nothing out of place. The old-fashioned red tiles on the floor were polished.

Like the front door, the back door had been bolted, and the Yale catch pushed into the lock position.

Crisp had followed him, but he said nothing. He had worked with Saltfleet for three years; he knew when he was expected to be silent.

He went back to the hallway, looking now for the telephone; it was not there. He found it in the small sitting-room next to the dining-room. The cord that connected it with the wall had been cut off. A pair of kitchen scissors lay on the table beside it.

He asked Crisp: 'Did you close the front door properly?'

'I think so.'

'There's an odd smell upstairs – sort of scent. I don't want it to blow away.'

They went back upstairs, both taking care not to touch the polished surface of the banisters. In the first-floor corridor, Crisp said: ' I think I can smell it now . . . It's probably floor polish.'

They checked the bedrooms, one by one; each one looked neat and unoccupied. The beds had been stripped.

'There ought to be a made-up bed somewhere.'

'Whose?'

'Her nephew, Manfred. She said he worked here. So he probably stayed overnight.'

The next flight of stairs was narrower; it led to what had probably been the servant's living quarters. Saltfleet went up first. The smell there was stronger. Crisp said:

'This place needs a good airing.'

Saltfleet opened the first door opposite the head of the stairs. The curtains flapped as it swung back. In the dim light, Saltfleet could see the bed had been made up.

'This must be it – his bedroom. And somebody's left the window open.' He switched on the light and crossed to the window. As he drew the curtains back, his eye caught the white object on the floor near the bed. He swore with surprise. A pair of feet, the toes pointing upward, were protruding. He dropped on his hands and knees. From there he could see that the man was naked; the face was turned toward him. The mouth was open, as if he had suddenly cried out in pain; the eyes, also open, were glazed. He gave the impression that he had picked up something he thought was cold and found it red hot.

Saltfleet said: 'Go down to the constable at the door. Tell him to get the Scene of Crimes Officer. As quickly as he can.' As Crisp went out, looking shocked and sick, Saltfleet called: 'Tell him to contact the Yard. We'll need Dilnot and Aspinal.'

Saltfleet was in charge of the case; but where corpses were concerned, he had to stick to the rule book. The Scene of Crimes Officer had been trained to observe and record every detail; it was essential that everything should remain untouched until he came. If anything was moved before his arrival, he would have some sharp things to say – even though he was only a detective-constable and Saltfleet was a chief-superintendent. So Saltfleet mastered the temptation to move the bed. Instead, he crouched on the floor, and examined the body with the aid of the pencil flashlight he always carried.

The arms, like the legs, were stretched out, although the fingers of one hand were clawed. It was the body of a man of about fifty, pale-skinned and flabby. The chest was covered with a mat of greyish-black hair. There was no blood, and no apparent cause of death. The body was lying on a black pile rug.

Saltfleet stood up, and moved to a position by the window; from there, he could survey the room carefully. The first thing he noticed was that the floor on the other side of the bed was thick with dust and a few feathers. The bedside table stood on the other side of this dusty area.

The wardrobe door stood partly open. He glanced in; it contained a dressing gown and slippers. There was another

33

door in the corner of the room, slightly ajar. He pushed it open. The smaller room next door seemed to be used as a dressing-room; it contained a wardrobe, a chest of drawers and a divan. On the divan, clothes were laid out neatly: a light grey jacket, trousers, silk shirt, underwear; shoes and socks were on the floor. On the chest of drawers there was a bow tie, and a pair of blue silk pyjamas, with a monogram on the pocket: the intertwined letters formed M.L. An empty dressing-case lay, open, on the floor by the divan. At his feet, there was a smaller zip bag, open; it appeared to contain nothing but a screwed-up paper handkerchief. Saltfleet picked this up; it was stained with lipstick. He dropped it back into the bag.

There was the sound of a car drawing up outside. He went back into the other room and looked out of the window; it was Coventry, with his assistant, Jackson. Crisp went out to meet them. Saltfleet leaned out of the window.

'Morning, George.' Coventry looked up. 'You'd better start down there. We've got a body up here and the Scene of Crimes chap isn't here yet.'

Coventry said: 'Oh, Christ.'

'Try the telephone and the table it's on. Crisp'll show you.'

As he withdrew his head, he heard Coventry say: 'Fine bloody time to find a body.' He knew what he meant. It was the end of any hope of a few hours' break that weekend.

He went into the corridor, closing the door behind him. There were three other doors on this floor. He pulled on his glove, then, using his fingertips, turned the knob of the nearest door. Coventry would want to test the doorknob for fingerprints. The room was a storeroom that had obviously been a nursery at some stage; the walls were decorated with pigs in sailor suits. A glance at the floor told him no one had been in recently.

The door of the next room stood partly ajar; he pushed it open with his foot. It was a small kitchen. On the table there was a loaf of French bread and two bottles of claret. The paper carrier bag on the floor contained more groceries: butter, cheese, stuffed olives in greaseproof paper, a pot of black caviare.

There were footsteps on the stair; it was the Scene of

Crimes Officer, Drake, with his assistant. Crisp came up behind them. Drake said cheerfully:

'Looks as if we should have broken in last night.'

Saltfleet nodded gloomily, acknowledging the implied reproach. 'It's in there.'

The assistant was carrying a camera. Drake said: 'I've got to take my own photographs today – the photographer's off. You coming in?'

'No. I'll check the other rooms.'

Crisp was looking into the kitchen. He said:

'Looks as if somebody intended to make a meal.'

'And for more than one. He'd started to take the food out of the bag when someone interrupted him.'

Again using the gloved tips of his fingers, he opened the door into the third room, and pushed it ajar. The room was bare, except for a double bed and a wardrobe. On the bare mattress there was a pile of clothes. Saltfleet said:

'Ah, that's what I was looking for. The girl's clothes.'

'Shall I call Drake?'

'No, don't interrupt him.'

He picked the clothes up, one by one. There was a tartan suit with a miniskirt, pink sweater, transparent bra, a short underskirt of dark blue nylon, and a narrow suspender belt with white nylon stockings still attached. One of the stockings had been burned; only half of it remained. On the far side of the bed, an electric fire was plugged in to a wall point, but not switched on. The bars were covered with a hardened, treacly material. The lead of the fire ran under the bed, and was plugged in to a point near the door.

Saltfleet went back to the other room. The Scene of Crimes Officer was photographing the body. He had moved the bed aside. Saltfleet waited until he straightened up, then said: 'We've found the girl's clothes. I think she was killed in the next room.'

'Clothes? She was wearing clothes.'

'Not the clothes she came in. She brought that schoolgirl outfit in that bag.' He pointed to the zip bag that was visible through the door of the dressing-room.

Drake moved the bed again, to get a shot of the body from the other side. His assistant was measuring the room.

35

'Do you think he killed her?'

'No. I think that whoever killed him killed her too. He probably killed him first.'

'What makes you think that?'

'He'd moved the bed over the body. You notice the bed must have been over there – from the dust and feathers on the floor? But why should he move the bed over the body?'

'In case someone looked into the room and saw it?'

'Quite. The girl. When she arrived, he was probably already dead. His murderer took her into the next room and told her to get changed.'

Crisp said: 'So he must have known her?'

'Perhaps. Not necessarily.' He beckoned to Drake. 'Come and look.'

Drake followed him into the next room. Saltfleet stood watching as Drake looked slowly round the room, taking in every detail. Drake looked through the clothes on the bed, and held up the suspender belt so the burnt stocking dangled. He pointed to the fire.

'Whoever killed her came up behind her, while she was sitting on the edge of the bed, taking her stockings off. He pulled her backward, and the stocking caught against the bar of the fire.'

Saltfleet nodded. 'Notice the position of the fire. The wall point's on the other side of the bed. But he put the fire over there so she'd sit with her back to the door.'

Drake said: '*If* he worked it out as carefully as that.'

'I think he did. This man thought everything out.'

Drake said: 'But what puzzles me . . . Look, Bob, go and sit on the far side of the bed.' His assistant, a fair-haired youth still in his teens, sat on the bed. Drake said: 'Look, I'm pretty tall. I come in quietly behind her, right? I lean over the bed, while she's leaning forward . . .'

Saltfleet shook his head. 'She's not leaning forward. She's already taken one stocking off. Now she's removing the other, with the suspender belt around her ankles. She's leaning back.'

'All right, then. Lean back, Bob. He grabs her from behind and pulls her backward.' He grabbed his assistant by

36

the throat from behind, and pulled. 'And look what happens.' His assistant doubled up, struggling to sit up. 'She'd drag the burning stocking across the bed, and leave some sort of a mark.'

'That depends. Bob was expecting you to pull him over, so he reacted immediately. She wasn't expecting to be attacked. He probably grabbed her by the hair – remember she had shoulder-length hair? Pulled her backward. And then hit her on the forehead before she knew what was happening. She had a bruise on the left temple.'

Crisp said: 'So he must have been left handed – not right handed, as we thought?'

From down below, a car hooted. Crisp looked out of the window. 'It's Doctor Aspinal.'

Drake's assistant said: 'I can't make out why she was wearing stockings. I don't know any girls who wear stockings now. It's all tights.'

Saltfleet said: 'Prostitutes favour them. I suppose men find them more sexy.' He asked Drake: 'Is it all right if Dr Aspinal comes up to examine the body now?'

'Yes. I've about finished. I'll get some photographs of this room.'

Saltfleet went downstairs. He found Coventry in the hall, carefully dusting fingerprint powder on a polished tabletop.

'Can I go up yet?'

'Yes, but I don't think you'll find anything. This chap was too clever to leave fingerprints.'

Aspinal came in through the open door, preceded by the blonde secretary. Saltfleet said:

'I'm afraid I've ruined your Saturday, Martin.'

'Not at all, I seldom have time to eat lunch anyway. Miss Crowther always keeps a stock of sandwiches.'

Coventry said with disgust: 'Not a bloody thing.' He was examining the tabletop through a magnifying glass.

'Have you tried around the telephone?'

'Not a thing there either.'

Aspinal said: 'Well, I presume you had a reason for sending for me.'

'Good heavens, didn't they tell you? There's another body – a man this time.'

37

'I'm not surprised. Suicide?'

'I don't know. But I don't think so.'

'A double murder? The case becomes complicated.'

Aspinal and his assistant followed Saltfleet upstairs. He asked: 'Can you smell anything?'

'No.'

Miss Crowther said: 'I can. A sort of flowery smell.'

As they mounted the stairs to the second floor, Aspinal said: 'Yes, I can now. What the devil is it?'

'Some sort of incense, I thought.'

He led them into the room. Someone had covered the body with a sheet. Aspinal leaned over and pulled off the sheet, tossing it on to the bed. He stood looking down at the corpse; its shocked expression somehow looked worse in the sunlight. Miss Crowther, Saltfleet noticed, had a look of fascinated repulsion. She opened her handbag, and Saltfleet thought she was fumbling for a handkerchief; but she only produced a notepad.

'Still a certain amount of rigor mortis.' Aspinal knelt down and touched the face of the corpse. 'Body at room temperature. I'd say he's been dead about thirty-six hours. I'll be able to tell you more accurately later.'

He raised the left arm. Its underside was pink, in contrast to the waxy whiteness of its upper surface. 'Normal hypostasis – the body has obviously been in the same position since death.' He bent over and sniffed the lips. Saltfleet asked:

'Poison?'

'No . . . I think not. I thought it might be cyanide – it produces this kind of redness.' He tried to turn the body over. 'He's quite a weight.' Saltfleet knelt down and helped him. The back was the same bluish pink colour as the underside of the arm. Aspinal looked carefully along the full length of the body. 'No sign of a wound.' When they let the body go, it rolled over on its back again. It was like handling a tailor's dummy.

There was a tap on the door; it was D.D.I. Murchison. He was a stocky man with a grey moustache and a deep voice.

'Sorry I wasn't there when you rang. Just got back from Hendon. Anything I can do?'

'Yes. Get the Scene of Crimes Officer's report, then go right through the house with a toothcomb. See if there's any sign of disturbance. At the moment, I need the answers to several questions. Whoever killed him – and the girl – carefully locked the back and front doors from the inside, to discourage anyone getting in, then got out through a bedroom window and closed it behind him with a piece of string. I want to find out why he did that, and why he left one body in the house and took the other outside. Why didn't he leave them both in the house? There must be some clue somewhere.'

'Well I'm damned if I can find it.' It was Coventry; he crossed the room and dumped the fingerprint case on the window-sill. 'I think he wore gloves all the time.'

'I don't think that's likely. I think the murderer spent some time with both victims before he killed them, and they might think it strange if he wore gloves all the time. You may find something in here.'

As Murchison turned to go, Saltfleet said: 'Any luck with this prostitute in South End Green – the one who dresses up?'

Murchison shook his head. 'I checked. She's in Holloway at the moment.'

Aspinal stood up; he told Miss Crowther: 'Phone for an ambulance. Have him taken to our morgue. Nothing more I can do here.'

'Any idea of the cause of death?'

'At the moment, not the slightest. From his expression, it was sudden and violent – that's what made me suspect cyanide. He could have been shot with a small calibre revolver, or even stabbed. He wasn't strangled anyway.'

'I can see that.' Saltfleet looked at the thick neck with distaste.

'Any idea who he is?'

'Yes. A chap called Manfred Lytton. Nephew of the owner of this house.'

'Indeed. That's interesting.'

'Have you heard of him?'

'Vaguely. One hears his name periodically.'

'In what connection?'

39

'I'm not absolutely certain . . . but I think I've heard his name in connection with Giles Gilmour, Franklin Bascombe, that set.'

'No, I don't know. What set?'

'Well, to put it bluntly, rather arty perverts. Gilmour's a novelist – goes in for rather nasty plots, a bit of sadism, a touch of black magic. A lot of his characters get burnt to death, I believe. Bascombe's a publisher and art collector, homosexual, with a taste for very young boys. Madge Rickwood's another of that group – rather weird lesbian.'

Saltfleet noted down the names, getting Aspinal to spell them. Aspinal was inserting a thermometer into the anus of the dead man when Coventry came in from the dressing-room.

'I've found a couple of prints on the handle of the bag – the girl's, I suppose. Otherwise, he seems to have done a pretty thorough job on wiping all the prints. What are you going to do about the clothes in there?'

'Send them to the forensic lab.' He told Crisp: 'Get them sealed in plastic bags – the girl's clothes too – and get them back to the yard. I'll get a lift with Dr Aspinal.'

Aspinal was peering at the dead man's chest from a few inches away. 'I need more light.'

'No sign of a stab wound?'

'None.'

Miss Crowther said: 'Could he have killed the girl, then died of a heart attack?'

Saltfleet shook his head.

'I'm pretty sure he died first. If he died about thirty-six hours ago, that makes it about one o'clock Friday morning. You said the girl died a few hours later.'

'Not much later. Incidentally, she'd eaten a meal some hours before she died – a rather distinctive meal.' Saltfleet took out his notebook. 'Herring salad, liver dumpling, sauerkraut, haricot beans. She'd also had some kind of orange cake. She'd eaten the meal about seven hours before she died – about nine in the evening probably.'

'German?'

'That would be my guess.'

'There aren't all that many German restaurants in London. We could get a photograph of her and see if anyone recognizes it.'

Aspinal withdrew the thermometer and examined it against the light. 'About five degrees above room temperature, but he was a fat man, so that's not unusual.' He dropped the thermometer in its metal case. 'Must remember not to put that in anyone's mouth.' Miss Crowther said: 'The ambulance is here.'

Aspinal said: 'Good. Are you ready to leave, Gregory?'

'Can you give me a couple of minutes? I want to talk to my C.I.D. man.'

He found Murchison in the room next door, examining the window catches.

'Listen Frank, there's got to be a green Aston Martin, sports model, parked somewhere in this area. It belonged to the dead man. Get your men to find it. Those kids hanging around the gate might have seen it.' He handed Murchison the keys. 'When you've finished, lock the place up and hang on to these. If you need me, I'll be back at the Yard in half an hour.'

He found Coventry in the kitchen, dusting a wine bottle for fingerprints; he was using a camel-hair brush to spread the fingerprint powder. He stood watching, while Coventry turned the bottle in the light of the window. He sighed. 'Not a damn thing. He must have spent at least an hour wiping off fingerprints.'

Aspinal stood by the table, looking at the food.

'He had good taste. Russian caviare. And the wine's Château Palmer. Evidently he intended to do something that would give him an appetite.'

'I think I can guess what.'

'Which reminds me. We have a bottle of Médoc in the car. Not up to this standard, but acceptable. I'm sure you need a drink.'

Three

Miss Crowther drove. Aspinal opened the leather-bound drink case; its three compartments contained a bottle of whisky, a bottle of brandy and a bottle of claret. He opened the wine, while Saltfleet ate an anchovy sandwich. Miss Crowther drove down East Heath Road, taking it slowly; the sight of the trees reflected in the water of Hampstead Ponds brought a twinge of nostalgia. Aspinal handed him wine in a metal cup.

'You once worked in this area, didn't you, Gregory?'

'That's right. 1954 to 1957.' They had stopped on the corner of South Hill Park, to allow a brewery lorry to pass. 'I was on duty the day Ruth Ellis shot David Blakely outside that pub there – 1955. And do you remember the Christophi case – the half-mad Greek woman who killed her daughter-in-law? That happened in a flat on the other side of the road.'

'Didn't she try to burn the body on a bonfire?'

'That's right. In the back garden, in full view of the neighbours. One of the neighbours thought it was a tailor's dummy on the fire.'

Aspinal said: 'Another sandwich?'

'Thanks. This is a nice wine.' He set the cup down on the small table that opened from the rear of the front seat. 'Both nice, straightforward cases. I wish this one was.'

'Isn't it? It doesn't seem very complicated to me.'

'Really?' Saltfleet chewed the sandwich, waiting.

'The girl was obviously a prostitute, specializing in customers with a yen for schoolgirls. Your murdered man was probably a pervert with a taste for schoolgirls. What does that suggest?'

It was Miss Crowther who said: 'Blackmail?'

'Quite. I would guess that the murderer's a blackmailer. At least, I think that's a good working hypothesis.'

'Then why should he kill him?'

'It was probably unpremeditated. He went to the house

42

expecting to extort money. There was a quarrel, and he killed Lytton – perhaps Lytton threatened to go to the police. He's just preparing to leave when there's a ring at the door bell – the girl has arrived. He could ignore it, of course. But if she's expected, then she'll wonder what has happened. She'll make inquiries. Lytton's body might be found within a matter of hours. There's only one thing to do – to let her in and kill her too. There is another possibility, of course – that she had a key to the house, and let herself in. In either case, she had to die.'

Miss Crowther said: 'Then why couldn't he leave both the bodies in the house?'

Aspinal poured himself more wine; he was enjoying himself. Miss Crowther was not aware of it, but this was a long-standing game he played with Saltfleet. It consisted in pretending that the police were hopelessly pedestrian, and that any crime could be solved with a little brilliant armchair theorizing, in the manner of Poe's Dupin.

'That is a little more difficult.' Saltfleet recognized his cue, and smiled sarcastically. 'It has to be approached logically. We know he carefully locked the house, and tried to give the impression that no one had been inside . . .'

'Except for the upstairs window,' Saltfleet pointed out. 'He left that open.'

'But that was hardly visible from the drive below. I noticed as we came out . . . Or perhaps he simply forgot about it. So he locked the house. He didn't want Lytton's body to be discovered . . . at least, not immediately. Which seems to point to two conclusions. One: he needed time – time to escape. He's probably on his way out of the country by now.' Saltfleet nodded gloomily; he had already reached that conclusion. 'Second: that the murderer should be known to some of Lytton's friends. Otherwise, he wouldn't bother to flee. You shouldn't have too much difficulty identifying your murderer. It may be more difficult to catch him.'

Miss Crowther said: 'But if he dumped the girl outside, he was inviting somebody to come and look in the house.'

Saltfleet said: 'Not necessarily. I wouldn't have been in any hurry to search the house if it hadn't been for the telephone.' He told Aspinal: 'When you said she'd been strangled with the telephone wire, I tried ringing the house. The phone was out of order.'

'Another proof that the murder wasn't premeditated. Otherwise he'd have taken a piece of rope to the house to strangle her.'

Saltfleet said: 'I agree but – it still doesn't explain why he didn't leave her where she was . . .'

'Unless, of course, he meant to take the body to some other place. Let us suppose, for example, that he had a car or van outside the house. He was carrying the body towards it when he thought he heard someone coming. He drops the body, leaps into the car, and drives off . . .'

Saltfleet said: 'Without leaving any tyre marks in the loose stones? Besides, he wouldn't carry the body across to the car. He'd back the car up to the front door, then put the body in the boot. So why was it twenty yards from the house?'

'Which takes us back to our first hypothesis – he had to separate the bodies for some reason . . .'

The car turned into the yard of University College. The ambulance was already there; the men were transferring the body, covered with a blanket, on to a trolley. Miss Crowther said:

'Would you like me to run you to the Yard? Or are you coming in?'

Saltfleet asked Aspinal: 'Do you intend to make another examination now?'

'Of course.'

'Then I'll come and watch, if I may.'

The post-mortem room looked like an operating theatre, with its white tiles and powerful adjustable lamps. One of its two tables was already in use; a young coloured doctor was bending over the abdominal cavity of an old woman. Her face was invisible, since the scalp had been pulled forward over the forehead; grey locks straggled out from under it, as from under a cap. The top of the skull had been removed, and the brain pan was empty. The brains were on a scale at

44

the end of the table. The young doctor saluted Aspinal respectfully. He said:

'You were right about the septicaemia.'

'Of course. I've seen those abcesses on the gums before.' He glanced down into the cavity. 'Pyelonephritis too, I see. No wonder she needed so much morphine.' He removed his coat and hung it on a locker, then donned a white smock. The trolley with the other body stood by the second table. Aspinal asked Saltfleet: 'Would you take the feet?' Together they slid the corpse on to the white-enamelled post-mortem table, the head towards the rounded end. Aspinal dropped the blanket on to the trolley. The upper lip of the body had caught against the teeth, giving the face a wolfish appearance. Looking at him, Saltfleet was again struck by the sheer deadness of dead bodies, the discarded appearance. Aspinal reached up and switched on the light, which extended from the ceiling on a long metal arm. He trained it on the face and began to examine it closely, peering at the skull through the thinning hair, raising the eyelids one by one, looking into the ears with an auriscope, and afterwards into the mouth.

'Nothing much. Contraction of the pupils. I'd like to look at the brain . . .'

He moved the light on to the chest, and began to examine it minutely through a large magnifying glass. He said: 'Aha.' He handed Saltfleet the glass. 'Come and look.'

Saltfleet bent over, peering at the spot above the heart that Aspinal had been examining. He pushed aside the greying chest hair. In the powerful light, the tiny puncture was immediately visible. It looked like a bruise, less than a quarter of an inch in diameter, with a V-shaped red line at its centre.

Aspinal said: 'Miss Crowther, go and get my instruments.' He took back the glass.

Saltfleet said nothing; he stood watching. Aspinal prodded the wound gently with his fingertips, then raised his head, staring at the opposite wall as he gently pressed and kneaded the flesh; Saltfleet observed again how long his fingers were.

The coloured doctor came over to watch. Aspinal said: 'Dr Rizal, would you mind telling me if you can feel anything?' Rizal pinched the flesh on either side of the wound, then probed the centre of the V with his little finger, pressing up and down.

'I would say . . . there is something there.' Evidently the presence of the great pathologist inhibited him.

Saltfleet had been struck by a sudden insight as he looked at the wound. The man who had committed these two murders was no amateur. This was not the first time he had killed.

Miss Crowther returned with the flat leather case. Aspinal selected from its array of polished instruments a pair of long forceps whose end tapered to a point. He pressed them into the wound, probing, still looking at the opposite wall, working by the sense of touch. He smiled imperceptibly, guiding the tip of the forceps with his left hand; then he gripped and pulled. Saltfleet watched, fascinated, as the thin metal spike came slowly out of the wound. 'From the angle, I should imagine it penetrated the left ventricle.' Aspinal held it up against the light. It was about three inches long and sharply pointed. At first glance, Saltfleet took it to be circular, like an ice-pick; but on looking closer, he saw that it had four flat surfaces.

'An awl?'

'I'd say so. The kind you could buy in any Woolworth's.'

Aspinal laid it on the white enamel in front of Saltfleet. Saltfleet leaned forward and peered at it. He took out a paper handkerchief, and wiped a drop of blood off its blunt end. The surface of the end was irregular.

'Snapped off in the wound, it seems. On purpose, would you say?'

'Probably not. It's not tempered steel. It probably snapped as he stabbed him.' He made a downward motion of his right hand, slowly, as if driving a blade into flesh. 'He was probably gripping it too tight.' Miss Crowther shuddered; it was the first time Saltfleet had seen her react strongly.

'Was he standing up or lying down when he was stabbed?'

'Lying down, almost certainly. From the angle of the wound. He's a tall man, six foot I'd guess. Unless the man who killed him was a dwarf – stabbing him from below – the blade would have entered at an angle of forty-five degrees if he'd been standing.' He crossed to the sink and washed his hands.

'Have you finished?'

'I think so. You know how he died.'

'I don't know why he lay down naked and allowed himself to be stabbed. He must have been conscious or his face wouldn't look so awful.'

'Presumably he wasn't expecting it. Your murderer was probably a masseur . . .' He called to a porter who looked around the door: 'Oh Barnes, don't go. I'd like you to stick this chap into refrigeration for me.'

Miss Crowther dropped him at the Yard. He asked the Duty Sergeant: 'Is the governor in?'

'No, sir. He's gone home.'

Although Lamb's office was in the new building, he still parked his car behind the old Yard.

His office was pleasantly cool; Crisp had opened the window to its limit, letting in an easterly breeze that seemed to smell of the sea. Crisp was looking through more criminal record sheets.

'Here's a likely looking chap. Been in gaol twice in Trinidad for molesting schoolgirls, now living in Camden Town . . .'

Saltfleet sat down heavily in his chair.

'Forget it. I doubt whether this chap's a rapist. The rape may have been an afterthought. We're more probably dealing with a blackmailer. Have you checked missing persons?'

'Ten minutes ago. They'll ring us if they get anything that sounds like her.'

'Get on to the Kilkenny police again . . .'

'I've already done it. Half an hour ago. I told them to notify Lady whatsername that they'd found her nephew in the house.'

'Good. Ring Mabel and see if I can have a cup of coffee.'

'How about a sandwich?'

'Had one with Aspinal, thanks. Did you get those clothes to forensic?'

'Yes.'

'Good. I've got another item for them.' He dropped the

47

small plastic bag on his desk; it made a clinking sound.

'What's that?'

'The spike that killed Lytton. It'd snapped off in his heart.'

While Crisp rang the canteen, he held the bag by its corner against the light. 'Not much to go on, is it? The kind of thing my wife uses for making moccasins. You can buy them anywhere.'

'And he's probably burnt the handle by this time. Still, it might turn up. Remember the Potter's Bar case.'

It had been the first murder case on which Crisp had worked with Saltfleet. The end of a knife had been found lodged between the vertebrae in the dead man's back. The forensic lab. – it was in Hendon at the time – said it came from a long knife that had been repeatedly sharpened. Saltfleet and Crisp had tried every butcher for miles around before they found one whose steak knife had disappeared on the day before the murder. The butcher's assistant – who had left at the same time – confessed to the murder; he had stabbed the victim as he sat in the kitchen chair.

'But we never found that knife, did we? He threw it away.'

'No. He hammered it into the turf of the golf course, and couldn't remember where. And we couldn't find it without ruining the course . . .'

He rang his wife as he drank the coffee.

'Look, I'm sorry, my dear, but you and Geraldine will have to go to Shepperton alone. I thought I might be able to get Murchison to take over, but it's hopeless. We've found another body. The guv'nor'll want me to stay on it now.'

'Whose body?'

'Oh, a chap called Manfred Lytton. I'll hope to be home before seven anyway.'

'Manfred Lytton? Isn't he the one who's mixed up in black magic?'

He was suddenly alert. 'Where did you hear that?'

'I'm fairly sure . . . It was in one of the Sunday papers. I used it for lining a cupboard – I saw it the other day.'

'Could you look it up now? And I'll get on to the newspaper.'

'I'd rather ring you back – I might have to search every

48

cupboard and drawer in the house.'

'All right, don't bother. Ring back if you find it. I should be back in the office later.'

When he hung up, Crisp said: 'Going out again?'

He sighed. 'Afraid so. I'll have to go and see this Mrs Beaumont Ames, and tell her her employer's dead.'

'She's probably guessed as much already.'

'I don't know . . . I'm inclined to doubt it.'

He found a parking space two blocks from Burnsall Street. Now he was feeling the faint tingling excitement that always came when a case began to grip him. He had a feeling that he was about to learn something.

He gave one short ring at the doorbell. Almost immediately, he heard her feet on the stairs, as if she had been expecting him. As she opened the door, she avoided his eyes.

He said: 'Shall we go in?'

She led him upstairs. He was aware of her nervousness, and he played on it.

'Do you have a photograph of your employer?'

Without speaking, she went into the next room, and returned a moment later, handing him a studio portrait in a frame. The face that looked out at him seemed younger, and was distinctly handsome; but it was certainly the man who now lay in Aspinal's freezer. Saltfleet examined the face for several seconds. It might have been an agency portrait of an actor; the eyelids were large, the eyes rather fine, distinctly romantic, Rudolph Valentino and that kind of thing. But the mouth was the giveaway, weak, with downturned corners, producing a sharkish impression. He looked a little too flabby, too soft, to be the great lover.

Saltfleet placed the photograph carefully on the desk. He said casually: 'I'd like you to come and identify the body.'

From the look of shock, he knew this was not what she had been expecting. It took her a moment to get her breath.

'He's dead?'

'Yes, he's dead.'

She took a very deep breath, then seemed to get control of herself.

'How did he die?'

49

'He was found stabbed – in the house in Hampstead. We found the girl outside in the garden – you know about that.' He had noticed a copy of the midday paper on the armchair. 'Have you any idea who killed him?'

She stared at the carpet, then shook her head.

'I don't know what he meant to do that day.' She sat down in the armchair. In spite of the attempt at self-control, he could see she was shaken.

'What about the girl? You know who she was, don't you?'

Without speaking, she stood up and went to the desk. She opened the top drawer, and took out a sheet of paper torn from a scratch-pad. On it was written neatly in pencil: Mary Threlwall, 12 Grafton Mews, Maple St, W.1.' There was also a telephone number.

'Why didn't you tell me this before?'

She made a querulous attempt at protest.

'I didn't know it was the same girl, did I?'

He grunted, placing the paper, folded, in his wallet.

'You thought he'd killed her, didn't you?'

She shrugged. 'Suppose I did?'

'You'd have been an accessory after the fact.'

She said rebelliously: 'You don't know *what* I thought.'

'It makes no difference anyway.' He sat in the chair opposite her, smiling to reassure her. 'We ought to understand one another. I don't think you've got anything to do with these murders. And in that case, you've nothing to lose by frankness. You help us and and we'll help you.'

His instinct had been sound; he had sensed that, under the hard exterior, she was feeling frightened. Now he could see her relax. She looked him directly in the eyes for the first time.

'I've nothing to be afraid of.'

'Of course you haven't. The girl was a prostitute, wasn't she?'

'Sort of. Not a pro.' She reached for a cigarette.

'Then what was she?'

'She called herself an art student, but I don't think she was still at art school. She was on drugs.'

'Where did she get the schoolgirl clothes?'

50

She looked surprised. 'I don't know. She had several customers.'

'Men who liked schoolgirls?'

She breathed in smoke with relief.

'That was her thing. The innocent virgin.'

'And your employer, Mr Lytton? He liked schoolgirls?'

She laughed. 'That was *his* thing. He loved them. Everything about them.' She opened the bottom drawer of the desk and took out an envelope. Saltfleet shook it on to the desk top. The photographs that fell out were what he had expected, the kind of thing that can be bought in almost any capital in Europe. In the strictest sense, they were not obscene; only the age of the children made them so. They were of girls of about twelve in gym slips and knickers, or getting undressed. The photographer had shown some ingenuity in the angles of the shots. Saltfleet turned one over; it was stamped with the address of a photographer in Copenhagen.

She said: 'He'd got others – worse than that.'

'And your job was to try and find him girls like this?'

She shrugged, pulling a wry face at him. She was completely at ease now.

'Where'd you think I'd find them? I'd soon land in gaol.'

'Then what *was* your job?'

'Oh, let's say, to look after him.'

'Which involved . . . what?'

She stood up restively, and walked to the window.

'Look, I told you. It wasn't just schoolgirls he liked. He was a very peculiar bloke.'

'What else did he like?' He had already guessed, but he did not intend to prompt her.

She opened a cupboard in the corner of the room. From the back of a shelf she took a black-bound book. Saltfleet took it from her. It was the carbon of a typescript. The title page read: 'The Ceremony of Innocence'. He turned to the opening page. *'This morning I had the most exquisite experience of my life. I shall tell it from the beginning. I woke up seething with lust, with an inexpressible, languid sweetness in the area of my loins. I had been dreaming of delicate white bottoms, reddening under the blows of a switch . . .'* Saltfleet glanced quickly over the next dozen

51

pages; the writer described a visit to a Hampstead girls' school to watch the headmistress administer the weekly flogging to the pupils. At the climax of the scene, he stands naked in the headmistress's study, watching through the keyhole as the girls are stripped and birched, while the assistant house mother, a woman with muscular arms, anoints his genitals and behind with cold cream.

Saltfleet looked at the title page. It was written by 'Robin Piggott-Smythe'.

'Did he write this stuff?'

'Yes.'

He turned to the end of the chapter. The hero was lying on the floor, being birched by the headmistress, while two sixth-form girls trampled on him with high-heeled shoes. Saltfleet had to repress a chuckle.

'He's no Dickens.'

She gave a stifled laugh.

'He's got a publisher friend who says it's real literature. He's going to bring it out.'

'Frank Bascombe?'

She looked surprised. 'Yes.' She was obviously wondering how much else he knew.

'So he liked being flogged?'

She sighed. 'Don't they all.' But the tone of ennui was overdone.

'Did you have to beat him?'

She laughed at him, raising her eyebrows flirtatiously; for a moment she was pretty.

'Oh, that was only one of the things. Incidentally, he never called me his housekeeper. It was always "house mother". He loved his little games.'

He wanted to ask if she had enjoyed it, but could think of no way of saying it. He asked: 'Didn't you mind?'

She looked almost surprised.

'Mind? At the money he paid me? I'd have been dotty. He didn't do anybody any harm. If he hadn't been rich, he'd have bought dirty books round behind Leicester Square and rubbed up against schoolgirls in the Underground. He could afford to pay for what he liked . . .'

'What made you think he'd killed Mary Threlwall?'

He had chosen his moment, when she was being frank. She glanced at him sideways, made up her mind, and said :

'I don't think he'd do it on purpose. But I've known him to get carried away.' She was pouring herself a gin. 'Sure you won't have one?' He shook his head. 'It's the way they play it. She has to pretend not to like it. They're supposed to be in a park, and he takes her in the bushes and tells her he's a doctor. You know the sort of thing . . . She has to keep on saying : "Oh please stop it. I'll tell my mother." That's what really got him excited. And he'd end by holding her down while he did it. Sometimes he held them by the throat. He had made one girl's eyes all bloodshot.'

He strolled restlessly around the room, looking into bookcases.

'Any idea who might have wanted to kill him?'

'One or two people didn't like him much. Frank Bascombe could tell you more about that. But I can't think of anybody who wanted to *kill* him.'

'Can you think of anybody who might have been blackmailing him?'

'What for? He wasn't doing anything against the law.'

'Didn't he ever try to get real schoolgirls?'

'Not in London. I think he did abroad.'

'Where?'

'Oh, Algiers, that sort of place.'

He stood beside her, looking out of the window.

'Did you send that girl to Hampstead?'

She hesitated a moment; he could see that telling the truth was not an ingrained habit with her; but the momentum of her frankness carried her on.

'Yes – I gave her the address.'

'Where was he earlier that day?'

'I'm not sure. He was supposed to go for a drink in Fleet Street – the Wig and Pen Club. Then he was due to meet Frank Bascombe for lunch. I think he was going up to Hampstead in the afternoon to do a bit of work . . . on his book, you know. The girl was supposed to be there at eleven o'clock and stay the night.'

'Why not here?'

'Too many nosy neighbours.'

'Did he know the girl already?'

'No.'

'Did you know her?'

'Yes.'

'How?'

She shrugged. 'That's my job. I've got a lot of friends around Soho.'

'And you heard about her?'

'Yes, from a friend. There were two girls in this flat near Fitzroy Square. They'd been on a cruise of the Med. with a pop singer, Johnny Bianci, and got hooked on drugs.'

'What drugs?'

'I'm not sure – could have been heroin, or just purple hearts . . . that sort of thing. They weren't pros, but they needed the money.'

'Did they have a ponce?'

'God, no. They were both scared stiff of getting into the hands of the Maltese brothers or something. My friend told me this girl looked about fourteen. That's why she'd gone on this trip – Bianci likes very young girls. But she wasn't a pro. When I told her Manny'd pay fifty quid for a night, she came and gave me a big kiss – came and hugged me. That's how glad she was.'

'What was the name of her friend?'

'Sheila something. I can't remember her other name.'

He wrote it down. 'Now let's get this clear. He left here some time before eleven o'clock on Thursday morning, and he told you he wouldn't be back until the next day?'

'No. He never told me anything. He didn't like to feel anybody expected him. He was always late for appointments because he said he felt trapped as soon as he had to be anywhere on time.'

'Was there anybody else who might have gone to the Hampstead house – anybody who shared his tastes?'

She shook her head. 'I don't know. You ought to talk to Frank Bascombe. He knew more than I did about that side of his life.'

She was obviously lying again, but he let it go.

Saltfleet sat looking at the bookcase opposite his eyes. There were titles like *Our Bible and the Ancient Manu-*

scripts, The Bible as History, Palestine Before the Hebrews.
He tried a question at random.

'Was he religious?'

She gave a high-pitched squeak of laughter. 'God, no.' She followed his gaze to the bookcase. 'He was interested in ancient things – archaeology, magic . . .'

'Magic?'

'He's got dozens of books on that.' She pointed towards the other room.

'Could I see?'

It was a small study or 'den', with two armchairs, a table, and the wall completely lined with bookshelves. On the table there was a skull with red eyes; when he looked more closely he saw they were semi-precious stones cemented in the eye-sockets. There was a round hole in the top of the skull, with a crack on either side of it.

'Somebody gave him a bash.'

'It's the skull of a murdered man. I don't know where he got it.'

The books on the shelves seemed to be mostly on magic and occultism: Frazer's *Golden Bough* in twelve volumes, *Magick in Theory and Practice* by Aleister Crowley, books on ghosts, vampires and poltergeists. There was also a case devoted to pornography, with titles like *Adventures of an Amorous Quaker, The New Ladies' Tickler*.

By the side of the armchair, on the carpet, there were four books bound in blue leather, with silver lettering. He picked up the top volume: *The Golden Dawn*, by F. I. Regardie. It was on expensive paper with colour illustrations. Between its pages there was a receipt; the sum at the bottom startled him: £305. The date, he noticed, was three days earlier: 21 April – the day before Lytton died. The address of the book-shop was printed at the top of the receipt: The Occult Book-shop, Red Lion Square, Holborn. Underneath, written with a ballpoint pen: Four vols Regardie: £100; 3 vols Crowley, *Equinox*, £215. Discount for cash: £10.

He folded it up. 'I'll take this, if I may.' He looked around the room. 'Any idea where the other books are – Crowley?' He was curious to see whether they were magic or pornography.

'I expect they're in his bedroom.'

'It doesn't matter.' But she had already gone. A moment later, she came back. 'No, that's odd. They were on the floor. He must have taken them out with him. They don't seem to be on the shelf either.'

'He took them out on the day he disappeared?'

'I suppose so. I'm not . . .'

'Why should he do that?'

'Perhaps he took them to the binder.'

'Do you have the address?'

'It's a man called Craigie, near the British Museum. He's in the phone book.' As Saltfleet reached out for the telephone directory, she said: 'I don't suppose he'll be able to tell you much.'

'Probably not. But we've got to trace his movements on the day he died . . .' He noted the address: 19A Bedford Square. 'What will you do now your employer's dead?'

'I don't know. Talk to Lady Edgton about staying on here.'

'She's his next of kin?'

'Yes.'

He closed the notebook. 'Thank you for your help, Mrs Beaumont Ames.'

'Is that all?'

'For now, yes. Could you come to University College on Monday to identify the body?'

She said gloomily: 'I suppose so. What time?'

'Eleven o'clock?'

'All right.' She was obviously relieved to see him go. He suspected she was holding something back. This didn't worry him. She would think about it after he'd gone, wondering if he'd find out anyway. Next time, she might tell him without too much urging.

Four

Crisp was hanging up the telephone as he walked into the office.

'Anything happening, Steve?'

'Yes. They've found the car – WP forty stroke ninety, green Aston Martin. It was parked a couple of streets away. Woman in the house said it's been there for two days.'

'Anything in it?'

'No. Usual tools, that's all.'

'No books?'

'No. He'd have mentioned them.'

'Get forensic to look at it. I'd like all the fingerprints checked. It's just possible he drove there with the man who killed him.'

Crisp said dubiously: 'Not very likely.'

'I know. But we've got to check. At the moment we've no leads – none at all.'

'Something's bound to turn up. It can't be long before they identify the girl.'

'I've done it.' He pulled out his notebook. 'Her name's Mary Threlwall. Art student. This woman, Beaumont Ames, sent her to the house to spend the night with Lytton. But that doesn't help much. It's a hundred-to-one chance against her knowing her killer . . . Have we heard from Lytton's aunt – Lady Edgton?'

'Not yet.'

Saltfleet pulled the phone toward him. "That's next on the agenda.' He asked the switchboard for the Kilkenny number, and hung up.

'Was this Beaumont Ames woman helpful this time?'

'Oh, as far as she could be, I suppose. She said she couldn't imagine who'd want to kill him. But I found one thing . . .' The telephone rang, startling him; he found it difficult to get used to the efficiency of the switchboard since most of the Yard staff had moved to the new building. 'Hello, could I speak to Lady Edgton, please?'

A moment later the precise voice snapped: 'Hello, who's speaking?'

'Chief-Superintendent Saltfleet. Have you heard about your nephew?'

'I've been told he's dead. Is that true?'

'I'm afraid it is.'

'Can you tell me how he died?'

Saltfleet hesitated, half-inclined to claim ignorance for the moment; then he decided she could take it.

'He was stabbed in the heart.'

There was a long silence. Saltfleet said: 'Hello?'

She said quietly: 'I see . . .' There was another pause, then: 'Have you any idea who . . . who was responsible?'

'Not yet, I'm afraid. I thought you might be able to offer us some kind of lead.'

'But I can't. I know nothing about my nephew's private life. Nothing whatever.' Her emphasis surprised him.

'I see. Did you know that he'd belonged to a witchcraft cult at one time?'

'I knew there was an article about it in one of the Sunday newspapers. But he told me it was all a joke.' After a pause, she said: 'He's a grown man . . . There was nothing I could do.'

'No, of course.'

'And what happens now? Do you want me to come and identify him?'

'That won't be necessary. His housekeeper, Mrs Beaumont Ames, can do that.'

'She's still with him, is she? He told me she'd left.'

'When was that, ma'am?'

'Oh . . . it must have been a year ago. I think he caught her out in some dishonesty.'

'I see.'

'I suppose I'd better come to London anyway. Shall I be able to make arrangements for the funeral?'

'Oh, certainly. You'll have to apply to the Home Office to have the body released. It becomes state property for the course of the investigation.'

'Yes, of course . . .' She sounded faraway. 'What a good thing his mother isn't alive.'

'Yes, ma'am.'

'And . . . I don't wish to tell you your job . . . but I would-n't advise you to trust that woman. She's a pathological liar.'

'I'll remember that, ma'am. Perhaps you'll contact me when you get into London?'

'Yes, yes . . .' There was a pause, then she said explosively, as if no longer able to contain it: 'He was such a *silly* man.' The line went dead. Saltfleet shook his head, then hung up.

Crisp asked: 'Upset?'

'No, not really.' He stared out of the window. 'I got the feeling she wasn't surprised. She said she didn't want to know about his private life – which sounds as if she had a pretty good idea of what went on . . .' He sat down, drumming his fingers on his desk. 'Well, that doesn't get us any further forward, does it? I've never known such a case.'

'What now?'

'I've one or two things more to check up.' He looked at his watch. 'You can take the rest of the day off. I know you like to take the wife out on Saturday.'

'Thank you, Chief.'

The telephone rang; it was the Public Information Officer's assistant. The *Sunday Express* had heard about the finding of a man's body in the house; would he confirm it, and how much did he want to tell the press? Saltfleet said: 'Tell them it's true, but I'd like it kept quiet for the moment – you know, information that might interfere with an inquiry in progress.' Saltfleet's relations with the press were excellent; publication of photographs and calls for information – 'the police wish to interview . . .' – had been crucial in solving many of his cases. The men in the press room knew he would always give the fullest information; and, in turn, they made sure there were no inconvenient leaks when Saltfleet had something he wanted to withhold.

He parked his car in the courtyard of the British Museum – a privilege he had gained by arresting Huevelmans, the thief of the Sahidic Codex of the Acts of the Apostles – and walked to Bedford Square. 19A was a basement; the front door stood open. There was a fragrant smell that he recognized as gum arabic. When he rang the bell, a short man in a leather apron limped to the door.

'Mr Craigie? I'm a police officer. I'm making inquiries about a Mr Manfred Lytton. Have you done work for him?'

'Ay.' He said it cautiously.

'Did he bring some books to be bound last Wednesday?'

He thought he detected a look of relief. 'No, I haven't seen him for a week or two.'

'You sure of that?'

'Quite sure. I've got some books for him to collect.'

'Could I see them?'

'Hold on a minute.' He was gone for several minutes. Saltfleet didn't mind the wait; it was pleasant to lean against the doorpost in the sunlight. Craigie came back with the three leather-bound volumes. Saltfleet recognized the wine-coloured bindings; he had seen identical bindings on Lytton's shelves. He glanced at the titles: *The Kabbalah Unveiled, Into the Occult, Cagliostro.*

'Do you bind many books for Mr Lytton?'

'Quite a few.'

'Mostly on magic?'

'Mostly.'

'Some on pornography as well?'

He got a defensive, hostile look.

'Sometimes.'

He said soothingly: 'That's all right. It's not against the law.' At least he had established why Craigie had seemed nervous. 'How many years had Mr Lytton been interested in magic?'

'Three or four.'

Saltfleet turned away. 'Thank you, Mr Craigie.'

'Is Mr Lytton . . . in trouble?'

Saltfleet decided it would make no difference if he told him. He said: 'Sort of. He's dead.'

One side of Grafton Mews was occupied by the rear end of a big store; opposite this there were garages, with flats above them. The door of number twelve had been newly painted blue. He pressed the bell, and heard it ring upstairs. No one came. A cat rubbed itself against his leg, mewing. He rang again, then stepped back from the door and looked up. A face disappeared from the window above. A door upstairs opened and there were footsteps on the stairs. The door opened six inches; the girl's face looked out cautiously above the doorchain.

'Is your name Sheila?' She nodded. 'I want to talk to you about Mary Threlwall.'

She went pale. 'Where is she?'

'I'm afraid she's dead.'

She stood staring at him, as if she failed to understand. Her face was not pretty, but the eyes were exceptionally large, making her seem a child. Then she said: 'Oh God, no,' She looked as if she were about to burst into tears, the lips twitching.

'May I come in?'

She unhooked the chain and opened the door. She was wearing a red dressing-gown; her feet were bare. She had obviously been in bed.

He followed her upstairs. He noticed she had a large purplish-brown bruise at the back of her left leg. The stair carpet was shabby but well brushed.

The walls of the room were papered with black wallpaper with red tinsel stars; the ceiling had been painted red; it made him think of a night club. There were two single beds in the room, one made, one unmade. The girl's clothes were lying on the armchair; he noted automatically that her underwear was there too, and that therefore she was probably naked under the dressing-gown. He observed also the man's tie that had fallen on the floor behind the armchair. On the far side of the room, a door opened into a kitchen, which looked as shabby and untidy as the living-room; beyond that there was another door, probably leading to the bathroom.

She sat down nervously on a wooden chair at the table.

'How did she die?' She asked it quickly; her fingers were trembling as she took a cigarette from her handbag.

'She was strangled.'

He was afraid she was going to cry or have hysterics, but she controlled herself. Without looking at him she said: 'If you want to know who did it, it was a man called Lytton, Charles Lytton.'

'Is that Manfred Lytton?'

'Yes.'

'He's dead too. Any more ideas?'

She turned the blank, uncomprehending stare on him.

'I don't . . . you must be wrong. How can he be?'

He said patiently: 'He was murdered. They were both killed by the same person, or persons.' He paused a moment to let it sink in. 'Can you think who might have been responsible?'

She shook her head dumbly.

'Why were you so sure Lytton killed her?'

'He . . . he liked hurting people. I warned her about him.'

'How did you know about him? Had you met him?' She nodded. 'How?' He had to repeat it: 'How did you meet him?'

'A woman came here. She offered me money to go to his house.'

'What did she ask you to do?'

'I had to take schoolgirl clothes . . .'

'Did you go to the house in Hampstead?' She nodded. 'When was this?'

'About . . . two weeks ago.'

'What happened then?'

'He came here to collect me. That's when he saw Mary . . . We drove to the house.'

He interrupted: 'Did he park outside?'

'No. He parked in the next street. He said the woman next door kept a watch on him . . .' Saltfleet nodded; that solved the problem of why the car was parked so far away. 'Then we went in and . . . what else do you want to know?'

'What did he make you do?'

She began to cough with the cigarette smoke. When she stopped, he repeated the question. While she hesitated, he heard a faint sound from the other side of the kitchen: the creak of the bathroom door. He said: 'Is there somebody in there?'

'Yes. My . . . my husband.'

A voice from the bathroom called: 'Who is it?' The man

62

had evidently heard the question. A moment later, he looked round the door. It was a good-looking, scarred face.

She said: 'It's about Mary. She's dead.'

'Oh no!' The man came out of the bathroom, across the kitchen. 'I am sorry to hear that.' He had a strong French accent. He was a big man, who had once had the figure of an athlete. Now he was running to middle-aged fat; but he still looked powerful, with a graceful movement that emphasized the hips. The white shirt he wore was immaculate, the sleeves held up by gold-plated bands. The grey trousers were knife-edged. Saltfleet noticed that he was carrying his jacket; evidently he had taken his clothes into the bathroom to dress. He spoke with perfunctory concern. From the air of casual self-confidence, it was clear he was a ladies' man. His voice was a pleasant baritone.

Saltfleet said: 'I understand you are this young lady's husband?'

The man looked surprised, and the girl blushed.

'No. My name is Taupin – Pierre Taupin.' He saw his tie, and picked it up quickly; as he bent, a scar along the line of the jaw whitened. He said, with apparent sincerity: 'I was convinced that something had happened to Mary. I am truly sad. She was a charming girl.' He smiled at the girl, laying his hand on her hair. 'You must not let yourself be too upset. It is sad, but there are many wicked people in the world.' Saltfleet noticed that she rested her head against his hand, like a cat being caressed. Taupin smiled at Saltfleet. 'But you want to ask her questions. I will come back later.'

She reached for his hand like a child. 'Don't leave me.'

A shade of irritation crossed his face. 'But I must, I am in the way.'

'Did you know Manfred Lytton?'

'No, but I have heard about him.'

She said: 'He's been killed.'

Taupin shrugged. 'I am not sorry. I think he deserved it.' He disengaged his hand and moved away.

'Why?'

'Have you seen what he do to her?' He took the top of the dressing-gown in his hand; she flinched defensively, then let him pull it open. He pulled it wide, showing her tiny flat breasts. The bruises on them were healing, but they still looked painful. Taupin said: 'She also has them on her stomach and . . . how you say, *les cuisses*?'

The girl said dully: 'Thighs.'

Saltfleet said: 'Yet your friend went?'

It was Taupin who said: 'He paid well.' He picked up his coat and slung it over his shoulder. 'And he do some other things that are filthy.'

She said: 'Please.'

He shrugged. 'He was a bastard. He deserved to die. It is a pity she had to die too.'

'Have you any idea who might have done it?'

Taupin stared him in the eyes. 'Of course not. Why should I? I don't even know them.' He turned. 'Now I am afraid I must go.'

She said anxiously: 'You'll be back later?'

He grunted; it could have been yes or no. The door closed behind him. Saltfleet said gently: 'Hadn't you better get dressed?'

She nodded, and stood up like an obedient child. The telephone bell rang, and she winced. She picked it up. 'Hello . . . No, I'm afraid he's just gone out. A few minutes ago . . . Goodbye.' She picked up her clothes in an armful. Saltfleet said:

'Would you like me to wait in the kitchen?'

'No, thank you.' She went out. He called:

'Mind if I use the telephone?'

'No. Please do.'

The lock of the bathroom clicked. Saltfleet dialled the Yard. 'Give me the C.R.O., please.' He closed the kitchen door quietly. 'This is Chief-Superintendent Saltfleet . . . Oh, hello, Ted. Ted, I want you to check on a Frenchman who calls himself Pierre Taupin.' He spelled it. 'Big man, about six foot three inches, age around fifty. Has a long scar running from behind the left ear along the line of the jaw. Black hair, swarthy complexion, eyes brown, the left one slightly green.' He had noticed this when Taupin had stared him in the eyes. The sergeant asked for his telephone number. He gave it and hung up.

There was something about the Frenchman that puzzled

him. He was handsome; he probably found women easy to get. This girl was attractive in a pale way, but there was nothing about her that would normally attract such a man. She was obviously completely in love with him; she would do anything he asked with total obedience. He was the sort of man who would find such devotion boring; that was obvious when she clung to his hand. So why was he interested in her? She had told Saltfleet he was her husband. It would have been just as easy to say 'A friend', or 'My boyfriend'. 'My husband' indicated wishful thinking; perhaps he had hinted at marriage. It was more than professional interest on Saltfleet's part; the girl aroused a paternal feeling of pity.

He picked up a photograph on a chest of drawers. It was of two girls, photographed against a background of the pyramids. One was Sheila; the other was Mary Threlwall. He could see why they had both attracted Lytton. They might have been sisters; neither looked more than thirteen.

She came back into the room, tugging at the bottom of her blouse. Her eyes were red, and there were damp wisps of hair round her ears. Saltfleet made her sit in the armchair. He sat opposite her on the wooden chair.

'What's your surname, incidentally?'

'Curtis.'

'Now listen, Sheila, I want you to tell me everything you know. Don't try to keep anything back.' She nodded. 'Why didn't you report Mary missing when she didn't return yesterday?'

'She was going away for the weekend to see her parents . . . in Banbury. I thought she'd decided to go straight there.'

'I see. How much was Lytton going to pay her?'

'A hundred pounds.'

'A hundred?' Mrs Beaumont Ames had mentioned fifty. The going-rate among West End prostitutes was a pound a stroke; but even so, a hundred sounded too much. 'Did he pay you that much?'

'No. Fifty.'

'Then why did he pay her a hundred?'

'She didn't want to go. She was frightened. She had a premonition.'

'That he was going to hurt her?'

'No . . . not exactly. He promised he wouldn't beat her.'

'No? Then what *did* he want to do?'

'There was some . . . funny business. He made her get ready for three days before.'

'Get ready? How?'

'He made her promise not to eat meat. And she had to take a bath in something that smelt bitter. And she had to rub a green ointment on herself before she went to bed.'

'Where? All over?'

'No. Here and there.' She indicated her breasts and genitals.

'Did he say what it was all about?'

'He said she had to be purified.'

'What did you think it was all about?'

She said helplessly: 'I just thought he was a bit mad.'

'Didn't you wonder what it was all about – what was in the bath salts, for instance?'

'Well, no, I mean . . . I didn't care.'

It was true, he could see: she did not care. Looking at her, he felt helpless; for a moment, he identified with her, and felt as indifferent and trapped as she felt. She looked at the world in a passive, helpless way; other people did things because they had reasons, but she had no reasons.

'Do you have any of the salts he made her put in the bath?' She shook her head. 'Or the ointment?'

'He told her to take it with her that night. He made her wear a thing round her neck too.'

'A thing?'

'A woman made of green stone like jade . . . some sort of goddess, the moon goddess, I think.'

'Was she wearing it when she left that evening?'

'Yes. She wore a gold chain with it.'

'He asked her not to eat meat, but she ate meat, didn't she?'

'I suppose so. She just carried on as usual. I mean, she thought it was all pretty stupid anyway.' She looked up at him suddenly. 'How did you know that?'

He was saved from answering by the telephone. He picked it up, saying: 'This may be for me.' It was the Criminal

66

Records Office. He turned to a clean page in his notebook, and wrote at the sergeant's dictation. He glanced up to see if she could read upside down, but she was staring past him, out of the window. He said: 'Thanks, Ted,' and hung up.

'Now, where were we? Oh yes. Did she use the bath salts as he told her to?'

'Only once. She said it made her skin taste bitter, so she stopped.'

'What happened on that last evening? Did Lytton collect her?'

'No. He said he'd collect her in The George, down the street. But he rang up at about nine and told her to wait here until she heard from him.'

'You're sure it was nine?'

'About then. Well, she was hungry, so she decided to go out and get a quick meal. I stayed in, in case he rang back. But he didn't ring back until . . . oh, a couple of hours after she got back.'

'What time would that be?'

'Let's see. Midnight, near enough.'

'You're sure?'

'Yes.'

'And what did he say?'

'He said he'd collect her at the corner of Grafton Way and Tottenham Court Road in about half an hour. She left here at twenty past midnight . . . we were watching the clock. We sat here talking about her brother – he's in the navy.' She began to cry, but continued to stare past Saltfleet, out of the window.

'And that was the last time you heard from her?' She nodded. She said, choking:

'Why should anyone want to kill her? She never did any harm . . .'

'They never have.' She looked up at him. 'Girls who get killed. It's a very dangerous profession. Do you realize that?' She nodded. 'Why don't you give it up?'

Her face brightened. 'I already have . . . At least, I'm going to.'

'What are you going to do?'

'Get married.'

'To that man Taupin?'

'Yes.'

He stood up and went to the window. He didn't want to look at her.

'How long have you known him?'

'Three weeks.'

'And he's promised to marry you?'

'Yes.' She was looking at him oddly, with a touch of defiance. After a pause she said: 'I know all about him.'

He looked round in surprise. 'You do? What did he tell you?'

'I . . . I can't tell you that. He wouldn't . . .' She stopped.

'Did he tell you that he and a Swede named Moberg run a brothel in Tunis? Did he tell you that his main business is running prostitutes out to the Lebanon?'

She looked less shocked than he expected. She just stared at him, as if he had asked her a question in a foreign language. He said, more gently:

'I don't know what he told you he was involved in – probably smuggling.' He saw from her face that he was right. 'He's not. His business is girls. He's not in love with you and he doesn't intend to marry you. He intends to get you out to North Africa and make money out of you.'

She was sitting slumped in her chair, her shoulders rounded, looking at her fingers in her lap. He felt a touch of exasperation at her passivity. He put a hand on her shoulder; she moved slightly, rebelling. He said:

'You say you've known him three weeks, yet he let you go off and get beaten by Lytton. You must have realized then that it's just part of his business? I suppose he took some of the fifty quid?'

She looked up at him; her eyes were angry. She said: 'Why not?' He dropped his hand and turned away. Of course she felt Why not? Why shouldn't a man fall in love with her? Why should she be stupid to imagine such things could happen? He picked up his notebook and said:

'He also called himself Guerin and Eddie Carossa. He's wanted by the French police. And he's served two terms in prison for gun-running during the Algerian war.'

68

'He told me that.'

'Yes, he would. His partner Moberg has been deported from England, France and Italy on morals charges – procuring girls for prostitution. Taupin hasn't been deported yet, but I'm going to see what I can do about it. Take my advice, my dear, go home to your parents for a month or two.'

'They wouldn't have me.'

He stood, looking at the photograph of the two girls against the background of pyramids, and experienced a sense of angry revolt. If she had been a minor, he would have taken her in, as being in need of care and protection. But she was obviously over eighteen; and it was difficult to get a care and protection order for anyone over sixteen. He said:

'Listen. Don't let him know you've found out. Wait and see what he suggests. But don't let him persuade you to leave the country with him. You don't want to end up in a brothel in Beirut or Tunis.'

He went to the door. 'Don't go away without letting me know at the Yard. Extension 91. I'll want you to come and identify her on Monday. Will you be in in the morning?' She nodded, indifferent. 'Do you have her parents' address?'

'Ten, Wilton Road, Banbury.'

He wrote it down. 'I'll call for you then. Goodbye.'

In the phone box at the end of the mews, he took out his diary, and looked up the number of the Vice Squad; now the Yard had the whole 230 exchange it was possible to dial direct. He asked for Superintendent Magill. The man said: 'Afraid he won't be in until later.' 'Who's that speaking?' 'Sergeant Mais.' 'Hello, Frank. This is Greg Saltfleet. I want you to take down a message for Bob. Have you got a pen? Ready? It's about a character called Eddie Carossa, C.R.O. 18655 stroke 38. He's in London at the moment. I saw him this afternoon at the flat of a girl called Sheila Curtis, 12 Grafton Mews, Maple St, W.1. I suspect that he intends to get the girl out of the country to a brothel in Tunis which he runs with a Swede named Moberg, who was deported as an undesirable alien. Carossa's wanted by the French police, but it's only for unlawful possession and dangerous driving, so I doubt whether they'll be interested in extradition. I think we might be justified in trying to get him deported. If

69

you've got time, Frank, you might take a careful look at his file – I only had a quick check done by C.R.O. . . . Got that? I'll be back later if Bob wants to contact me.'

Five

He walked back through Bloomsbury. He could have brought the car, but he was glad of the chance of exercise. It was after four, and the afternoon was becoming cooler. He had been hoping to spend this afternoon with Miranda and Geraldine at a garden fête and jumble sale in Shepperton. But the quiet of Bloomsbury on a Saturday afternoon was some compensation. The organ grinder outside the British Museum played the Anvil Chorus from *Trovatore* in a rhythm Verdi would not have recognized. In Bloomsbury Square, the air was filled with the drowsy hum of a lawn-mower.

The Occult Bookshop looked new, its frontage painted emerald green; Saltfleet recollected that it had been an Oxfam shop. A large jade Buddha occupied the centre of the window. The books around it were on subjects as varied as the Loch Ness monster, astrology and primitive cave paintings. On the other side of the doorway, a notice in a glass case read: Exhibition of Paintings and Drawings by Aleister Crowley and Max Engelke.

The inside was larger than he would have supposed. Rows of books stretched from floor to ceiling. There were a dozen or so customers browsing. Saltfleet approached the girl who stood behind the counter; she wore a white dress, and her blonde hair came to her waist. He opened his wallet and took out the receipt he had taken from Lytton's flat.

'Pardon me, miss. Is the owner here?'

'He is upstairs at the moment. Can I help you?'

'Perhaps. I'm trying to find out about some books that were bought here by someone I know.' He showed her the receipt . . . She peered at it short-sightedly, then looked up at him, startled. She looked away quickly.

'Wait here, please.' She hurried to the door, then hesitated. 'What name shall I say?'

'Saltfleet.'

The door led into a small art gallery. He wandered

through and looked around. In one corner there was a small coffee bar with an Expresso machine. The girl who stood behind it bore a remarkable resemblance to the one who had gone upstairs, except that she wore a black dress; they were probably sisters.

One wall contained a huge photograph of a bald-headed man, with sunken, magnetic eyes and folded arms; he recognized it as Crowley. Drawings and watercolours were arranged around it. The paintings seemed to be of lurid subjects, or subjects treated luridly: women melting into decay, bulls, skeletons, monkey gods with immense teeth, wraiths holding knives.

On the opposite wall, facing the Crowley portrait, there was a large mirror, tinted green. The objects on the wall around it were not, strictly, paintings; they seemed to be made of burnt objects stuck on canvas: books, pieces of wood, the top of a shoe, the half-melted face of a plastic doll. He peered more closely at the nearest one, and was startled to find a pair of eyes looking at him; a moment later he realized they were his own. He moved his head to one side; his reflection vanished, and he found himself looking into a taut, thin face with insane green eyes and pointed red teeth. It took him a few minutes to work out the trick. The painting had been photographed with a three-dimensional camera, so it appeared to stand out from its background. The lines comprised a plastic viewing screen of convex vertical strips; from a slightly different angle, they became a mirror.

The blonde girl came down the stairs, followed by a man. Saltfleet went to meet them. The man was remarkably ugly, with a receding jaw and forehead; his face seemed wedge-shaped. He was small and slightly built, hardly bigger than a ten-year-old child. He said: 'Are you the gent who wanted to see me?' The accent was glottal, and he seemed to have something wrong with his palate, so the words clicked.

'That's right. Chief-Superintendent Saltfleet, C.I.D.'

'George Widdup. What can I do for you?'

'I believe you knew a Mr Lytton – Manfred Lytton?'

'Of course I know him. Is something wrong?'

'I'm investigating his death.' Although he was speaking

72

quietly, he could see that the girl behind the coffee counter had caught the words; she looked startled.

'Bloody hell,' Widdup said. He looked quickly around the gallery, as if afraid someone might have overheard Saltfleet. 'You'd better come upstairs.' He pronounced it 'Coom oopstairs'. As they passed the counter he said: 'Bring us a couple of coffees, will you, love?'

The room above was evidently his living quarters. Although it was a large room, it was so crowded with books and curious objects that it seemed small. There were stuffed birds and animals in glass cases, globes, a huge brass telescope, flasks and retorts, and strange measuring instruments, including an enormous egg-timer filled with red sand.

'Have a seat.' He flung himself into the swivel chair behind the desk; Saltfleet took the chair opposite. 'So the poor sod's dead, is he? How did he die?'

'He was stabbed.'

Widdup made a sharp, wincing noise between his teeth.

'That's nasty. He was only in here the other day . . .'

'He bought some books?' Saltfleet placed the receipt on the desk. Widdup glanced at it without interest.

'That's right.'

'Did he take them with him?'

'Ay.' He pushed a box of cigarettes across the desk; Saltfleet shook his head.

'How long had Lytton been interested in magic?'

'Oh . . . years, as far as I know. Have you got on to Wally Steinhager yet?'

'No. Who's he?'

'Ah, well he's the bloke you ought to talk to. He's known Lytton for a long time.'

'What does he do?'

'He runs what he calls a "magical order" – the Golden Dawn. Lytton used to be a member.'

'Have you got his address?'

'No, but it's in the phone book.' He was searching through a pile of books beside his desk; he found the one he was looking for and opened it. 'Here's a bit about it.' He marked a paragraph with his thumbnail, and passed the book to Saltfleet. Saltfleet read:

*'The group that seems to have the greatest claim to pre-
cedence is the New Order of the Golden Dawn, founded in
1946 by Walter Steinhager, a member of the Dion Fortune
group. They claim to practise magic according to the "Eno-
chian system". Steinhager himself seems to possess some
genuine knowledge of astral projection and alchemy. But my
impression of the other members, when I attended a meeting
two years ago, was that they are more attracted to the
mystery and glamour of running a secret society, wearing
impressive robes, etc, than in serious occult training, with
its rigorous disciplines.'*

Saltfleet glanced at the title: *The Golden Dawn and Its
Derivatives* by Austin Curry.

'Did Lytton really practise magic?'

Widdup smiled. 'If that's what you can call it.'

'What would you call it?'

Widdup blew out a cloud of smoke. 'Well, if you ask me,
I'd have said self-deception was a good word.'

Saltfleet looked around the room. 'But you make a living
selling books on it?'

'Of course. I'm a bookseller. Before that I ran a restaurant
in Slough. I make more money at this, I can tell you.'

The girl came in with the coffees. There were also tiny
cress rolls. Widdup said: 'Thank you, love.' He gave her
behind a friendly slap.

She said: 'That strange lady is in the shop again, Mrs
Galletti.' Saltfleet noticed she didn't react to the slap.

'Does she want to see me?'

'Yes. Ingrid said you were engaged.'

'Tell her I'll see her in ten minutes.' He said to Saltfleet:
'Now there's a real witch if you're interested. Very weird
female . . .' He reached into a drawer and came up with a
bottle. 'Like a spot of this in your coffee?'

'What is it?'

'Navy rum. Marvellous stuff.'

'Just a bit.' Saltfleet knew the value of relaxed conversation over a drink. 'What about these books you sold him –
did they contain magical rituals and all that?'

'Oh yes, I'll say.' He was carefully pouring the rum; the
smell carried across the desk.

Saltfleet said: 'We can't trace the books. This thing called *The Equinox* is missing.'

Widdup looked puzzled. 'Yes, but . . . so what? I mean, it's probably around somewhere . . .'

'No. His housekeeper thinks he took it out with him on the day he was killed. Of course, he could have lent it to someone.'

Widdup said: 'I doubt that.'

'Why?'

'He'd been trying to get a copy for six months. He enquired about them every time he came in. He paid for three advertisements in the *Clique* before I found them. He wouldn't lend them the day after he bought 'em – especially at that price.'

'So it's possible his killer took them.'

Widdup frowned, sipping his coffee; Saltfleet said:

'You think that unlikely?'

'I wouldn't say that. But it'd be a stupid thing to do, wouldn't it? Narrows your field of enquiry.'

'He may be a stupid man. A lot of killers are. What about the binding of these books? Was it distinctive?'

Widdup smiled. 'Very distinctive. Red leather stamped with gold pricks.'

'Pricks?' Saltfleet assumed it was some term in heraldry.

'Penises. It was the way Crowley signed his name.' Widdup drew on a pad with a ballpoint pen. 'He made the A look like a penis with a pair of balls.'

'Hmm. I see. Was the whole edition bound like that?'

'I'm not sure. I could find out for you.'

'I'd be grateful. Was there anything else distinctive about these books – a name written in them, for example?'

Widdup brooded about it, then shook his head. 'Not as far as I can remember.'

'Any idea who might have taken them?'

Widdup laughed. 'I can't think of anybody bloody daft enough to commit murder to get them.'

'That's not what I meant. Lytton was killed for some other reason, and whoever killed him knew something about magic. Or was deliberately playing on Lytton's interest in magic.'

Widdup looked at him over the coffee cup, his eyebrows raised.

'I suppose that could make me a suspect?'

'It could. But it doesn't.'

'Why not?'

'I don't know. I go by instinct. Somehow I don't think you're the killer type.'

'You can say that again. The sight of blood makes me sick.' He chewed a cress roll; it made him look more like a ferret than ever. He asked: 'Was Lytton fully dressed?'

Saltfleet hesitated, then decided it would make no difference to tell him. 'No. He was naked.'

'I guessed as much. You know he was a right perv?'

'I'd heard something of the sort.'

'So isn't it more likely he was killed by some other perv? One of his boyfriends or something?'

'Was he homosexual?'

'Well, I only heard rumours . . . but as far as I know, he was just about every bloody thing. I always found him a nice enough bloke – bit pompous . . . I'll tell you the chap to ask – Franklin Bascombe, a publisher, Green Lyre Press.'

Saltfleet wrote it down. 'I've already heard about him.'

'He knew Lytton as well as anybody . . .'

'But you can't think of anybody connected with magic – somebody who might have stolen those books?'

'No. But then, he was only a customer. I didn't know him very well. All I know is that he was interested in sexual magic.'

'*Sexual* magic? What the hell's that?'

Widdup sighed deeply. 'Hard to explain . . . But a lot of magic makes use of sex. There's what's called Tantric Yoga, for example. Crowley did a lot of it.'

'So, in fact, Lytton could have been practising magic *and* sex when he was killed?'

'Oh yes, of course. Although I'm not sure that . . .'

There was a knock at the door; Widdup called sharply: 'Hello?'

A woman looked in the door. 'I hope I do not interrupt?' She had a foreign accent.

76

Widdup said: 'As a matter of fact, you do, Juanita. Can you give us another five minutes?'

Saltfleet stood up. 'No, it doesn't matter. I'd finished anyway.' He looked up at Widdup. 'Unless there's something else you wanted to tell me?'

'No, no . . .'

The woman came into the room. She was small and plump, with large brown eyes. Her teeth were very white. She smiled charmingly at them. Widdup said, with a touch of severity:

'This is Inspector Saltfleet from Scotland Yard.'

If he was hoping to make her apologetic, he was unsuccessful. She smiled at Saltfleet, and held out her hand; it felt cool and firm. Saltfleet noted that she had a way of widening her eyes, as if about to make an exclamation of surprise or admiration. In this case, it seemed to be admiration. She said:

'I am delighted to meet you, Inspector.' To his surprise she retained his hand, and turned it palm upward.

'You have the hand of a soldier, Inspector. Were your ancestors soldiers?'

Widdup said apologetically: 'She does horoscopes for us.'

She ignored him, looking into Saltfleet's eyes. He said:

'Farmers, I think.'

She allowed his hand to drop. 'Are you interested in magic, Inspector?'

Widdup gave an involuntary cackle of laughter. Saltfleet said cautiously:

'Well, I suppose you could say I am at the moment.'

She asked Widdup coldly: 'What is funny?'

Widdup said breezily: 'Nothing, nothing at all . . . The Inspector's making enquiries about a friend of yours – that chap Lytton.'

Saltfleet asked her: 'Do you know him?'

She said irritably: 'He is no friend of mine.'

Widdup said: 'I was joking. She hates his . . .' He corrected himself: 'She can't stand him.'

'Why?'

She said: 'I would rather not say.'

77

Widdup said: 'He pinched her behind in the shop one day.'

'He tried to do more than that . . .'

'How well did you know him?'

'I didn't know him. I didn't want to know him. I refused to let him come to my house for a horoscope – I told him: I don't want your money.' There was a silence. She looked from one to the other. 'He is dead, no?'

Saltfleet caught Widdup's eye. He said: 'How did you know that?'

She shrugged. 'I can tell.'

Widdup said: 'She's got second sight.' He avoided Saltfleet's eyes.

She said dryly: 'I could tell from the way you were speaking about him. It does not surprise me. I had a feeling when I first looked at him.'

'That he'd be killed?' He kept his face impassive.

'That he *could* be.'

Saltfleet waited for her to go on, but she seemed to have finished. He said: 'Why?'

'Oh, he is . . .' She sighed, and waved her hands. 'It is hard to explain. He is the sort of person who can be swindled because . . . because he wants to believe.'

'You mean gullible?'

'In a way, yes. Not obviously.'

Widdup said: 'I'd say that's a good assessment.'

Saltfleet said: 'But you've no idea who might have killed him?'

Widdup shook his head, frowning. 'Well . . . no. I only knew him as a customer. I knew nothing about his private life . . . Well, just a bit, not much.'

Saltfleet said: 'But Lytton used to come to this shop? He met people here. You've got a coffee bar downstairs. He could have met his killer here.'

Widdup nodded. 'I suppose he could have. But if he did, I don't know anything about it. You could ask the twins – the two Swedish girls downstairs. They're always here. They might know.'

Saltfleet turned to the door. 'All right, thanks. What are they called?'

78

'Ingrid and Sigrid. Ingrid's the one behind the coffee bar.'

'Have you got a phone book? I'd like to look up the address of this man in Highgate.'

'I'll do it.'

Juanita Galletti asked him: 'Are you driving to Highgate?'

'Yes.'

'Now?'

'Yes.'

'Could you give me a lift? I live in Regent's Park.'

She opened her handbag, and took out several long envelopes; she placed them on the desk. 'These are the horoscopes. I want to talk to you about Mrs Edwardes, but it will do another time.'

Widdup looked up from the phone book. 'Steinhager's address is: 28 Northwood Park, N.6.'

'Thanks. And thanks for your help. Do you mind if I ask these girls a few questions?'

'No, please go ahead. I'll come down with you.'

He led the way downstairs. Madame Galletti came behind. Saltfleet was aware of her presence. He had been strongly aware of it ever since she shook his hand. She seemed to use her femininity as a kind of radiation, an air of soft helplessness that invited male protection. He found it disturbing, but not unpleasantly so.

The two Swedish girls were talking at the coffee bar; as Saltfleet came downstairs, one of them started to walk away. Widdup called : 'Sigrid, don't go.' She turned and stood there, without moving. Widdup said: 'This gentleman wants to ask you something.' She moved reluctantly back to the counter.

Saltfleet smiled at them. He said: 'You know Manfred Lytton's dead.' He made it a statement, not a question; it was obvious that Ingrid had told her sister.

The girl behind the counter nodded very slightly: otherwise, neither of them showed any sign of having heard.

He said: 'You both knew him.' Again, it was a statement. 'How well did you know him?'

It was the girl behind the counter who said: 'We knew him by sight, that is all.'

'Did he speak to you?' One of them started to speak, then stopped. The girl from the shop said: 'Only to buy books.'

It was obvious there was no point in pressing them further. He said: 'Thank you.' They were still looking at him impassively as he walked away.

He rejoined Widdup and Madame Galletti. 'They couldn't tell me much.'

Widdup said dryly: 'No, I don't suppose they could.' Saltfleet wondered if he meant more than he said. As if to change the subject, Widdup said: 'What do you think of the exhibition?'

'I like these.' He indicated the paintings on the opposite wall. 'I'm not so sure about these.'

'Still, they're interesting, don't you think?'

'I suppose so. But it's basically a gimmick, isn't it – painting on mirrors.' Widdup shrugged, smiling. Saltfleet said: 'Do you think they're any good?'

Widdup glanced up at him slyly:

'Do you want my frank opinion?'

Madame Galletti said softly: 'Not too frank. That is the artist over there.'

Widdup looked round. 'Oh, yes. That's Max Engelke. Do you want to meet him? He knew Lytton better than I did.'

'In that case, I'd like to.'

'I'll get him.' He said to Madame Galletti: 'I hope you're not in a hurry?'

She smiled up at him. 'Of course not. I have all afternoon.'

Widdup was talking to a small, powerfully-built man in a bright check shirt and well cut flannel trousers. They came across the room. Widdup said:

'This is Max Engelke. Inspector Saltfleet . . . that's right, isn't it?'

Saltfleet said: 'More or less.' His first impression of Engelke was of a sullen and bad-tempered face. When he said 'How d'you do?', Engelke nodded, but made no attempt to shake hands. He seemed very young, but there was something tough, almost brutal, about him.

Widdup said: 'The Inspector's investigating a murder.'

Engelke said: 'Oh.'

80

Saltfleet said: 'I wonder if you knew the man. His name was Lytton – Manfred Lytton.'

Engelke said: 'Oh, him.'

'*Did* you know him?'

'Slightly. He's no great loss.'

'Why not?'

Engelke looked as if he were about to walk away; he said reluctantly:

'Oh, he's a . . . a fool. The sort of person who was likely to get himself killed sooner or later.' He had a slight foreign accent, but less perceptible than Madame Galletti's.

'Can you think of anyone who might have wanted to kill him?'

Engelke said, with an air of bored irritation: 'Of course. Dozens of people. But I can't think of anyone who would risk ten years in gaol for the sake of killing him. Now, if you'll excuse me . . .' He turned and walked towards the coffee counter.

Saltfleet asked Widdup: 'Has he ever had any brushes with the law?'

'I dunno. Why?'

'He gives me the impression he doesn't like coppers.'

'Oh, he's all right.'

Saltfleet said: 'What do you really think of these . . . paintings, or whatever he calls them?'

Widdup grinned. 'Oh, not much.'

'Then why do you exhibit them?'

'Do you really want to know? I don't mind telling you.' He lowered his voice. 'He arranged for me to use the Crowley paintings. He's got the contacts . . . I said if he could get me the Crowleys on loan, I'd exhibit his stuff as well. Mind, I don't think his stuff's all that bad. As you said, it's an interesting gimmick.'

Madame Galletti said: 'I think they are very good. He told me what they mean. They mean that most people only see their own faces when they look at a work of art.'

Widdup winked. 'She's his strongest supporter.'

'That is not true. But I think he has talent.'

Saltfleet said: 'I think I'd like another word with him.'

Engelke was signing the autograph book of a freckled

girl in torn jeans. Standing behind him, Saltfleet noticed that he had written a long message above the autograph. The girl smiled happily. 'Great. Thanks.'

Saltfleet said: 'It must be nice having admirers.'

Engelke shrugged, but said nothing. Saltfleet said:

'Just another question, if you don't mind. You said you knew dozens of people who hated Lytton. Anyone in particular?'

Engelke took his time replying, staring across the gallery. He said:

'I have no right to speak for other people. But *I* didn't like him.'

'Why?'

'You don't need a reason. You can dislike people without a reason. It's chemical.'

'But you didn't dislike him enough to kill him?'

Engelke smiled up at him; it was a superior smile, as if he had seen through an attempt to trap him. He said patiently, as if talking to a stupid child:

'I disliked him enough to *want* to kill him.' He looked challengingly at Saltfleet; Saltfleet said nothing. 'If you dislike somebody, that means you wish they weren't alive – that they didn't exist. Do you agree? If you could make them disappear with a wave of your hand, you would. That means you're willing to kill them – to destroy them. If you're asking me whether I'd kill Lytton, if I could do it without risk to myself, the answer is: probably yes.' He paused; his face had coloured. 'Does that answer your question?'

Saltfleet said: 'It doesn't tell me why you disliked him so much.'

Engelke said irritably: 'I've told you. I had no reason. Do I need a reason?'

'I'd have thought so.'

Engelke smiled sarcastically. 'You don't particularly like me, yet you've known me only a few minutes. Do you have a reason?'

For a moment, Saltfleet was taken aback; it was true that he felt an instinctive distaste for Engelke; it was because he seemed spoilt and arrogant. He was tempted to say so; then decided against it.

82

'I've no reason to like or dislike you. But if I did, it wouldn't mean I'd want to kill you.'

Engelke said with contempt: 'You mean you wouldn't admit it. It wouldn't do for a policeman to admit he feels like everybody else.' His irritation was so genuine that Saltfleet was not offended. He looked at Engelke with a kind of wonder.

'Are you saying that whenever somebody dislikes somebody else, they want to kill them?'

Engelke said contemptuously: 'You know I'm not. Most people aren't worth the effort.' He pointed out of the window at the street. 'Suppose half those people out there just vanished into thin air, would it make any difference to you?'

'It might, if I knew any of them.'

'And supposing you didn't – supposing you couldn't possibly have any sort of connection with any of them. Would it matter then?'

Saltfleet said: 'Perhaps not . . .' He was about to qualify it, but Engelke interrupted:

'Of course it wouldn't. So it doesn't make any difference to you whether most people are alive or dead. You don't really care about them. They're just strangers. But supposing you meet one of them and take an immediate dislike to him? What then?'

Saltfleet said, with deliberate mildness: 'I still wouldn't want him dead.'

'You're contradicting yourself. You just admitted you don't care whether most people exist or not. So if you dislike somebody, isn't that the same as wishing he didn't exist?'

Saltfleet laughed. 'In a few cases, perhaps . . .'

Engelke said: 'You laugh because you don't want to think about it. Be honest with yourself, and you have to admit it's true.'

Widdup had crossed the room toward them. He heard what Engelke said, and laughed.

'So he's got you arguing, has he?' Engelke glanced at him irritably; it was obvious he resented the interruption. Widdup ignored the look. 'He'll argue all night.' Engelke shrugged angrily and half turned away. Then he turned back to Saltfleet.

'Tell me one thing. Why do you want to catch the man who killed Lytton?'

'It's my job.'

'And suppose someone proved he was such a swine he didn't deserve to live?'

'It'd still be my job.'

Engelke shrugged. 'Isn't that what the guards in the concentration camps said?'

Widdup was alarmed; he said: 'Here, hold on.' He said to Saltfleet: 'He doesn't mean it.'

Saltfleet laughed. 'It's all right. I've had worse things said to me.'

Widdup said to Engelke: 'Anyway, Max, who are you to decide who deserves to live?'

Engelke said: 'I'm not going to argue with you. You are an idiot.' But he said it without heat. He turned and walked away.

Widdup showed no sign of offence. He grinned at Saltfleet.

'That makes two of us, eh?'

He was glad to relax in the car; his feet were beginning to ache. The car was cool; he had parked it in the shade. Madame Galletti smoothed her skirt over her knees; her hands, like her legs, were plump and shapely.

He had expected her to chatter; but after he had helped her fix the seat belt, she relaxed with a kind of child-like contentment and stared out of the window. It was not until they had turned into Euston Road that she spoke.

'What time do you expect to finish today?'

'I don't know yet. There are no fixed hours on a murder case. You just work on as long as there's anything to do.'

'I am glad I am not the man you are looking for.'

'Yes? Why?'

'You will catch him. I know that.'

'How do you know?'

'Sometimes I have an instinct. I just know things.'

'What else do you know about me?' He was not really

84

interested; it was a pleasant way of passing the time. In general, he preferred not to talk about himself.

She looked up at him. 'When is your birthday? No, don't tell me. I think it is . . . it is in March.'

He looked at her, startled. 'Right!'

She smiled, pleased with herself. 'Let me see . . . It is probably between the 21st and 27th.'

He glanced at her in astonishment. 'How the hell did you know that?' He was trying hard to remember if she had any way of finding out his birthday; but it seemed impossible.

'What *is* the date?'

'March the 23rd.'

'Yes, the cusp of Pisces-Aries. You are the type.'

His tiredness had vanished. 'But *how* did you know?'

'It is not difficult when you do it every day. I spend a lot of time making horoscopes . . .'

'Yes I know, but . . .' He tried to find a more tactful way of putting it. 'I don't want to seem insulting, but . . . I never took it very seriously.'

She said: 'No, of course.'

He was afraid he had offended her. 'Do you mean that people really fall into types, according to their birth date?'

'Not always, perhaps. But you, yes.'

'And you could tell just by looking at me?'

'And by talking to you.'

'What *is* the Aries type?'

'They are strong and good at organizing. They are very determined. I can see you are a kind man who is interested in people – that is another Aries characteristic. But because you are on the borderline of Pisces, you are fond of beautiful things. Is that true?'

He said doubtfully: 'I suppose so.'

'And you love the countryside.'

'Yes.'

'You are capable of being bad tempered, but you feel ashamed about it a few minutes later. Is that true?'

He laughed. 'If I hadn't just met you, I'd say you'd been talking to my wife.'

'Perhaps I don't need to talk to your wife; I feel I already know you very well.'

The words were innocent enough, but again he felt the disturbing twinge of attraction, as if a kind of static electricity had flowed between them. He said:

'Where do you live?'

'Prince of Wales Terrace. Turn left at the next traffic light.'

Neither spoke as he overtook a stationary bus. He said:

'Widdup said you were a witch. Would you say that's true?'

She gave a gurgling laugh. 'That is something you will have to decide for yourself.' She pointed. 'It is the house over there, the one with green railings.'

He pulled up outside the house. A passing policeman recognized him, but gave no sign of it until Saltfleet smiled and nodded. It was a rule for a man in uniform never to recognize a man in plain clothes; if he was following a suspect, it could blow his cover.

She said: 'Will you come in?'

'I . . . don't think I'd better.'

'Don't you want to see what a witch's study looks like?'

'Just for a moment, then . . .'

He followed her up the front steps, and into a large hallway. The house had once been fashionable and expensive, but it had been allowed to deteriorate. The walls needed painting; the stair carpet was shabby. Somewhere, upstairs, a baby was yelling. The hall smelt of burnt fried fish.

She inserted a key into the lock of a battered green door, and pushed it open. There was a curtained alcove on the other side.

'Please go in.'

He pushed aside the curtain, and was pleasantly surprised by the room beyond. It was large and well furnished. The walls were papered in green and silver, and the carpet was a bluey-green. The large mahogany table in the centre of the room was polished so that its surface seemed almost transparent. The rest of the furniture was modern and comfortable. The room had a faint chemical odour that reminded him of seaweed.

'Very attractive.'

'Thank you.'

Although the windows were covered with green, gauzy curtains, the room had a feeling of airiness that he found pleasant. In the corner of the room, an altar covered in green velvet contained a large bronze Neptune. On the shelf there were ornaments of sea creatures – Tritons and mermaids.

'It's like being under water.'

She took it as a compliment. 'I am a Cancer, and Cancers have an affinity with the sea.'

In the centre of the mantelpiece there was a block of blue crystal, as clear as glass. He stood staring at it.

'It's beautiful. Is it valuable?'

'No. Except to me. It comes from the mines at Falun, in Sweden, nearly a thousand feet under the earth. Once it was under the sea.' She took it off the shelf, and set it on the table. It was like looking into the water of a deep pool, with a few tiny specks, like bubbles, disturbing the clearness. Around it, the wood of the table seemed to be a different kind of water, the brown water of an Irish bog.

She went out of the room. He sat on the chair, where he could look into the crystal. He was still experiencing the odd excitement he had felt in the car. It disturbed him; he could think of no reason to be excited, but it sometimes happened when an intuition was trying to find its way into his consciousness. He sat looking around the room. It was obvious that Juanita Galletti made a comfortable living, but there was no evidence to show how she did this. There were no crystal balls or astrological charts.

When she came back, she was wearing a green tunic that fitted loosely. She had released her hair so that it spread over her shoulders. She was wearing sandals; her arms and legs were bare.

He pretended not to notice the change. 'What do you use the crystal for?'

'It concentrates the mind. Would you like to try it?'

'If you like.'

'Sit here.' She placed a stool near the table; it was lower than the chair. She moved the crystal until it was under his eyes. 'Now look into it, and let yourself relax.' He looked down into the blue depths, and thought that the sea smell

87

had suddenly intensified. She stood behind him, and he could feel her body pressed against him.

'What am I supposed to do?'

'Just relax.'

He could feel the outline of her thighs against his back, and the breasts against his shoulders. He thought of the smooth, silky knees and the short skirt she had been wearing earlier, and the excitement made him uncomfortable. From the warmth that radiated through the jacket he sensed she was wearing very little under the tunic. He said:

'That's not as easy as you think . . .'

She understood him. 'Just look into the crystal and let yourself go. Stop holding on to yourself.'

He could see the reflection of her arms in the table, looking as if they were immersed in peaty water. The blue crystal seemed to have a hypnotic effect, filling his mind. As he relaxed, he began to feel sluggish. She pressed against him, and placed her hands on his arms; he had a dreamlike impression that an electrical fluid was flowing from her fingertips into his muscles. He was breathing slowly, but with a certain tension, as if he was wading into the sea. He wondered whether she was exerting some hypnotic power, or whether he was doing it himself.

He said: 'What am I supposed to see?'

'You are not supposed to see anything. Let your unconscious mind do the work . . .'

The blue of the crystal merged into the warmth of her body; then, just as he was beginning to believe it was self-hypnosis, his brain was suddenly flooded with impressions. There was a feeling as if he was falling slowly, a sharp smell of autumn, an impression of something sad, and also of something cold and alien, like a lizard.

'Do you see anything?'

He shook his head.

'Do you feel anything?'

He nodded. She said:

'I am trying to give you my power. What do you want to know?'

He shook his head again; her questions were disturbing him. The autumn smell was so clear that he could have believed he was in a wood on an October afternoon; he wanted to enjoy the sensation. The thought of Manfred Lytton seemed irrelevant and unpleasant.

She said: 'Have you anything connected with the murder?'

He shook his head, then remembered. 'There's a glove in my pocket.'

'Take it in your hand.'

He groped in his pocket and found the glove; as he touched it, the unpleasant feeling increased; there was a smell of decay. For a moment he felt sick, then the feeling passed. He realized Madame Galletti had sat down on the chair beside him. Her face was so pale he felt alarmed.

'Are you all right?'

She nodded. 'Just tired.' In fact, she seemed to have aged. He put the glove back in his pocket.

'Can I get you anything?'

She opened her eyes.

'Why didn't you tell me there were two of them?'

He felt too tired to be surprised.

'How did you know that?'

'The glove belonged to a girl, didn't it?'

'Yes.'

She stood up and went over to the settee. She lay down, with her head against the cushion. He said:

'I'm sorry.'

She smiled. 'No, it was my fault.' She shivered. 'I told you to take it in your hand. I didn't realize it would be so strong.'

'What?'

She was silent for several moments, breathing deeply. She said:

'He pulled her backwards and hit her with something heavy.' She touched her left temple. 'After that he strangled her . . . She was still half conscious.'

He said: 'Any idea who did it?'

'No. She hardly saw him . . . Why did he kill her? She was only a child.'

'What?' He looked at her sharply. She opened her eyes, startled by his tone.

'Wasn't she?'

89

He shook his head. 'She was in her mid-twenties – a prosti-tute.'

'I had a strong impression she was a child.'

'She was wearing schoolgirl clothes. She'd put them on for Lytton. He liked schoolgirls.'

Her face wrinkled with disgust. 'It makes me sick . . .'

'But how . . .'

She said: 'Excuse me a moment. I am cold.' She went out of the room. He walked over to the window. He wanted to smoke his pipe, but guessed she wouldn't like the smell. There was a telephone on the window-sill, and he called out to her:

'Do you mind if I use your telephone?'

'Please do.'

A woman's voice answered; she had a distinct Scottish accent. When he asked for Steinhager she said: 'I'm afraid he's not here today. Can I give him a message?'

'When will he be back?'

'Late tonight.'

'I'll try again in the morning. I'd like to come and see him.'

'Very well. Who shall I say called?'

'My name is Saltfleet.'

Madame Galletti came in, wearing a dressing-gown and slippers; he could tell she was tired – the vitality had gone out of her. He said:

'Look, I don't want to be a nuisance, and I know you want to be left alone . . . But can you tell me more about your im-pressions?'

'There was nothing besides what I have told you.'

'Suppose I brought you something belonging to Lytton? Do you think you might get some impression of the man who killed him?'

She was already shaking her head before he had finished.

'I am sorry. I don't think I could do it again . . .'

'You might be able to help us find the murderer.'

'You don't understand.' He waited for her to explain, but she only said: 'Please, don't ask me . . .' She murmured something that sounded like 'I don't like it'.

'No, of course. I understand. Just one more question. You

90

said you thought she was a child. But she wasn't. How do you think you made the mistake?'

'I don't know.'

'Have you seen a newspaper this morning?'

'No. I don't take a newspaper.'

'The early editions said it was a schoolgirl. You could have seen a placard.'

'I don't think so. Perhaps I picked it up from your mind. This often happens . . .' She trailed off.

'And you got no impression of the man who killed her.'

She smiled tiredly. 'Only one, but it will be of no use to you.'

'Tell me all the same.'

'Hitler.'

'What?' He stared at her. 'You mean he looked like Hitler?'

'I'm sorry. I don't know.'

'You mean the word "Hitler" came into your head? Or an impression of someone like Hitler?'

'I don't know.' Her voice was suddenly strained. 'Now please . . .'

'Yes, of course. I'll go now. Thank you very much. You've been very helpful.'

She came to the door with him. 'Have I?'

He smiled. 'Well, let's say you've given me a lot to think about.'

As she closed the door, she said:

'I'm sorry. If you need me, you know where I live.'

'Thank you.'

The baby was still crying upstairs. The front door stood open, but the hall still smelt of fried fish. It seemed an age since he had gone into her room; in fact, it had been seventeen minutes.

Six

Saltfleet was usually up at seven o'clock on Sunday mornings, winter and summer. But he was still asleep at 8.15 when Miranda brought in a tray with coffee. She drew the curtains while he sat up and rubbed the sleep out of his eyes.

'Did you sleep well?'

She already knew the answer.

'No. I woke up at two and couldn't get to sleep again until after it was light.'

'Why don't you take some of those sleeping tablets, just for a few nights? You've been working too hard lately . . .'

'No I haven't.' The smell of the coffee made him feel more cheerful; his mouth was dry. 'It's this bloody case.' She said nothing; she never questioned him about his work. He said : 'There's no lead, no lead at all.'

'Does it matter? It's often happened before . . .'

'I know. It's happened in plenty of cases where the murderer didn't know the victim – sex cases, robberies. But in this case, he knew him all right. That's what worries me. We ought to have twenty suspects by this time. We haven't got one.'

He stirred the coffee; it was a relief to talk.

'There are still plenty of possibilities. We haven't checked his bank account yet. If he's been withdrawing large sums, it could mean he was being blackmailed. Or it might have been jealousy. His housekeeper says he wasn't involved with anyone, but I find that hard to believe. There must be someone . . . Did you find that newspaper – the one with the piece about Lytton?'

'No. I thought I'd seen it in a drawer, but it must have been thrown out.'

He sighed. 'You see what I mean? It's just one of those bloody awkward cases where nothing goes right . . .'

He was drinking his second cup when she came back, ten minutes later. She was carrying a torn newspaper. She said accusingly :

'I knew I'd seen it somewhere. It was on your bench in the shed. It's been there for ages.' She laid the newspaper on the eiderdown. It was stained with oil and boat varnish.

'Good God. I must have seen it a dozen times . . .'

The headline across two pages read WITCH CULTS EX-POSED. There were photographs of naked men and women, most of them apparently middle-aged, performing ceremonies with candles and swords. At the bottom of the page there was a small inset picture; the man was scowling over his shoulder at the camera. The caption said: 'Manfred Lytton: He searches for secret masters.' The newspaper was dated February 1971. 'Our investigator discloses how young girls are lured into secret rituals. A married couple allow their children to take part in Black Masses.'

'Feeling more cheerful now?'

'Thank you, my dear.' He caught her hand and kissed it. 'That's a good start to the day. Perhaps it's an omen. Any more hot milk?'

When she came in a few minutes later, he had dropped the newspaper on the floor; he was frowning as he stared out of the window.

'Nothing?'

'A little. Nothing much about Lytton. It's mainly about a couple called Dalgliesh who run some kind of new religious cult down at Hastings. I'll have to check on them. But it's all a long time ago.' He picked up the newspaper, and tapped the picture. 'That's almost an invitation to cranks and confidence men. Especially as the story calls him a wealthy playboy. He seems to have been mixed up with this pair.'

'Wouldn't Ted Sparks know about them?'

'He might. I'm going to ring him after breakfast.'

It was a bright, clear morning; the wind that blew from up-river smelt of fields. It was on mornings like this that he almost regretted being a policeman. He ate breakfast with the windows wide open. It was nearly half past nine when he looked up the home number of Chief-Superintendent Ted Sparks of the Hastings police. The phone rang for several minutes; he was about to hang up when Sparks's voice answered.

'Hello, Ted. This is Gregory Saltfleet. Sorry to bother you on a Sunday morning.'

'Hello, Greg. I was in the greenhouse. What's the news?'

'Piece of information you might be able to give me. Do you know anything about a couple called Alan and Marjorie Dalgliesh?'

'Oh yes. Are they in trouble?'

'Not as far as I know. I've got a press cutting here that says they ran a sort of religious group down there.'

'Religion my arse. It was a witch cult – sex and black magic. A really nasty pair. Why are you interested?'

'I've got a murder case – a man called Manfred Lytton. This report says he was a member of their group. I'm trying to trace people who knew him.'

'What makes you think they knew him?'

'It says so in this newspaper. It says they got their rituals from some secret masters in Turkey, and that Lytton intended to go and try to make contact with these masters. You say it wasn't a religion?'

'Well, that's a matter of opinion. I think it was just an excuse for sex and sadism.'

'Sadism?'

'Listen, I'll tell you. There's a little girl, daughter of a farmer near Beckley. She went in one day and told her mother she'd seen people dancing naked in the woods. Her father went down and had a look, but he couldn't find anything. A few weeks later she said she'd seen these naked people again, so this time he rushed down with a shotgun. He didn't see them, but it was obvious they'd only just left – I can't remember what they'd left behind but it was something or other. The next day, their Alsatian dog came into the house and dropped a pig's head on the rug – the head of a baby pig. And from then on, for the next year, they kept finding pigs' heads around the farm, usually on the doorstep.'

'Their own pigs?'

'No. We never found out where they came from. But it was nasty. Sometimes the heads were still warm. It worried them – they've got three kids. They were talking about selling out and leaving the area when it suddenly stopped.'

94

'Any idea why it stopped?'

'Yes. Because the Dalglieshes went to America.'

'Are they still there?'

'As far as I know – Los Angeles. They run the same kind of thing there – they call it the Church of the Dragon. They're supposed to worship monsters – you know, like the one in Loch Ness . . .'

'Do you know the approximate date when they left?'

'Oh, it was . . . February or March 1970. What makes you think they might be connected with this murder?'

'Suspicions of black magic . . . all kinds of things. Do you know if there are still any members of this Church of the Dragon around Hastings now?'

'Couldn't say. They kept it all fairly secret. Do you want me to try and find out?'

'It might be a help. I can't find any leads so far.'

'O.K. I'll probably ring you back tomorrow. How's the wife?'

As he hung up, five minutes later, Miranda asked:

'Any luck?'

'Not much. These people went to America two years ago. But there's a new possibility. This cult sounds pretty vengeful.' He told her the story of the pigs. 'If they'd do that to get revenge on a farmer who'd interrupted their rituals, they might kill Lytton if he'd betrayed their secrets. It's worth following up.'

She said comfortingly: 'I'm glad it wasn't a total loss . . .'

'Nothing's ever a total loss . . .' He was dialling Steinhager's number, with quick, decisive movements of his index finger. Suddenly, he was experiencing a sense of real involvement in the case.

The Scottish woman answered. When he asked if he could come and see Steinhager, she said he'd be at home all day. Saltfleet said he'd be there in about an hour.

The house had a large front lawn, with a fishpond in the centre. It was detached from its neighbours, and partly concealed by tall bunches of veronica and sea holly. Near the front door, facing the path, there was a notice: 'No visitors except by appointment.'

He rang the front door bell. The morning was warm and peaceful, with distant sounds of traffic, and the hum of bees in the wallflowers: the first he had seen this year. After a few minutes, he rang again. A plump, red-cheeked woman opened the door; she said: 'I hope ye haven't been ringing long – I was down the garden.'

'Not long. I'm Chief-Superintendent Saltfleet.'

'Yes, he's expecting ye. But he said I was to ask ye if it was anything I could help ye with? He doesn't like to be disturbed.'

'It's about Manfred Lytton. I believe Mr Steinhager knows him?'

'Oh yes. He knows him all right.' She glanced at him meaningfully. 'Is he in trouble?'

'Yes.'

'I thought so. I knew he'd land himself in it up to his ears one of these days.' She led him through the house; it was well furnished and spotlessly tidy. 'Can ye tell me what it is?'

'I don't see why not. Somebody murdered him.'

'Great God!' She stared at him incredulously. 'You'd better go and see my husband right away.' She opened the back door and pointed to a low brick building at the end of the garden. 'He's in his laboratory.'

He followed her down a stone-flagged path: the flower beds were full of japonica and flowering currant.

'You must have a good gardener.'

She said dryly: 'Yes, me.'

'Doesn't your husband help?'

She had time to say 'Och, him!' before they arrived at the door. From a distance he would have taken the building for a workhsop or garage; but the door was massive, studded with old-fashioned nails. She noticed his look of surprise and said apologetically: 'It's from an old castle or something.'

'Dracula's, I should think.'

She raised her finger to her lips. 'Sshh.' She knocked sharply on the door. There was a sound like muffled swearing inside. She turned the ring that raised the latch, and went in. An angry voice snapped: 'What do you want, you stupid woman? Haven't I told you I don't like to be disturbed? Get out and leave me alone.' It had a distinct foreign accent. The

woman's voice, also indignant, but lower, replied; he could-
n't catch what she said. The man's voice said angrily: 'What
do the police want with me? I won't see *anybody* . . .' There
was more hushed talking, then the man said: 'Dead! *Mein
gott* . . .' The door opened, and the woman looked out.
'Would ye step inside, Superintendent.' She was the first person who had got his rank approximately right.

She pushed aside a curtain; it was thick and velvety. The
room was in semi-darkness, except for a glowing purple
globe on the table. After the bright sunlight, the room
seemed as dark as the inside of a cinema. A man's voice
said: 'I'm Doctor Steinhager. What's your name again?'

'Saltfleet. Chief-Superintendent, C.I.D.'

'I'm sorry I can't put on the light. It would ruin my experiment. Sit down here.' A hand guided him to a chair. 'My
wife tells me that Lytton is dead.'

'That is so.'

Steinhager made a grunting noise, then said: 'Idiot.'

'I gather that he was a member of a magic circle that you
ran.'

'He was, until last November. Then he left.'

'Why was that?'

His eyes were becoming accustomed to the darkness. The
man was standing in the centre of the room, near the table;
he was very tall and thin. He was wearing a white shirt,
which glowed purple in the light from the table. This came
from a great globular bottle, of the kind that used to stand
in windows of chemists' shops. It had a glass stopper. The
light that illuminated it was a beam of sunlight that came
through a small, square window in the ceiling, and was
focused by a magnifying glass that seemed to be held by
metal clamps. The beam fell straight through the purple
liquid in the vessel, making a shimmering patch of colour on
the tabletop, and on a pyramid of white powder.

Steinhager said: 'It's a long story. He wanted to make
certain basic changes in our rituals.'

'Important changes?'

'Does it matter?'

'It might be relevant.'

Steinhager said impatiently: 'Unless you understand the

Kabbalah you couldn't possibly grasp what it was all about.'

'I'd be grateful if you'd try to give me a rough idea.'

'Oh, very well.' Saltfleet had instinctively hit the right tone of humble inquiry. 'Do you know anything about the Order of the Golden Dawn?'

'No.'

He sighed. 'I see . . . Well, I'd better start from the beginning. In 1880, a clergyman named Woodford somehow came into possession of a number of manuscripts in cipher. They turned out to be descriptions of various magical rituals. And these rituals were used as a basis of the original Golden Dawn, founded by Woodford, Wyn Wescott and Liddel Mathers. The purpose of the Golden Dawn was the study of ancient magical knowledge – a knowledge that has always existed in secret. I became a member of that original order in 1928. It broke up just before the Second World War. But I held on to many of the vestments, as well as magical documents, and I started it again in 1958.'

'And you study magic?'

'Yes, you could say that. You just referred to us as a magic circle, but that makes us sound like stage conjurers. Our group is basically a kind of religious order. And we take it very seriously.' He paused and stared at Saltfleet, as if expecting him to challenge this. Saltfleet said nothing. Steinhager went on, less aggressively: 'I must be frank with you. The original Golden Dawn was not always as serious as it should have been. Mathers was a clown, and Westcott was a romantic trying to deceive himself. Most of them were interested in personal power, and it ended by destroying them. The aim of our group is the scientific exploration of the hidden powers of the mind.'

'Was Lytton interested in the hidden powers of the mind?'

'Oh, Lytton!' He seemed impatient that Saltfleet had reintroduced the name. 'That man was a damn fool. He was another who wanted personal power.'

'What kind of power?'

'Sexual, mainly. He was infatuated with some silly girl in a Camden Town grocer's shop, and he wanted to try and seduce her with magic. He actually persuaded me to go in to see her on one occasion . . .'

'What was she like?'

'Just a girl, like any other girl.'

'How old?'

'Oh, nineteen, twenty, I don't know.'

'Do you know her name?'

'I'm afraid not. In any case, it's hardly worth your attention. An ordinary little cockney, rather pretty in a commonplace way – long blonde hair down to her waist . . .'

'She looked like a child?'

'I suppose so.'

'And why did he want you to see her?'

'There *are* ceremonies for gaining sexual power over a particular person. Lytton wanted me to help him get this girl. I told him he was an idiot . . .'

'Why didn't he simply offer her money?'

'She wasn't that kind of a girl. She was engaged to a boxer. And Lytton – it was completely typical of him – he was just like a spoilt child – he decided he wanted her, and he *had* to have her. That's the kind of thing that made me so angry with him. He finally lost her – she simply left and got married. Lytton seemed to have rather an obsession about girls with long blonde hair . . .'

'Were there others?'

'I believe so, but I couldn't be bothered to pay attention to all his infatuations . . .'

'And why did he finally leave the group?'

'We threw him out, frankly.'

'Can you tell me why?'

'If you like. He wanted to introduce Crowleyite rituals, and I flatly refused. You see, Crowley nearly destroyed the original Golden Dawn, back in about 1900.'

'What are Crowleyite rituals?'

'Mostly sex.'

'You mean sexual intercourse?'

'Quite. You see, while the western religions insist on purity, there are many religions that regard sex as holy – in India and Central Africa, for example. I am not saying they are wrong – one of the rules of our order is to be tolerant of all religions. But I couldn't allow Lytton to import Tantric disciplines into our rituals. It's an entirely different approach.'

'Can you . . . describe the kind of changes he had in mind?'

'I could, but I don't see that it would help you to find out who killed him.'

Saltfleet said patiently: 'I'm trying to build up a picture of Lytton – the sort of person he was . . .'

'Very well . . . Well, to give you an example, there's a ceremony to enable a man to identify with his true will. It culminates in pouring a few drops of milk on to the altar – preferably milk squeezed from a mother's breast. Lytton wanted to substitute male semen. Now you can see, this was simply a reversal of the meaning of the ritual – male semen is surely the opposite of mother's milk . . . Then he wanted to introduce an act of flogging into the ritual of the third grade – he said it was to subdue the flesh. But we all knew he enjoyed being flogged.'

Saltfleet hoped his smile was not visible in the half-light. 'And what happened then?'

'I told him in no uncertain terms that he could go. That was after a particularly nasty exhibition – he arrived at a meeting one day stinking of brandy, and kept trying to paw one of the girls – a young adept . . .'

'A blonde?'

'Yes.'

'And what happened after he left?'

Steinhager said irritably: 'I heard he'd joined a coven run by a couple of frauds – down at Brighton or somewhere like that. My wife read about it in a newspaper . . .'

'A coven? That's a group of witches?'

'Quite. These things have sprung up like mushrooms in recent years. They're mostly followers of Gerald Gardner – which is why Lytton was interested.'

'I don't follow you. Why?'

'Because a lot of Gardner's covens went in for sexual rites. He was a crank who wrote a book claiming that witchcraft is an ancient religion called Wicca. A lot of these people do their ceremonies in the nude. And their Great Rite consists of sexual intercourse between a high priest and a priestess. Some of them even go in for whipping – which is why Lytton was so interested . . .' He turned away, as if in total disgust.

100

'Did Lytton have any enemies in your group?'

'Most people didn't like him much. But he had no real enemies.'

'And you've no idea who might want to kill him?'

'None whatever. And now I must continue with my experiment, so if you don't mind . . .'

'Of course.' He stood up. 'Thank you for giving me your time.' He leaned forward and peered at the purple liquid, which seemed to vibrate in the sunlight. 'What *is* the experiment?'

'It is too complicated to explain.' Saltfleet expected the brush-off. But Steinhager seemed to relent. 'This powder contains various chemicals that are sensitive to sunlight, and a small amount of one of the salts is gold. The purple dye in the flask is some of the original Tyrian purple, dating from the days of Carthage – 900 BC. I got the method from the manuscript of the alchemist Fulcanelli – the only man in this century to make a small quantity of the Elixir.'

'But what are you trying to make?'

Steinhager stared at him for several seconds before speaking. 'I have told you. The Elixir . . .'

Saltfleet said: 'Ah.'

'And I will tell you something else. Fulcanelli is still alive, although he is more than a hundred. If he can do it, so can I.'

'Yes, I see . . .' Saltfleet paused at the door. 'How do you know he's still alive?'

Steinhager gave a thin chuckle. 'Ah, now you are asking for secrets.' He opened the door; the sunlight was dazzling. 'You can find your own way out, I hope?' Saltfleet found himself outside, and the door closed behind him. He had to stand still for a moment, his hand over his eyes. Then he made his way up the garden path, between the neatly cut lawns.

From behind him, the woman's voice said: 'I'll come and see you out.' She emerged from a small greenhouse. She was wearing gardening gloves.

He said: 'Oh, don't bother.'

'No bother at all.' She walked up the path ahead of him. 'Would you like a cup of coffee?'

'No thank you very much. I have to go now.'

She led the way through the kitchen. 'I don't suppose there was much he could tell you?'

He recognized the note of curiosity. 'Not much. I gather you haven't seen Lytton for some years anyway.'

'Oh yes.' She paused at the front door. 'He came to the house at Christmas.'

'He did?' He stared in astonishment. 'Your husband didn't mention that.'

'Och, he probably didn't think it was important. He wouldn't talk to him anyway. He walked out and went to his laboratory.'

'So they didn't exchange a word?'

'Oh, he wasn't rude – not as rude as he can be, anyway. He just made some excuse and went out.'

'Have you any idea what Lytton wanted?'

She removed the glove to scratch her nose. 'It was a name – an odd name . . . He wanted to ask Walter about some man.'

He said: 'Please try to remember.'

She concentrated for a moment. 'It's no good. It won't come back . . .'

He said patiently: 'Can you describe to me what happened? Did Lytton just knock on the door?'

'Yes. I suppose he knew Walter wouldn't see him if he rang up. I opened the door, and he said he wanted to see Walter for just a moment. He said he wanted to ask his advice. So I let him in.'

'What time was this?'

'Oh . . . nine o'clock in the evening. Walter was in the sitting-room . . .'

'Was Lytton sober?'

'Oh yes, quite sober. In fact, he looked rather miserable. So I let him into the sitting-room. He was quite polite to Walter – you gather they parted on rather bad terms . . . He said he wanted to ask what he knew about . . . this odd name. I wish I could remember . . .'

'Do you think your husband might remember?'

She said quickly: 'I'll ask him later. But I daren't disturb him again now.'

'It could be important . . .'

She said coaxingly: 'I'll ask him as soon as he comes out. Give me your telephone number, and I'll ring you.'

He wrote his home telephone number on the back of a card. 'I'll be home later today. My office number's on the other side. Did *you* speak to Lytton after your husband went out?'

'Only a few words. He said he wanted Walter's help, and I said I'd talk to him about it later.'

'Did he say help? Or advice?'

'Help, I'm pretty sure.'

'Did you get any idea of *why* he needed your husband's help?'

'Well, no. To tell the truth, I wasn't too curious, I assumed it was something to do with magic . . .'

Her tone made him ask: 'You don't believe in magic?'

She avoided his eyes, then smiled. 'No, I think it's a load of nonsense. But I don't tell him so. It keeps him happy.'

He parked his car at the old Yard building and walked across Parliament Square to Broadway. The day was becoming uncomfortably warm. In the Criminal Records Office he checked on Steinhager; but, as he expected, there was no listing. Neither was there anything on Engelke.

It was after twelve-thirty. Passing the Tank – the ground floor bar – he had noticed that it was open; usually it was closed on Sunday, but today the Commissioner was showing a group of prominent European police officials over the Yard, and lunch had been laid out in the corner of the bar. He ordered a light ale, and drank it standing at one of the tall tables near the door. The room was pleasantly cool and almost empty. While he was drinking, George Forrest, head of the Flying Squad, came in, followed by Peggy Larkhill, the secretary he shared with Saltfleet.

'Working today?'

'Unfortunately. Big job in south London for Interpol. Bloke named Jacques Gerrin. What would you like, Peggy?'

While Forrest was at the bar, Saltfleet asked her:

'How do you spell Gerrin?'

'G-U-E-R-I-N, I think. Accent over the E.'

103

'He doesn't call himself Carossa, does he?'

Forrest, returning with the drinks, overheard him.

'Yes, he does. Why?'

'And Taupin?'

'Yes. What do you know about him?'

Saltfleet said: 'He's not in south London. At least, he wasn't yesterday afternoon. He was at the flat of a girl called Sheila Curtis, at 12 Grafton Mews, W.1. I left a message with Frank Mais of the Vice Squad to check on his file. They should have told you in Criminal Records.'

Forrest swore, then apologized to Miss Larkhill. 'Sorry, but isn't that just bloody typical!'

'What do you want him for?'

'The Dutch police want him on a murder charge. They found the body of his partner, a Swede named Hedberg, in an oil drum at the bottom of the harbour. He's suspect number one.'

'Sure it wasn't Moberg?'

'No, Hedberg. You'd better tell me about this. We're due to raid a house in Walworth Road in two hours!'

While Saltfleet was explaining, someone tapped him on the shoulder. It was Detective-Inspector Coventry of Fingerprints. He said: 'Don't go before I've had a word with you.'

'Right.' He turned back to Forrest. 'You'd better check with Bob Magill before you do anything else. I left a message for him with Sergeant Mais when I left the flat. You may find he's still at that address.'

'It'd save a lot of trouble if he was.'

He excused himself, and went across to Coventry, who was standing at the bar. 'Anything new?'

'We didn't find any fingerprints. Somebody had been around and wiped almost every smooth surface. It must have taken over an hour. But I tell you what we did find. Wax on the curtain.'

'Wax?'

'That's right. Right near the bottom of the curtain, a foot above the floor. A blob of greenish wax.'

'Wax? Candle wax?'

'Could be. Struck me as a bit odd. There were no candles in the place, as far as we could see. And another thing – it had a funny smell. Didn't you say you noticed a funny smell when you went in?'

'That's right. Like geraniums.'

'This wasn't like geraniums. It was more like . . . oh, I dunno – a sort of perfume.'

'Incense?'

'Could be.'

'What did you do?'

'Took the curtain down and sent it to Forensic.'

'Nice work, George. I'll ring them now.'

'That's no use. I gave it to Fred Naylor, and he won't be in today. Ring him in the morning.'

'O.K. Thanks.'

'Like another drink?'

'No, thanks. Got to get back to work.'

He walked back to his office, but the In Tray was empty. The crime reports of the weekend would be saved until Monday morning. He looked up the telephone number of the Occult Bookshop in the directory, then rang it. There was no reply. He checked under 'Widdup', and found another number at the same address. He rang this; for several minutes there was no reply; he was about to hang up when Widdup's voice said irritably, with its nasal Lancashire accent: 'Who is it?'

'It's Saltfleet – C.I.D. Hope I didn't wake you up.'

It was supposed to be a joke, but Widdup said: 'You did, as a matter of fact.'

'Sorry. There's a question you might be able to answer . . .'

'Go on.'

'You know about magic ceremonies . . . Do they use any special kind of candle? Something made of special wax?'

There was a silence, then: 'I . . . I'm blowed if I know.' Another silence. 'I'll tell you who might be able to 'elp you – Eileen Fox. She's a witch. Hold on a minute, I'll give you her number . . . No, wait a minute. Perhaps it'd be better if . . . Listen, where are you?'

'At the Yard.' He gave the number. 'Extension 91.'

'I'll ring you back in ten minutes. Right?'

'That's very kind of you.'

'That's all right. I'd do as much for any copper.'

While he was waiting, he rang his wife. She said:

'There was a telephone call for you half an hour ago. A Scottish lady with a funny name.'

He said excitedly: 'Steinhager? Yes?'

'She just said to tell you – hold on a minute – to tell you the name you wanted was Norbert Tinkler.'

'What?'

'That's what she said. Shall I spell it?' She did. He said: 'What a name.'

'Yes. When will you be home?'

'I'm not sure. It looks as if I've reached a dead end here. With a little luck I might be back by mid-afternoon. If it's early enough, we'll take the boat out.'

Another voice shouted: 'Oh, hurray! Try and get back, won't you?'

Miranda said: 'Geraldine, I wish you wouldn't listen on the extension. Get off.'

'All right. Try to make it, Daddy, won't you?' There was a click.

He said: 'I'd better ring off. I'm waiting for a call.'

He spent five minutes looking through the London telephone directories for a Norbert Tinkler, without success. He decided to ring Mrs Steinhager, but as he reached out, the phone rang. He recognized Widdup's voice. He said: 'You're back soon.'

'Ay. Without much joy, I'm afraid. She said the traditional candles of black magic were made of human fat, and set in ebony candlesticks made in the shape of a crescent. But modern witches use ordinary candles – the sort you can buy anywhere. She said they might use coloured candles – the expensive kind you buy from Harrods – but it didn't make any difference to the rituals.'

'Any idea about incense? Do they burn incense during the ceremonies?'

'Oh yes. I'm sure they do. If you'd like to hang on a minute I can look it up.'

'Please.'

Widdup was away for about five minutes; then he said: 'Sorry to keep you. I've found it. It says here: Incense might be of any odiferous woods and herbs, such as cedar, rose citron, aloes, cinnamon or sandal, reduced to a fine powder and mixed with church incense or storax . . .'

'Any idea where you'd buy incense?'

'No, but I could find out for you. Max Engelke knows a place.'

'Oh . . . that's interesting. Any idea where?'

'No. He wanted to burn incense in the gallery during his exhibition, but I wouldn't have it. I'll ask him for you. I should see him tomorrow.'

'I'd be grateful if you would. Incidentally, how long have you known Engelke?'

'I dunno . . . a few months. You don't suspect him, do you?'

'Not particularly. But I've got to check on everyone.'

When he'd finished speaking to Widdup, he tried to ring the Steinhagers' number; there was no reply. No doubt she was still in the greenhouse.

He dialled the switchboard. 'Have you got anybody there who could look up a number for me?'

'I could.'

'It may take some time. I want to try and trace the number of a man called Norbert Tinkler.' He spelt it. 'I don't know where he lives, but he's not in the London directory. Try the home counties first, then Kent and Sussex.'

'I'll see if I can find it. If not, Mavis is due back from lunch in ten minutes.'

'Thank you, m'dear.'

He was tempted to ring Widdup back, to ask if he'd heard of Tinkler, but decided against it. Where possible, he preferred to ask his questions face to face; the telephone was the lazy way. For the same reason, he decided to call on Mrs Beaumont Ames on his way back home.

He opened the window to its limit, pulled the swivel chair over, and lit his pipe. There was a sound of pigeons, and a boat hooted on the river. Relaxed in the sunlight, he found it easier to put the case out of his mind. Besides, his detective instinct told him that the case was at last beginning to yield, even though there were no obvious grounds for thinking so. It was a kind of innate knowledge, like birds at the approach of spring.

He was considering whether to start another pipe when the telephone rang. The girl said:

'I've found a Mr Tinkler in the Surrey directory. He lives at Chilworth Green.'

'Does it give his first name?'

'No, but the initial's N.'

'Excellent.' He wrote down the number and thanked her. After that, he took down an atlas, and looked up Chilworth Green. It was a few miles from Haslemere, not far off the Portsmouth Road. He could try ringing the number; but if Tinkler was the man they wanted, it would only alert him.

It took him less than a quarter of an hour to get to the house in Chelsea. He was able to park outside the front door.

Mrs Beaumont Ames was wearing a flowered, summery dress that was too young for her, and she had combed her hair loosely down her back. As she preceded him up the stairs, he observed that her legs were bare.

'Want a gin?'

'No, thanks.'

'Whisky?'

'No, thanks.'

'Don't you *ever* take any time off?' From the slur in her voice, it was clear that she had already had several drinks. The gin bottle on the table was almost empty, and there were four empty tonic bottles.

'Not on a murder case. Did Lytton ever mention someone called Norbert Tinkler?'

'Yes – once.'

'What did he say?'

'Nothing much. Just that if a man called Norbert Tinkler rang up, he'd be at his club.'

'And did he ring?'

'Yes.'

'Can you recall what his voice was like?'

'Not really. He might have had a slight foreign accent, but I couldn't be sure.'

'And he never referred to him again?'

'Never.'

'Thanks. You've been helpful.'

108

'Going already?'

'I've got to work. Why don't you go out? It's a lovely day.'
She sat down, sighing.

'I'm bloody bored, that's why. And I've got nobody to go out with.'

Suddenly, he had a glimpse of the emptiness of her life, the boredom of an empty afternoon that seemed to stretch forever. He sat down opposite her.

'I know what you mean. It must seem strange . . . to have nothing to do.'

She responded quickly to the sympathy in his voice.

'I never thought I'd miss that spoilt little bastard. But I keep wondering what to do with myself . . . Oh, it'll only last a day or two. I'll find something to do . . . Sure you won't have that drink?'

He said: 'All right. I suppose a weak gin wouldn't do any harm. I'll get it.' He helped himself to a small gin, and drowned it in tonic. 'Cheers.'

'Cheers . . . Do you think this Tinkler might be the man who did it?'

'It's impossible to say. But he's another name to check up on.'

'Have you tried Bascombe yet?'

'No. He's out of town until tomorrow.'

'I doubt whether he can tell you much anyway. Just the names of a few of the girls he went to bed with.' She put her glass down. 'That reminds me . . .' She got up, and went into the next room. She came back with an envelope. 'I don't suppose these are of any use, but they might be . . .'

He took the envelope, and shook it; a batch of photographs fell out. He looked at the first and felt his heart tighten. It showed two girls removing their brassieres. He recognized them as the Swedish girls from the Occult Bookshop.

He asked: 'Do you know them?'

'No. Never seen them. I found those in his bookcase, behind the books.'

'Do you think they fell there? Or did he hide them?'

'Probably fell. Why should he want to hide *them*?'

The first half-dozen photographs showed the girls removing their clothes. There was an attempt to make the striptease titillating, but their boredom was obvious. Other photographs showed the two girls in various lesbian poses, but again the lack of conviction was apparent; the intertwined bodies looked as innocent as if they were female wrestlers. Mrs Beaumont Ames stood by his chair and looked over his shoulder.

'They're not much good at it, are they?'

The remaining photographs – a dozen of them – showed Lytton with one of the girls; they had evidently taken it in turns to use the camera. All showed a slight but definite sadistic tendency: the girl on her knees, performing fellatio, while Lytton towered above her, his head thrown back, his hands on his hips, looking like a Nazi stormtrooper having his boots cleaned; the girl bent back, her body arched against the mantelpiece, while Lytton clasped her buttocks, looking like a hairy crab.

She asked: 'Getting excited?'

'Yes. But not for the reason you think. I've seen these girls before. They told me they hardly knew Lytton.'

'They could have been telling the truth.' She laid her finger on a picture of Lytton with his face hidden between a girl's thighs. 'That's hardly knowing him, is it?'

'Did he often arrange these things for himself?'

'I think so. I sometimes didn't see him for days.'

'Did he like blondes?'

She laughed. 'I don't know whether you could call it that.'

'Why?'

'Well, he wanted to . . . hurt them. They seemed to bring out the worst in him.'

He put the photographs in the envelope. 'I'll take these with me, if I may.'

'Going?'

'Yes, I'm sorry.' He emptied his glass. 'You've been very helpful.'

She said, sighing: 'I'm always helpful. That's the story of my life.'

He resisted the temptation to pat her on the arm. He had a suspicion she wanted to cry.

It was nearly four o'clock when he arrived home. Miranda was working in the greenhouse. His daughter Geraldine and a friend had wheeled the thirteen-foot speedboat on to the lawn, and were touching up the varnish. He felt a contraction of the heart as he looked at her; with her long blonde hair, and long slim legs, she looked like a model in an advertisement for expensive cigarettes. But when she turned round, he saw her face had caught the sun, and the nose was peeling. She rushed at him and kissed him.

'If we're taking the boat out, can Jenny come? She's been helping me to paint it.'

'I'm sorry, darling. But we can't take it out today. I've still got another job to do.'

'Oh damn.' But she took it easily; she was a happy child.

Miranda overheard him. 'What have you got to do?'

He said: 'I thought we might drive down to a place near Haslemere for a drink a bit later. I've got a call to make.'

He changed into old clothes and, for the next two hours, wandered around the garden, cutting weeds out of the lawn, replacing a broken pane in the greenhouse. At six o'clock he poured himself a cold beer, and switched on the television to watch the news. The last item concerned a policewoman who had been dressed up in the clothes of a murder victim – a hitch-hiker – to try to jog the memory of motorists who might have seen her on the day she was strangled and raped. He experienced a moment of relief, reflecting that his own case was more straightforward than that. The casual sex murder was the policeman's nightmare.

Geraldine said: 'Can I come with you?'

'I'd rather you didn't. You'd have to sit outside the pub . . .'

When they were in the car, he told Miranda:

'That wasn't the real reason I didn't want Geraldine. I'm going to try calling on a suspect, and I don't want to take any unnecessary risks.'

'Could he be dangerous?'

'I doubt it. It's this Norbert Tinkler you took the message about. I'll inquire in the local pub first. If there's any element of risk, you'll have to wait there for me.'

'Who is he?'

'Somebody who knew the murdered man, I think. And I've got to check on everybody...'

When they arrived at Chilworth Green, forty minutes later, she said:

'I must say, it doesn't look the kind of place where you'd find a murderer.'

He was inclined to agree. The curved main street was quiet and deserted. It was too narrow for parked cars; with its old houses and cottages, it looked exactly as it might have looked a century ago. The small front gardens were full of greenery and rose bushes. The pub, the John Blogg, was a red-brick building that no one had thought of modernizing; there was only one car in its small park.

He ordered a large vodka and bitter lemon for Miranda, and a vodka and tonic for himself. He would have preferred beer, but not before an interview.

The public bar was empty except for three old men in a corner playing dominoes. In the lounge, visible on the other side of a wooden partition, a group of well-dressed men and women, probably on their way back from the coast, ate sandwiches and talked about golf.

He asked the barmaid: 'Could you direct me to Mr Tinkler's house?'

She turned to the landlord, who was in the next bar. 'Where does Mr Tinkler live?'

The landlord came in. 'You go straight out of the village toward Linchmere, and it's the last cottage on the left. You can't miss it – sort of sham-Elizabethan place. Red creeper all over the chimney.'

'Thank you.' He offered the barmaid a drink; she said she'd have a pineapple juice. Saltfleet said cheers. They sat in the corner of the bench seat, next to the bar. He asked the girl:

'Do you know Mr Tinkler by sight?'

'Can't say I do. He never comes in here anyway.'

The landlord said: 'And if he knows you've been in here you won't be very welcome.'

'No? Why not?'

'He's a right 'un. Lord's Day Observance people. He'd have me shut down tomorrow if he could.'

112

'Ah, I see . . .'

When the barmaid moved away, Miranda said: 'I think you've got the wrong one. I can't see a type like that getting mixed up with this man Lytton.'

He said gloomily: 'I'm afraid you're right.'

As they went out, the landlord said with irony: 'Give him my regards.'

The cottage was, as the landlord said, instantly recognizable. The Tudor beams had been recently tarred, and the wall spaces in between newly whitewashed. The pungent smell of the tar mingled pleasantly with the smell of lilac blossom. The end was covered with virginia creeper.

He rang the doorbell. After several minutes, there was the sound of a stick. A woman in her sixties opened the door.

'Yes?'

'Does Mr Norbert Tinkler live here?'

'Yes.' She smiled at them. 'Do come in.'

He glanced at Miranda. 'Don't you want to know what I want?'

'Is it about the prosecution?'

'No.'

'Well, he'll be back from church in a moment. Would you like to wait inside?'

'Er . . . thank you.'

She led them through a hall that smelt of scented polish, into a neat sitting-room at the rear of the cottage. Through the leaded window they could see the back garden, surrounded by a wall. There was a well in the centre of the closely cut lawn.

He asked: 'Are you Mrs Tinkler?'

'Miss. I'm Norbert's sister.'

'I'm Chief-Superintendent Saltfleet. This is my wife.'

She smiled pleasantly, without curiosity. 'How do you do. Hasn't it been a beautiful day?'

Miranda said: 'What pretty water colours! Who did them?'

She smiled with pleasure. 'I did. They were mostly done in Germany and Switzerland. I used to travel quite a lot before I got this arthritis . . . Oh, here's Norbert.'

They heard the front door open. A voice called 'Hel-lo',

113

making it sound like a clock chiming. The old lady went out. They heard her say: 'Norbert, dear, there's a gentleman from the police to see you.'

'Ah, good.' Saltfleet and Miranda exchanged glances; they were thinking the same thing: that a man who said 'Ah, good' like that had nothing on his conscience.

Tinkler came into the room. He was about five feet tall, and had a head that was too large for his body. The round eyes produced an effect like a startled goblin. He shook hands warmly.

'I'm so glad you've come so soon. Do sit down.' The voice was high-pitched. 'I'm sorry to cause you so much trouble, but on this occasion I really *do* think it's justified. You see, I've known that bookshop in Guildford for years – they used to have an excellent theology section. And I went in the other day to see if I could get a copy of *Honest to God* by the Bishop of Woolwich, and the first thing I saw was a revolving stand with half a dozen volumes of the most abominably filthy limericks. I protested to the young lady in charge, but she said their traveller was responsible for the stands. So I've decided that if the police won't take action, I'll have to start a private prosecution . . .'

Saltfleet said: 'Excuse me for interrupting you, Mr. Tinkler, but I'm not from your local police.'

'Oh . . . Better still.'

'I mean I'm not here about your complaint. This is a murder inquiry.'

Tinkler and his sister stared at one another. He said: 'I don't understand.'

'I'm investigating the death of a man called Manfred Lytton. We found your name in his address book.' It was less involved than the true explanation.

'Indeed. You surprise me. I have no recollection of him. Have you, Agatha?'

She shook her head. Tinkler sat down, pressing his finger-ends together, nodding magisterially.

'It seems to me unlikely that there could be another person of the same name. It is hardly commonplace. In fact, I have never come across the surname outside Scotland. Tinker is common, of course, but not Tinkler. Our father, Superin-

114

tendent, was the Scottish artist Alastair Tinkler, who painted the Dying Stag.' Saltfleet looked suitably impressed. 'His daughter inherited some of his talent. I, unfortunately, inherited only his religious temperament and his impatience with fools. How did this man die?'

'He was stabbed.'

'Mmm. In the heart?'

Saltfleet said resignedly: 'Yes.'

'I've often thought it must be fascinating to be a detective. You meet with such extraordinary problems. For example, what on earth could this man be doing with my name in his address book?'

'And you've no idea at all?' He looked at Tinkler's sister. Both shook their heads. She said:

'Of course, Norbert's well known to quite a lot of people. He's always writing to the newspapers to protest about immoral books and plays. He had a letter in *The Times* last week.'

Saltfleet asked casually: 'Do you often have letters in *The Times*?'

'Occasionally. And *The Telegraph* and the Church newspapers. Not, of course, in a left-wing rag like the *Guardian*. I keep a book of them. Would you care to see it?'

Miranda was trying to catch his eye, but he said: 'Yes, if I might just glance at it . . .' There was always the remote possibility that he might stumble upon the reason that Lytton knew a man called Norbert Tinkler. There had to be a reason.

But when he left, half an hour later, he had still not found it. Tinkler had presented Miranda with a signed copy of a pamphlet written by himself: 'The Story of Lot's Wife.'

As they drove out of the village, he asked her:

'What would you say about his voice?'

'Rather high and thin.'

'Quite. If he'd spoken to you over the phone, you'd remember it. But Mrs Beaumont Ames said that Norbert Tinkler had a completely nondescript voice . . . except for a slight foreign accent.'

Seven

When he got to the office the next morning there was a note by the telephone: 'The Chief would like to see you before ten.' Crisp was already going through the routine reports from the divisions.

'Anything important?'

'Yes. Another attack on a schoolgirl at Hendon. It sounds like the North Circular bloke.'

'Is she hurt?'

'Not badly. A few scratches. But she was raped.'

He glanced over the notes on his desk: Crisp had taken them from dictation over the phone. Gillian Stone, aged 12, doing a newspaper round at 7.15 that morning, dragged into Sunny Hill Park by a man who approached her on a bicycle. After the assault, he warned her not to tell anyone and rode off. Although he had insisted on binding a scarf round the girl's eyes while he raped her, she had described him as being in his mid-twenties, fair haired, blue eyed, very sensual mouth. This was obviously the North Circular man. The Identikit pictures constructed from earlier assaults showed a thin face, brush-like hair, wide-apart eyes.

He glanced quickly through the other reports. Two burglaries, one of them through a skylight with the use of a rope; that sounded like Freddie Carstairs, who had been released on parole a month ago; he would get the local man to check on him. An Islington doctor had been coshed and robbed of his black bag – obviously someone after drugs. A nurse attacked on her way home from night duty at Barnet hospital on Sunday morning; but the man had been frightened by her screams, and ran away before completing the assault.

He told Crisp to ring N Division and get their man there to check on Carstairs. 'And ask him if there's anything yet about that bank raid in Poplar.' He tried to ring George Forrest at the Flying Squad, but his sergeant said he wasn't in yet.

He told Crisp: 'If anyone wants me, I'm in with the Commander.'

Lamb's door was open. He was sitting at his desk with his chief aide, Chief-Inspector George Harper, on one side of him, and his personal assistant, Detective-Sergeant Truscott, on the other; they were going through the morning's reports. Lamb was an impatient explosive man who would have been a bully if he had not also possessed an innate fairness of temperament. Physically, he was not big; it was interesting that he was often described as a big man, simply because his tremendous drive conveyed the impression that he was a kind of steamroller. He was inclined to suspect people's motives and think the worst of them, which is why he was so impressed by Saltfleet's natural patience and charitableness. There was something about Saltfleet that made him uncomfortable, so that he tended to leave him to get on with his own work with a minimum of interference.

'Morning, Greg. Have a chair. Smoke? Truscott, see what you can find out about this chap who calls himself Aristide Weber. Get on to Jackson on the Fraud Squad. And cross-check under credit card swindles – I've got a feeling he did a stretch for something of that sort.' Harper moved back to his own desk in the outer office when Truscott went out. Lamb started in without preamble.

'*The Sun* wants to splash this story about the second body in Hampstead. Could there be any connection with this North Circular case?'

'No, definitely not.'

'How can you be so sure?'

Saltfleet paused while he lit his pipe. 'The dead girl wasn't a schoolgirl. She was a kind of amateur prostitute called Mary Threlwall. And she was definitely killed in the house, soon after the man was killed.'

'But she was raped.'

'Apparently, yes. But I think that was to throw us off the scent. Lytton was the intended victim. The girl was an afterthought.' He summarized all he had found out so far. Lamb liked these interim reports on a case; he also knew that it often helped the officer in charge to sort out the details in his own mind. Saltfleet knew this, and he unfolded the details

117

deliberately, in their proper order. Lamb listened with his hands interlocked under his chin, without interruption. At the end, he nodded approvingly.

'It sounds as if it was pretty carefully premeditated. That means your problem is to dig into Lytton's past until you find out who'd got a motive to kill him . . .' He lapsed into silence, staring out of the window. Saltfleet sucked at his pipe and said nothing. Lamb said: 'I'd say one of the key questions is: Why did he kill the girl? She must have known him . . .'

'Not necessarily. He may have killed her in a panic.'

'Do you think so?'

Saltfleet said: 'No. I think Lytton was murdered soon after he made the phone call to the girl's flat. I think the killer then took Lytton's car and went to collect her. He'd decided to kill her before he killed Lytton. But that doesn't mean he knew her, or she knew him. He may have been afraid that Lytton had mentioned his name to her, or said something that might give us a clue.'

'He sounds a pretty cold-blooded bastard – a psychopath, from the sound of it. Probably on drugs.'

'That still wouldn't explain why he dumped the girl's body outside instead of leaving it inside.'

'No.' Lamb stood up and looked out of the window at the buildings of Victoria Street. 'That *is* strange . . . Any ideas?'

'I can only think of one possibility. If he left her inside, her flat-mate might notify the police. They'd soon check on the Hampstead house – they'd find out about it from the house-keeper – and find both bodies. On the other hand, if she's found outside, and it looks like a sex murder, then the police have no reason to look inside the house – at least, for a day or so.'

Lamb said: 'In which case he's playing for time . . .'

'Quite. And he's probably out of the country by now.'

Lamb shrugged. 'Then we'll have to bring him back. When we find out who he is.'

'We may need Interpol anyway. His housekeeper said he kept a Swiss bank account. We'll have to check on that.'

'Do you think the housekeeper's in it?'

'I doubt it. She looked genuinely shocked when she heard he was dead.'

'What about his friends – intimates?'

'He didn't seem to have many. I'm checking on the main one today – chap called Franklin Bascombe.'

'And what about this bloke with the odd name . . . Bellman?'

'Tinkler. That's the strangest thing so far. The real Tinkler's a highly respectable type who lives near Haslemere. He's one of these moral vigilantes – always writing letters denouncing dirty books to the newspapers. It looks as if the killer stole his name as a joke.'

'Christ! A joke!'

'I can't think of any other reason.'

'Then the killer must know Tinkler to some extent.'

'Not necessarily – he may have seen one of his letters in *The Times* . . .'

One of the three telephones on Lamb's desk rang. He said: 'Hello. Good, put them on . . . International Bureau? Hello, je veux parler à Monsieur Sicot, s'il vous plaît. Commander Lamb, New Scotland Yard . . . Eh bien, j'attend jusqu'a il est pret.' His French was Anglicized but fluent. He looked at Saltfleet. 'O.K. Greg, you'd better carry on. Check that bank account. I'll get Motherwell to deal with your routine stuff from Divisions . . . Hello.' Saltfleet nodded and went out.

Back in his office, he rang Forrest at the Flying Squad again. This time he was in.

'Hello, George. What happened about Guerin?'

'Not a bloody thing. We drew blanks all three times.'

'Did you see the girl – Sheila Curtis?'

'No. I sent Cartmel over there. He stayed with her for an hour, in case she rang him and warned him.'

'Sorry to hear that. I've got to see her this morning. I'll let you know if I find anything out.'

Next he rang Mrs Beaumont Ames.

'Did Lytton have an accountant?'

'I don't think so.'

'Where did he keep his cheque-book stubs?'

119

'In a drawer in his library.'

'Can you bring them with you this morning?'

'I doubt it. The drawer's locked, and he always kept the key.'

'On him?'

'I think so, but I'm not sure.'

'Force it, if necessary. And I'll also need the names of his banks, and, if possible, the account numbers.'

'I can give you the names now.' He wrote them down.

After that, he rang Lytton's Chelsea bank, and asked to speak to the manager. He identified himself, and told him that Lytton was dead.

'What I want to know is whether Mr Lytton withdrew any unusually large sums over the past six months – especially since Christmas. Could you check on this for me?'

'Of course. I'll be glad to do anything I can. Would you like to hang on now?'

'No. But I'd be grateful if you could ring me back here at the Yard.' He gave his extension number. 'My sergeant can take the message if I'm not in.'

As he was leaving the office, the phone rang again. Crisp said: 'It's the Press Officer.'

'You talk to him. Tell him to try to get the newspapers to play it down. Say we haven't established cause of death yet.'

It was twenty past ten when he left the Yard. Crisp stayed behind; he didn't like post mortems.

He drove to Grafton Mews. It was jammed with parked cars, and he had to park on a yellow line at the end of the street. When he rang the doorbell, he half-expected no reply. But her footsteps came down the stairs, and when she opened the door, he saw she was in her street clothes. She said:

'Have you arrested Pierre?'

'No. He's probably out of the country by now.'

She said, with suppressed anger: 'What had he done?'

He looked at her for a moment before answering; it could make no difference if she knew.

'His partner's been found dead in Amsterdam. The Dutch police want to question him.'

She looked at him searchingly, as if doubting his word. Then she said:

'He didn't do it.'

'He behaves as if he did.' They were walking down to the car.

'Why?'

'When I came on Saturday afternoon, he probably felt the police were getting too close. So he skipped.'

She said nothing, climbing into the passenger seat. He said: 'I don't want to seem heartless, my dear, but you're lucky to be rid of him.' She said nothing. He glanced at her tired, set face, and decided to say no more.

It was ten minutes to eleven when they pulled into the yard of University College. A young man in a white smock, whom he recognized as one of Aspinal's assistants, came over to the car and opened the door for the girl.

'Good morning, sir. Nice to see you again.'

'Morning, Peter. Were you waiting for me?'

'Yes, sir. The doc says you're to go right up.' To the interns, Aspinal was 'the doc'; the medical students called him Gilbert, the name referring to a comic strip character called Gilbert the Ghoul.

Saltfleet said: 'The young lady's here to identify the girl.'

The assistant said: 'Hello,' the tone conveying recognition. Saltfleet said: 'You know one another?'

'I tied up her hand one day. She'd given herself a nasty cut on a breadknife. How is it?'

'Healed up now, thank you.' She produced the ghost of a smile.

'Did you . . . know the dead girl?'

'We shared a flat.'

'Oh, I'm sorry . . .' He led them along the corridor to the morgue. As they stopped outside the door, Saltfleet observed that her face had become very white.

'Do you feel all right?' She nodded. 'This won't take a moment.' The body was on a trolley. When the assistant pulled back the sheet, she stepped back a pace, and Saltfleet had to steady her elbow to prevent her from falling. He was glad the dead girl's face looked peaceful. The ligature mark was still visible around the neck, but the worst of the congestion had vanished. The face looked as if she was deeply asleep.

'Is that Mary Threlwall?'

She nodded. The assistant said:

'She seemed a pretty girl.'

This seemed to touch some spring of realization; the girl burst into tears. The assistant put an arm round her shoulders and tried to soothe her. Saltfleet said:

'Listen, there's something I've got to ask you.' She looked up at him, the tears running down her face. 'It's possible that the man who killed her was afraid she'd recognized him. Think hard. Can you think of anyone she knew who could have done it?'

She thought for several seconds, then shook her head.

'There's no one.' She staggered, and would have fallen except for the assistant's arm. Saltfleet asked him: 'Can you get her home?'

'Of course. Where does she live?'

'On the other side of Tottenham Court Road.'

'I'll take her. It'll be no trouble.'

It was eleven o'clock when he got down to the hall again. Mrs Beaumont Ames was talking to the porter. He said:

'Sorry I'm late. Did you bring the cheque stubs?'

'In here.' She touched her handbag.

'Good. Let's go up.' He knew the body would be in Aspinal's post-mortem room. Miss Crowther was waiting outside. She said: 'I was just going to ring your office. Dr Aspinal's waiting...'

Aspinal's post-mortem room, adjoining his laboratory, was barely ten feet square. When they went in, he was pulling on rubber gloves. Lytton's body lay on the table, the mouth now held closed by a cloth tied round the head. Saltfleet watched Mrs Beaumont Ames out of the corner of his eye. She was obviously fascinated, unable to keep a kind of happiness from her face. She went to the table and looked down at the upturned face, then at the rest of the body. She said casually, without emotion:

'Yes, that's him all right.'

Aspinal, who was fitting a blade into the scalpel, said:

'Would you like to watch, or would you prefer to go?'

Mrs Beaumont Ames glanced at Saltfleet.

'Will it be all right if I stay?'

'Of course. If Dr Aspinal doesn't mind.'

She gave a short laugh. 'It's not every day you see your boss cut up.'

Aspinal said, with grave courtesy: 'It must be a liberating experience.' Without further ado, he sliced into the skin below the Adam's apple, and then made a clean incision down the inside of the breast. The skin parted like stretched rubber, revealing a greyish, fatty layer. Aspinal continued to cut with small strokes, like a dressmaker cutting stitches, stopping just above the pubic hair. After this, he started at the top again, and made a deeper cut, down through the subcutaneous fat. Then he laid down the scalpel, and carefully pulled the skin apart at the breast bone, exposing the reddened cage of the ribs. He worked quickly, in a businesslike manner, like a butcher dissecting a carcase. He used the scalpel so swiftly that Saltfleet was afraid he might cut his finger.

Aspinal took up an instrument that looked like pruning shears. He said conversationally:

'These are my old plaster shears – for cutting plaster of Paris. They're much better than bone shears.' He began cutting up the ribs, starting at the centre of the bottom left side. Each snap of the shears cut through a bone. When he reached the shoulder blade, he started on the other side. Finally, he lifted out the section of ribs like a grating. The death-smell began to permeate the room. Saltfleet had never liked it: the sweetish, decaying smell that reminded him of old farm lavatories in the days before disinfectant. The exposed lungs were a blackish-grey colour. Mrs Beaumont Ames asked:

'Is that through smoking?'

'No. Through breathing the soot in the air. Only babies have pink lungs.' He turned to Miss Crowther. 'I think we might need the camera again.' He told Saltfleet: 'I'd like to get a picture of the puncture in the lung, for my book on legal medicine. We took half a dozen shots of the body, by the way – just in case you need them.' This was leg-pulling; it was established procedure to photograph the body before

123

a post mortem, and Saltfleet had not bothered to ask about it. Aspinal smiled at Mrs Beaumont Ames: 'You could have one too, if you like. As a keepsake.'

The smell was bothering her. She shook her head violently: 'No, thanks. I saw enough of him while he was alive.'

Aspinal said: 'Not as much as this, I imagine?'

She said dryly: 'You'd be surprised.'

Aspinal bent over, and sniffed the chest cavity above the right-hand lung. Then he made a careful incision in the lung, and bent close again to sniff. Saltfleet also bent over, the smell making his stomach heave.

Aspinal said: 'Notice anything? No? I'd like to bet there's a trace of some anaesthetic. Miss Crowther . . .' She held out a jar, the screw-cap removed. Aspinal removed the lung and dropped it into the jar. She screwed on the cap.

'What could it be?'

'Not ether or chloroform, I'm fairly certain. My guess would be halothane, but I shan't know until after the gas chromatography.'

'What is halothane?'

'A general anaesthetic – trade name for fluothane. It's non-inflammable.'

'You think he'd been anaesthetized when he was killed?'

'Not necessarily. Perhaps just drowsy.'

'What does halothane smell like?'

'Miss Crowther, pass that bottle.'

He uncapped the brown bottle; the smell was not unlike formaldehyde.

'And it's non-inflammable?'

'Yes.'

Their eyes met. Saltfleet did not want to say more in front of Mrs Beaumont Ames.

Aspinal pointed to a dark spot on the surface of the heart. 'There's the wound – neatly central in the left ventricle, as I thought. Miss Crowther, could you get a photograph?' He gestured with disgust at the coronary arteries. 'As I thought. Look at this mess.' He looked at Mrs Beaumont Ames. 'Did you know he was suffering from fatty degeneration?'

'No. Was it serious?'

'It would probably have killed him within two years.' He

124

looked at Saltfleet. 'Do you want to see the brain?'

'Not particularly.'

'Well, I think I'll take a look, just for curiosity. I've seen massive cerebral embolisms developing from stab wounds in the left ventricle. It's also possible, of course, that death didn't follow instantaneously.' He began cutting carefully under the chin and behind the ears. Saltfleet said to Mrs Beaumont Ames: 'Are you ready to go?'

'Go?' She looked startled, then laughed. 'Oh, you mean leave this place. I've got death on the brain. Could I just see how you get at the brain?'

'Your enthusiasm does you credit,' Aspinal said gravely. 'Pass me the saw, Miss Crowther.' He finished the incision across the top of the scalp, then pulled the scalp forward over the eyes, exposing the bone. 'I'm afraid this part of the job is just sheer hard work, like sawing wood.' He rested the saw against the forehead, steadying it with the other hand, then began to cut. Saltfleet said:

'I'll see you, Martin. Let me know the result of the chromatography test as soon as you can.'

In the corridor outside, he met the assistant, Peter.

'How is she?'

'Oh, fine. Badly shaken, poor girl. She needs looking after. Excuse my asking, sir, but what does she do for a living?'

Saltfleet said quickly: 'She's a model. Why?'

'My sister wants to spend a few months in London. I thought I might ask this girl if she wants someone to share her flat.'

Saltfleet smiled at him, to hide his indecision.

'Why don't you ask her about it?'

'Thanks. I will.' He went into the post-mortem room. Saltfleet was glad Mrs Beaumont Ames didn't know what they were talking about.

She asked: 'Are you going anywhere near Chelsea?'

'I can, after I've made a couple of calls.' He wanted a chance to talk to her. 'Why don't you come too?'

'I'm in no hurry.'

They went out together, into the sunlight. He had parked his car in the shadow of the building; it was still pleasantly cool inside.

125

As they drove down Gower Street, he said:

'I suppose you'll have to start looking for another place now?'

She hesitated before answering. 'Not necessarily.'

'Why not?'

'He promised to leave me the lease of the house in his will.'

'That was generous of him. Why?'

'Well, we had a terrific row about a year ago. I was going to leave. So he offered to give me the lease of the place if I'd stay on . . .'

'I don't quite see the point. He didn't expect to die, did he?'

'Oh no. Some fortune-teller told him he'd live to be eighty. But that was typical of him. A kind of gesture that meant nothing. Just to keep me quiet.'

'How long has the lease got to run?'

'Twenty years.' She glanced sideways at him. 'But if you're thinking that gave me a motive for killing him . . .'

'I wasn't. You couldn't have killed him. It was a man.' But he was not being entirely frank; it certainly gave her a motive for being involved in his death.

As they drove through Russell Square she asked: 'Where are we going?'

'To the Occult Bookshop, near Holborn. Do you know it?'

'I know *of* it.'

'Did Lytton spend a lot of time there?'

She said smiling: 'He spent a lot of money there.'

'You haven't answered my question.'

'No. I don't think he went there a lot.'

He said, with a kind of exasperation: 'Then where the hell did he go in the last few months of his life?'

'I . . . I don't know. He spent a lot of time at home . . . reading in his study. He was excited about something – I could tell.'

'Did you get the impression he was seeing a lot of somebody?'

She shook her head. 'I honestly wish I could tell you. He was up to his neck in something, but I couldn't tell you what.

126

He was always very close . . . you know, secretive.'

'So what makes you think he was up to his neck in something?'

'He stopped seeing his old friends. One day Franklin Bascombe rang up – the publisher. He wanted to talk to Charles . . .'

'Charles? Was that Lytton's real name?'

'One of them. His friends called him Charles or Charlie. You couldn't really call anybody Manfred, could you?'

'And you called him Charles?'

'Yes. It wasn't exactly a formal relation . . . Anyway, Bascombe rang up one day and got talking to me. And he said "What the hell's Charles doing with himself these days? We never seem to see him." So I gathered he was up to something.'

'Weren't you curious?'

'Oh, I suppose so. But he was always getting mixed up with a lot of odd people. Frank Bascombe could tell you more about that . . .'

They had turned into Red Lion Square. He stopped to allow a car to pull away from the kerb, then backed into the space by the parking meter. He said:

'Could you make me a list of the books he was reading in the past few months?'

'I suppose so . . .' She sounded dubious.

'Try to remember as many as you can.'

'All right. But what good would that do?'

'It might give us a clue about what he was up to . . .'

'I can tell you one thing. He read several books on Hitler and the Nazis. I don't know whether that means anything . . .'

'Since Christmas?'

'Yes, round about that time. They're still in his bedroom. I could tell you the titles when I get back . . .' She reached out and held his sleeve. 'Hey!'

They were looking in through the window of the bookshop; one of the Swedish girls leaned into the window from inside to get a book.

'She's one of the girls in the photograph!'

'That's right.'

'So this is where he found her . . .'

They went into the shop. At that moment, Widdup came out of the door of the art gallery. He said:

'Hello, Inspector. How's it going?'

'Not too badly. Have you got a minute to spare?'

'I expect so. I'm just off to lunch. Feel like a quick one in the pub at the corner?'

'That's a good idea.'

Mrs Beaumont Ames said: 'The best yet.'

They followed Widdup into the saloon bar of the pub. It was almost empty.

'This is Mrs Beaumont Ames, Lytton's housekeeper.'

'How'd you do? I'm George Widdup. What will you have?'

Widdup brought their drinks over to the table. Saltfleet had a pint of bitter. It tasted good; his throat was dry. Widdup also had a pint. Mrs Beaumont Ames drank gin and tonic. She gave a sigh of pleasure as she set down the glass.

'I can't get that rotten smell out of my throat.' She explained to Widdup: 'I've just been to see my late employer sliced up. I didn't realize there was such a lousy smell . . .'

Saltfleet took the envelope out of his inside pocket, and dropped it in front of Widdup. Widdup glanced up at him suspiciously, then opened it. He glanced at the first photograph.

'Oh. My little pets.' In spite of his casualness, Saltfleet could see he was startled. He thumbed through them. He said: 'Oh, him.'

Saltfleet said: 'They told me they hardly knew him.'

Widdup finished looking through the photographs without speaking. Then he said:

'I'm not surprised.' He tossed the envelope back.

'Who are they? How long have you known them?'

'Six or seven months – since the shop opened. They're from Stockholm – their father's a civil engineer.'

'How did you meet them?'

'Through Max Engelke. He brought them to the opening.'

'Ah . . .'

Widdup looked at Saltfleet over his beer. 'You think Maxie's mixed up in this, don't you?'

128

Saltfleet shrugged. 'If they knew Lytton better than they said, perhaps he did too.'

'That's possible. They've just given notice.'

'The girls? When are they leaving?'

'End of the month.'

'Did they say why?'

'They just said they're going back to Sweden.' He tapped the envelope with his index finger. 'But I don't see they prove anything. Lytton had got money. They let him take pictures . . .'

Mrs Beaumont Ames said: 'Yes, but he didn't pay them.'

Saltfleet stared at her. 'What?'

'He didn't pay them. I know because he told me.'

'What did he tell you?'

'He showed me the photos, and I said: "I bet they cost you a nice packet." And he said: "Oddly enough, they didn't cost me a penny."'

Saltfleet said: 'You didn't tell me you'd seen the photos before. You said you'd found them behind some books.'

'That's right. You didn't ask me if I'd seen them before.'

Saltfleet looked at Widdup. 'What do you make of that?'

Widdup said decisively: 'I'd say Lytton wasn't telling the truth. I mean, for Christ's sake, why *should* they let him . . . do things like that? He wasn't exactly God's gift to women.'

Saltfleet looked at Mrs Beaumont Ames. She said: 'I suppose he *could* have been lying. But I don't see why he should.'

Widdup was shaking his head. He said: 'No, it's bloody daft.'

Saltfleet said: 'How well do you know Engelke?'

Widdup shrugged. 'Not all that well, I suppose. He's not a close friend, if that's what you mean.'

Saltfleet said, as if changing the subject: 'By the way, did you find out where they sell incense and candles?'

'Oh yes.' He reached into his inside pocket.

'From Engelke?'

'No. I saw Eileen Fox – the witch I told you about.' He produced a sheet of folded paper from his wallet. 'She says she uses this one at the top – The Brass Bottle, in Pedley Street, behind Brick Lane. This one's in Clapham, this one's in Maida Vale, and this one's in Noel Court, behind Poland Street . . .'

'Marvellous. Many thanks. I didn't realize there *were* such places . . .'

'There weren't until recently.' He emptied his pint. 'I've got to get a move on. I've got a traveller coming at half past.'

Saltfleet said: 'Just one more thing. Ever hear of a man called Norbert Tinkler?'

Widdup said promptly: 'No, never.'

When he'd gone, Mrs Beaumont Ames said: 'Who is this Engelke?'

'A painter.'

'Oh yes?' He could tell by her tone that she was interested.

'He has rather an odd gimmick. He paints on a kind of three-dimensional perspex with a mirror behind it, so you suddenly find yourself looking at your own face. Ever heard of him?'

She shook her head. 'No. Charles *did* meet some artist sometime recently – at least, I suppose it was recently . . .'

'What happened?'

'I don't know. Some kind of a quarrel, I think. Charles was going to buy one of his paintings, and found out it was a fake, or something . . .'

'How could it be a fake if it was one of his own paintings?'

'Oh, I don't know . . . He didn't tell me much about it. Ask Bascombe, he can tell you . . .'

'Does he know the man's name?'

'Probably.'

He stood up. 'Look, I've got to call at this shop in White-chapel before lunch. Would you like me to send you home in a taxi?'

'No. I'll come with you. I've nothing else to do.'

He emptied his glass. 'Ready?'

She rolled her eyes roguishly. 'For anything.'

He parked at the side of the Shoreditch Underground station. Children were playing hopscotch on the cracked pavement. Saltfleet knew the Whitechapel area well; he had spent two years at the Commercial Street station as a Detective-Sergeant. In those days, he and Miranda had lived in an ugly block of concrete flats in Tower Hamlets. It felt strange to return here fifteen years later: as though a lifetime had passed.

The shop was halfway down Pedley Street. He seemed to recollect some kind of second-hand shop there, devoted to battered prams and bicycles. Now it was unrecognizable. The plate-glass window was new; the front was newly painted in two shades of green. The sign above the door showed a genie emerging from a brass bottle. On either side of the window stood two large wooden totems, not unlike Easter Island statues. Between these there was a display of books, some in Oriental languages, and of wooden objects of folk art. In the centre of the window, in the foreground, there was an object that looked like a human hand in a glass case.

When he pushed open the door, there was a silvery chiming sound. Mrs Beaumont Ames said: 'Christ, fairy bells.' The smell in the shop was strange, but not unpleasant: a mixture of curry and some kind of musky scent. On the wall behind the counter there were a number of shrunken heads hanging by the hair; looking more closely, he saw they were made of wood.

The bead curtain parted; the woman who came in was bigger than Mrs Beaumont Ames, but had the same long, straight black hair. The complexion and profile made her seem like a Red Indian; but when she spoke, the accent was cockney:

' 'Ello, what can I do for you today?'

Saltfleet said: 'I was interested in candles.'

The woman grinned at him in a friendly way. 'Yeah, you look as if you're interested in candles.' She gave a throaty laugh. 'What kind of candles.'

Saltfleet said: 'A rather special kind. A kind that gives off a scent as it burns.'

'Scent? What kind of scent?' Before he could reply, she said: 'Anyway, we don't have nothing like that.'

'Are you sure?'

'Sure. If you mix things with wax, it makes it splutter. And that ain't no good for a candle, is it?' She pulled open a drawer under the counter. 'Look, we got every other kind.

131

Wax tapers. The kind you burn in Catholic churches. Tallow candles – these are very popular now. Some of our candles were on TV the other night in a film about witches. Now these pink ones have got a kind of scent, a bit like roses.' She picked up an elaborate pink candle and raised it to her wide nostrils. 'But you can't smell it when it burns.' Saltfleet shook his head. She said: 'You're not thinking of incense, are you? We've lots of different kinds.' She pulled open another drawer. It was full of labelled boxes.

'I'm afraid not. This is a green coloured candle, with a strong smell.'

She shook her head contemplatively.

'No, 'fraid I can't 'elp you. You're sure it *is* a candle you want?'

'I think so. Why?'

'I'll tell you . . . There used to be 'ands of glory in a green wax, and that gave off a very funny smell.'

'What's a hand of glory?'

'You know, er . . . a hand. We 'aven't got any left now. They used to make 'em a couple of years ago – kind of Hallowe'en novelty.'

'Did they burn?'

'Oh yes. Like candles. You set the fingers alight. They was supposed to be murderers' 'ands.'

Mrs Beaumont Ames said: 'Yes, I've seen them. They're supposed to be a real hand pickled in saltpetre . . .'

'That's right. We had a boxful of 'em, but we sold 'em all a few months ago.' She rummaged under the counter. 'There used to be a broken one somewhere . . . ooff.' She gasped as she knelt down. 'Yes, I thought it was still 'ere.' She pulled out a cardboard box, and straightened up painfully. Inside, there was a wax hand, the green fingers broken and crumbling. Smears of red paint or sealing wax simulated blood.

He said: 'May I?' He lifted it carefully to his nostrils. The smell was strong and distinct, and he recognized it immediately. The bubble of exultation rose in him, making him want to laugh aloud, but he suppressed it as a matter of course. He said: 'Yes, that's what I wanted.'

'Ah, I'm sorry we can't 'elp you. I'm pretty sure they don't make 'em any more.'

132

'Could I buy that one?'

She looked startled. 'Well, that ain't much good . . .'

'How much were they new?'

'Fifty pence each.'

He found a fifty-pence piece and put it on the counter. 'All right?'

'I s'pose so. Don't seem right, charging you full price. We'll make it five bob.' She rang open the till, and handed him change. 'It's a pity we sold all the others. We 'ad 'em a year, then someone bought the lot.'

'Did you sell them?'

'Yes.'

'Can you remember what he looked like?'

'Wasn't a man. It was a girl . . .'

'Pretty?' An instinct already told him that he was on the right track.

'Yes. Blonde.'

'Swedish?'

'Foreign anyway.'

He reached into his pocket and took out the packet of photographs. He pulled the top one halfway out, so that only the upper halves of the girls were visible, and showed it to her.

'One of these?'

'Yes.' She glanced up at him. 'You're a copper, aren't you?'

'That's right.' He picked up the box from the counter. 'And you've been very helpful.'

She said dryly: 'Hope I 'aven't got her into trouble?'

He smiled at her. 'No, not trouble exactly. Thanks again.'

Outside, he put his arm across Mrs Beaumont Ames's shoulders, and gave her a squeeze.

'Come on, I'll buy you a drink. I think we both deserve one.'

Eight

A squad car turned into the wide gateway of the old Yard; as he pulled into his parking space, Eric Lamb climbed out of the rear door.

'Hello, Greg. Any luck?'

'Yes, I think so. How's it with you?'

Lamb came over. 'Pretty good. We've got the bastard who did poor Jeff Crimble. American army deserter, pushing drugs in Soho.'

'Good. That's marvellous news.' Crimble had stopped a car that was driving too fast through Hammersmith; the driver had lowered the window and shot him at close range. Fortunately the bullet had travelled upward, missing the brain, and exiting at the centre of the skull. Crimble was not going to die, but he had gone blind in one eye. It was the kind of crime that made every policeman dream of violent revenge. 'Where did you catch him?'

'Tilbury. We got a tip that he was coming in from Stockholm with heroin. What's happening with you?'

'I think I know who killed Lytton. But I've no solid evidence yet.'

'Good. Listen, I've got to go and see George Forrest. I'll drop into your office in ten minutes. Get some tea up.'

Crisp's desk, and the floor around it, was piled high with files.

'Hello. What's this?'

'We've got another Identikit picture of the North Circular rapist, and I'm damned sure I know him. So I've had the C.R.O. send up some of the files on sex offenders.'

'Why didn't you go down there?'

'Didn't like to 'til you came back.'

Saltfleet looked down at the Identikit picture on the desk; it was certainly better than the other one they had. But this was no guarantee it was accurate.

'You can't have the file of every sex offender in the London area. They'd fill the office.'

'I know, but I've been working it out. He's spread these assaults over a wide area. Why should he do that? Because he wants to avoid his home territory. Don't you think?'

'It's possible.' He didn't feel it was worth while to raise objections; if Crisp had an idea, he should test it.

'Well, look at the map. Here's the North Circular, and these are the places where he committed assaults. Now suppose he lived here – around Golders Green. He's close to the North Circular, and it explains why he's committed assaults in Ealing, Neasden, Enfield, Hendon, Waltham . . .'

'If it comes to that, he could live in Finchley, Barnet or Haringey.'

'Right. So I'll check them too . . .'

Saltfleet patted his shoulder. 'Good work. Anything from the bank manager?'

'Oh yes. He wants you to ring him back.'

'Get some tea sent up, would you? One for the Chief too – he'll be in soon.'

Crisp looked at his watch. 'You've got this bloke Bascombe coming in at three o'clock. I contacted him this morning.'

It was now half past two. He dialled the Chelsea bank and asked to speak to the manager. When he identified himself, the manager said:

'Ah yes, this information about Mr Lytton's account. I've been through it fairly carefully, and as far as I can tell, his outgoings over the past six months have been rather less than usual.'

Saltfleet said: 'Ah, I see.' His voice expressed his disappointment.

'But that in itself struck me as a little odd . . . Let's see. I've checked back as far as 1968, and Mr Lytton's average expenditure has been over twelve thousand a year. In 1969 it was eighteen thousand. Yet between last November and 8 April, he's spent only two thousand eight hundred pounds.'

'What about payments into his account?'

'They've also been low. Less than three thousand, compared with seven thousand in the same period last year.'

Saltfleet was now smiling. He wrote down the figures. 'I see . . . Which looks as if he may be using a foreign account?'

'Precisely. So if I were you, I'd check with the Chase Manhatton Bank at Third Avenue in New York, and the Credit Lyonnais in Lausanne, the main office.'

'Where did his income come from?'

'Foreign investments mostly. Made by his father. He lost a great deal when the Malayans took over the tin mines, but he still had a pretty healthy income.'

'Thank you, Mr Pearson. That's very helpful indeed.'

Crisp asked: 'Any luck?' Before he could answer, the phone rang again. It was Aspinal.

'Gregory. I've just got the result of the gas chromatography test.'

He said quickly: 'Yes?'

'It *was* halothane.'

'You're quite certain?'

'Absolutely. We're doing a spectro-photometric test as well, but I've no doubt about the result.'

'He breathed it immediately before death?'

'He must have done. At least, within an hour. There was a high concentration in the adipose tissue, as well as in the arterial blood. If he'd gone on breathing normally, he'd have got rid of it in six hours. My guess is that he was stabbed soon after inhaling it.'

Saltfleet said nothing for a moment. Aspinal said:

'Are you there?'

'Yes. I'm just thinking . . . If the man intended to stab him in the heart, why bother with the anaesthetic?'

'To make sure he didn't struggle.'

'Wouldn't he struggle as the pad was pressed over his face?'

'I don't believe it was, Gregory. Remember the incense smell? He could have left the halothane to evaporate in an open dish.'

'Wouldn't that have knocked out the killer too?'

'He probably wasn't in the room. Lytton was probably supposed to be meditating, or repeating a magic formula, or something.'

'How long would it take for halothane to knock him out?'

'In a room of that size, perhaps five minutes. A concentration of three percent is enough to cause unconsciousness.'

136

'Is there any way of testing the room for halothane? Would it linger in the curtains, for example?'

'I doubt it. Not after three days.'

Crisp's telephone rang. Crisp picked it up, said thank you, and hung up. He said:

'Bascombe's downstairs.'

'Good, get him sent up.' He said into the phone: 'Sorry, Martin. I've just heard that Bascombe's arrived.'

'Try and give him a fright. He deserves it.'

'Why?'

'He's been getting away with too many things for too long. Ask him about Wendy Bateson.'

'Who's she?'

'A twelve-year-old girl who got involved in this Hellfire Club of Bascombe's.'

'Does it really exist, this club?'

'It did. They used to meet in the house of a lesbian called Madge Rickwood, out at West Wycombe. Not far from Dashwood's place – that's where the original Hellfire Club used to meet. This Madge Rickwood got involved with a woman called Cheryl Bateson – her husband had left her. And Cheryl Bateson moved into the house at Wycombe with her daughter, this child Wendy. They said she was the Egyptian goddess Angerona, or something like that – she was supposed to be the eyeless goddess they worshipped. Then one of the Sunday papers did a series about witchcraft a couple of years ago, and Cheryl Bateson agreed that her daughter had taken part in the ceremonies – witchcraft rites and all that. When the article came out, the mother threatened to sue the newspaper. She wanted twenty thousand pounds. At this point the reporter found out that the child was going to the local doctor for a skin rash on her thighs and buttocks. And they bribed the doctor to examine the child to find out if she was *virgo intacta*. And she wasn't. So the whole case was quietly dropped.'

'Any idea who was responsible?'

'No. But I can tell you one thing. Lytton and Bascombe share the same taste for young girls . . .'

There was a knock on the office door. Saltfleet said:

'Thanks for the tip, Martin. I'll be in touch with you.'

Crisp had opened the door. The man who came in was much as Saltfleet had imagined him: overweight, late middle age, the face shiny with perspiration. He said:

'I say, this is shocking news. I was absolutely shattered. Who on earth could have done it?'

The public-school voice was higher than one would have expected from a man of his bulk. Saltfleet asked him to sit down, and offered him a cigarette – he kept a box in his drawer for this purpose. He thought Bascombe's manner was slightly shifty; perhaps it was merely nervous. He glanced through the papers on his desk to give Bascombe time to recover. He said:

'At the moment we don't have much idea. Do you think he could have been blackmailed?'

Bascombe was lighting one of his own cigars; his hand trembled slightly. He shook out the match, then said:

'I would say that, in my opinion, he was almost certainly *not* being blackmailed.'

'How can you be so certain?'

A peculiar smile twisted Bascombe's plump mouth; a projecting front tooth lent the smile a certain schoolboy charm.

'I knew him quite well, you know.'

'But not well enough to have any idea who might have killed him?'

'Put it this way.' Bascombe now seemed at his ease. 'Lytton and I were very close friends for years – very close. In the past eighteen months we haven't seen much of one another, for various reasons. But we've remained fairly close. His vices, such as they were, were not of the kind that would attract the attention of the police. And if he *was* in that kind of trouble, I'm pretty sure he'd have told me. I had lunch with him last Thursday, and he didn't seem to have anything on his mind.'

'He was a member of your Hellfire Club, wasn't he?'

'Oh yes. You could call it that.'

'I could call it what?'

'A member. You see, the so-called Hellfire Club is . . . well, it's almost a joke. One of my authors lives very close to Medmenham Abbey, where Sir Francis Dashwood's original Hellfire Club used to hold their meetings. She did a lot of research on it for a book I published. We all got rather interested and had a few picnics by moonlight on West Wycombe Hill – where the Hellfire Caves are situated. But it was all rather a lark. Never a real club.'

'This club was the subject of an article in a Sunday newspaper?'

Bascombe went red. 'Yes. Some scum of a journalist invented a lot of nonsense. We had to threaten to sue him.'

Saltfleet said : 'But you didn't sue?'

Bascombe evaded his eyes. 'Er . . . no. It was settled out of court.'

Saltfleet was not willing to let him get away with it. He said : 'You mean they paid damages?'

'I'm not sure of the details. I wasn't directly involved.' Bascombe was evidently alarmed at the way the conversation was going; his face flushed until he looked as if he was on the point of a heart attack. The cigar in his fingers trembled. At that moment there was a knock on the door. It was the girl with tea. Eric Lamb stood behind her. Saltfleet said :

'Ah, come in, Chief.'

'Am I intruding?'

'Not at all. You'd probably like to meet Mr Bascombe. He was Lytton's closest friend. This is Commander Lamb.'

'I'm pleased to meet you, sir.' Bascombe shook hands effusively; he was probably grateful to Lamb for interrupting.

Crisp pushed up a chair for Lamb. Saltfleet said :

'Mr Bascombe was just saying that he was sure Lytton wasn't being blackmailed.'

Bascombe said : 'Although, of course, we'd been out of touch in the past six months.'

Lamb said : 'Why was that?'

'Oh . . . I didn't ask him . . . No, no tea for me, I never touch it . . . No, frankly I assumed he'd developed some other interest.'

'What kind?'

'Sexual, of course.'

Lamb said : 'Why "of course"?'

'Because, my dear sir, all his interests were sexual. He was

139

what the medical textbooks call a satyr. Of course, he had other interests – music, painting . . .'

Saltfleet said : 'Magic?'

Bascombe took this in his stride. 'Yes, magic. And incidentally, I imagine you'd find it worth while to interview a man called Steinhager who runs a witch circle at Highgate.'

'I've seen him. I'm convinced he knew nothing about it.'

Bascombe looked disappointed. 'Oh, you surprise me. You surprise me very much indeed.'

Lamb asked : 'Do you know of any other groups he got mixed up with?'

'Oh, dozens, over the years.' Bascombe chuckled. 'We used to call him Toad of Toad Hall because he was always getting involved in some new craze. Apart from Steinhager there was – let's see . . . the Maharishi for a period, and a sort of Kensington yogi called Narendra Ghosh – that was in the mid sixties. There was a couple who ran some kind of witchcraft cult down at Brighton – I've forgotten their name . . .'

'Dalgleish,' Saltfleet said.

'Ah, you've found out about them . . . Then, let's see, there was Steinhager's lot. And at one point he got mixed up with a crowd of gypsies who lived out near Watford – he was talking about buying a caravan and moving in with them to study gypsy magic.'

Saltfleet said : 'Do you know anything about a painter he got to know fairly recently – around Christmas?'

'Ah yes, I can tell you something about that too. About three weeks ago, I went to call on him, and he had a painting called "The Killer from the Stars". It was an impressive sort of thing – a sort of night-time landscape with mountains, and this great Thing hovering in the sky, like some demon on a horse. Well, for some reason he was terribly cagey about it – wouldn't tell me the name of the artist or how much he paid for it. Well, I kept looking at this thing, and I was sure there was something familiar about it . . . but I couldn't tell what. Then, a couple of days later, I remembered where I'd seen it – it was almost a copy of a painting by a Mexican called Siqueiros, part of some series illustrating war. I found it in a book on Mexican art. So I sent the book to him in the post, with a note just saying see page so and so. His house-keeper told me he was furious about it and sent the painting back to the artist ... I asked him about it the last time I saw him, but he didn't want to talk about it. Probbaly didn't like to admit he'd been duped.'

'Did the painting have a signature?'

'No, I don't think so.'

'And you've no idea at all of the name of the artist?'

'No. He clammed up completely.'

'Didn't you see him again between sending him the book and meeting him last Thursday?'

'No. I'd been in Ibiza for ten days.' He looked at his watch. 'Say, do you mind if I rush off? I've got a board meeting at four o'clock.'

Saltfleet stood up. 'Not at all. You've been most helpful. If we've any more queries, I'll ring you.'

He shook the plump hand, and noticed that the palm was now wet – a sign of tension.

When Crisp had escorted him out of the room, Lamb said:

'Have you checked him in C.R.O.?'

Saltfleet knew him too well not to suspect it was more than a casual query.

'No. Have you?'

'Yes. He's got two convictions for soliciting males in public lavatories – 1948 and 1957. The second time he got three months in gaol because it involved gross public indecency.'

This was typical of Lamb. Saltfleet had mentioned Bascombe's name to him only once, in the course of casual conversation; he had taken the trouble to check in Criminal Records.

'Well I'll be damned. That's interesting. Lytton's house-keeper told me he liked being flogged ...'

'Lytton? Or Bascombe?'

'Lytton ... Of course, it doesn't prove anything about Lytton. Homosexuality may have been a taste they didn't share.'

Lamb said broodingly: 'I'd like to bet on it ... Who's this suspect of yours?'

'A painter called Engelke ...' He nodded. 'Yes, he's probably the one who tried to sell Lytton the forged picture.'

'Which might provide some kind of motive for the murder. Tell me about this Engelke.'

Saltfleet took the packet of photographs out of his pocket and gave them to Lamb. Lamb glanced through them.

'Mmm, nice. Is this Lytton?'

'Yes.'

'Where did you get them?'

'Lytton's housekeeper found them. The two girls are Swedish – they work in this Occult Bookshop I mentioned to you. Engelke introduced them to the bookshop owner – they're probably his mistresses. Now the odd thing is that, according to the housekeeper, Lytton didn't pay the girls for posing for the pictures . . .'

'I see . . .'

'Quite. So Lytton probably got them to do it for nothing. And I've got another piece of evidence. Coventry found green candlewax near the bottom of the curtain in the room where Lytton was found. It had a distinctive smell – flowery, a bit like geraniums. I noticed the smell when I went into the house. This morning I found the shop that sold it – not an ordinary candle, but a thing shaped like a human hand. I've checked at the Forensic Lab, and the wax is identical. And one of those two girls bought the last six of these hands . . .'

'Tremendous! That's excellent work, Greg. So you think you might have a case against this Engelke?'

Saltfleet shook his head. 'Not yet. Not by a long way. I'm not even certain yet that he's the man we want.'

'Why not?'

'There's this problem of the man who calls himself Norbert Tinkler. Just before Christmas, Lytton went to the home of this Walter Steinhager – the one who runs a magical order – and wanted some advice about Norbert Tinkler. That makes it sound as if Tinkler was mixed up in magic. Unfortunately, Steinhager wouldn't speak to Lytton – they'd quarrelled earlier – so all we know is that Lytton was worried about somebody who called himself Norbert Tinkler. Now the real Tinkler's never heard of Lytton . . .'

Lamb said: 'So Engelke *could* have used the name.'

'He could have. But there's a complication here. Both

142

Engelke and Lytton used the Occult Bookshop, and Engelke's got an exhibition of paintings on there at the moment. They must have met in the shop. In which case, it wouldn't take Lytton very long to find out that Engelke's name wasn't Norbert Tinkler.'

'How long has this shop been open?'

'Six months – since last November.'

'How long has Engelke been using it?'

'Ever since it opened. The owner said he was at the opening.'

'How long has Lytton been using it?'

'I'm not certain. The only person who could tell me is Widdup, the owner, and I don't want it to be too obvious that Engelke's the chief suspect. Not that I think Widdup would warn him. But there's no point in taking risks.'

Crisp had come to Saltfleet's desk to place some papers in the 'In' tray; he stopped to look at the photographs. He said:

'I can tell you where that was taken.' He was looking at the picture that showed Lytton entering the girl as she leaned back against the mantelpiece.

'Where?'

'That place in Hampstead. That's the bedroom at the top of the stairs. Look.' He placed his finger on a design at the corner of the mantelpiece. 'I'd recognize that anywhere.'

Saltfleet nodded. 'Yes, that's logical. That's the obvious place for him to take the girls. Unfortunately, that doesn't get us any further. What we need is some connection between Lytton and Engelke.'

'That doesn't sound too difficult.'

'It is. Damn difficult. One of the first things these magic circles do is make you swear an oath of secrecy. I think Engelke made Lytton swear an oath. And then I think he went to great lengths to make sure there was no obvious connection between himself and Lytton. They probably met at the Hampstead house with nobody else present. Perhaps other places too . . .'

'But if Lytton claimed to be practising magic, wouldn't there be other members of the group?'

'I suppose so. On the other hand, Engelke may have told him some story . . . perhaps claimed to represent some Ger-

143

man group . . . I wish Steinhager hadn't refused to speak to Lytton at Christmas . . .'

'What about money? If Lytton gave Engelke money . . .'

'I've checked with his English bank. No large sums went in or out over the past six months. But he's got American and Swiss bank accounts. I'll have to check on them.'

'There shouldn't be any trouble getting the details of his American account. The Swiss might be a bit more awkward . . . Have you got the details? Write them down for me. I'll see what I can do through Edgar Meyerstein."

'That'd certainly help.' He scribbled on a sheet of scrap paper and handed it to Lamb. 'There's not much, but it should be enough.'

Lamb stood up. 'What do you intend to do next?'

'Try and find out what I can about Engelke's past. I'll check with Interpol to see if he's got a criminal record. If he hasn't then I don't know where to start. Perhaps Widdup . . .'

'Why not ask Engelke?'

'Do you think it's wise at this stage?'

'Why not? I don't see it makes any difference if he knows you suspect him. He can only skip the country. But if he thinks you've got nothing on him anyway, he'll probably sit back laughing at you.'

Saltfleet nodded. 'You could be right. But if I'm going to come out in the open, I think maybe I'll talk to the girls first.'

When Lamb had gone, Crisp said: 'So you're sure it's this Engelke?'

'It's *got* to be. Or I'm losing my grip. What I'd really like to know . . .' He sank into brooding, staring at the blotting pad. Crisp said: 'What?'

'Oh . . . just why Engelke should choose Norbert Tinkler as an alias – if he did. It was downright careless. Tinkler wrote letters to the newspapers. Lytton only had to set eyes on one of those – denouncing pornography – and he'd know somebody was pulling his leg.'

'Perhaps Engelke didn't know about the letters to newspapers.'

'Then he didn't know Tinkler very well. It's the first thing he talks about.' He sat, doodling on the blotting pad.

144

'Didn't you say Engelke's a painter? Perhaps Tinkler said nasty things about his paintings.'

Saltfleet sighed. 'I suppose there's only one way to find out.'

He took out his wallet, and found Tinkler's phone number. The lines were bad; it took him ten minutes to get through. It was Miss Tinkler's voice that finally answered. He said:

'Sorry to bother you. Do you know if your brother ever met a painter by the name of Engelke?'

'The name isn't familiar. I'll ask him when he gets home. I've never heard him mention it.'

'Does your brother normally have any contact with painters?'

'Not normally. *I* meet more painters than Norbert does.'

Saltfleet said: 'Of *course*. Your paintings . . . I shouldn't have forgotten – we both admired them very much. But you've never met this man Engelke?'

'What does he look like?'

'Smallish. Blond. Rather good-looking, in a sullen sort of way. Speaks with a foreign accent.'

'Oh yes, I know *him*. If it's the same man. He and Norbert had the most awful set-to at the Landscape Exhibition. '

'Can you tell me what happened?'

'It was at the opening of the exhibition of modern British landscape painters, last April or May, I forget which. I had a few small things in it. This rather objectionable young man was standing there with a fairly pretty girl and making sarcastic remarks about the paintings. As he was drinking champagne, I suppose he must have been there as a guest. So Norbert said something to him, and they got into an argument. Then Mr Smythe came over – the organizer of the exhibition – and tried to smooth things over. But I'm afraid he wasn't very successful. Norbert got terribly angry.'

'Was this young man a painter?'

'Oh yes. He told Norbert he'd just finished a painting of the Queen and the Archbishop of Canterbury dancing naked on a tightrope. Norbert told him he had a twisted sense of humour.'

'You haven't seen him since?'

'No, and I hope we never see him again. Do you think he's connected with this murder?'

'It's just possible.'

'Norbert said he thought he was a drug addict – it was something about his eyes. Do you think that's possible . . .?'

Saltfleet let her talk on for several minutes more, grunting agreement or disagreement as it seemed necessary; he felt grateful to her, and was unwilling to interrupt her. He finally broke off the conversation by claiming there was a call on the other line. He hung up.

'Well, there's the connection with Tinkler. They had a quarrel at the opening of an art exhibition. One more link.'

'Do we pick him up yet?'

'No. There's still no real evidence. Even if we searched his place and found the other five hands of glory, it still wouldn't be evidence. He'd point out that they can be bought in half a dozen shops in London.'

'So what's the next move?'

'Back to the Occult Bookshop to talk to those girls.'

'Want me to drive you?'

'No. You stay here and keep looking for the North Circular bloke.'

As he walked out of Red Lion Square, the sky clouded over; the wind became cooler, smelling of rain. The first large drops hit the pavement and spread out. He reached the doorway of the bookshop as the downpour began. The rain whitened the road, the drops falling with such violence that they ricocheted like bullets. He stood watching it for five minutes, enjoying the clean, dustless smell, before he went into the shop.

There was a different girl behind the counter; this one was thin and dark. But the other twin was in the gallery, serving coffee. Her eyes met his for a moment, in recognition, then she looked away.

He mounted the stairs and knocked on the door. Widdup's voice called:

'Come in.'

He was standing by the window, which was open to its limit, watching the rain. He said:

'Isn't it lovely, watching the rain? I could stand here for hours.'

'Wish I could.' Saltfleet meant it.

'Have a seat. What can I do for you?'

Saltfleet said: 'This man Engelke – we're going to check on him pretty carefully.'

Widdup sat down. 'Yes, I thought so.' He scratched his nose, frowning at a stuffed owl on his desk. 'I think you're probably wrong, but that's your business.'

Saltfleet said slowly: 'If those girls slept with Lytton for nothing, then somebody told them to, and that somebody could have been Engelke.'

'I don't believe they did it for nothing. Perhaps he told that woman he did. But I don't believe it. He probably had his own reasons for lying to her.'

'I thought of that too. She was his procuress – that was part of her job – to get him girls. And she probably took a percentage. Yet I don't think it's likely he'd lie to her.'

'Why don't you ask the girls?'

'That's what I want to do. There's only one downstairs at the moment – the one in the coffee bar.'

He looked at his watch. 'Yes, it's Ingrid's turn for a late lunch today.' He picked up the telephone and pressed a switch. He said: 'Miriam, ask Sigrid to step up for a moment, would you?'

Saltfleet said: 'I'm afraid I'll have to ask you to leave us alone for a few minutes. If I questioned her in front of you, she'd have grounds for an official complaint.'

'Oh, sure. Why don't you take my seat? Press that red switch when you're ready, and I'll come back up. I'll be in the shop.'

He met the girl at the door and said:

'Sigrid, the Inspector wants to ask you a couple of questions. Do you mind?'

He caught a shade of nervousness in her face; but she shrugged and raised her eyebrows.

'Of course not.'

147

Saltfleet adjusted himself in Widdup's chair. It was very comfortable. He said:

'Would you like to sit down?'

She looked as if she were going to refuse, then sat down cautiously on the edge of the chair. Saltfleet said:

'How well did you know Manfred Lytton?'

She hesitated before replying. 'I used to see him in the shop, that's all.'

Saltfleet took the envelope out of his pocket; he took one photograph out and laid it on the desk. The girl looked away from it. He guessed she had been expecting something of the kind; her expression remained unchanged. Saltfleet said:

'Why did you lie about knowing him?'

She turned to look at him; her face was open and un-alarmed.

'You know why I lied.'

He allowed the silence to lengthen, then said:

'All right, we'll try again. How well did you know Lytton?'

'And I've told you the truth. We hardly knew him at all.' With the slight foreign accent, her voice had a charming schoolgirl lilt. It was hard to associate her with the photographs.

He said: 'He was murdered, and we're trying to find his murderer.'

'I know. I can't help you.'

'Why did you do it?'

'For money.' It sounded spontaneous.

'How much?'

'Fifty pounds.'

'How often?'

She hesitated before answering: 'Five or six times.' It told him what he had wanted to know. She had considered the possibility of lying about it.

He said: 'Tell me how it happened. When did he approach you?'

'I can't remember the exact time. I think it was just before Christmas.'

'Tell me exactly what happened.' He smiled at her with friendly encouragement.

'There isn't much to tell. I came back from lunch one day and found him talking to Ingrid . . .'

'That was the first time you'd seen him?'

'Yes.'

'The first time he'd been in the shop?'

'Yes, I think so.'

'What happened?'

'Nothing. He talked to us both. He was very polite. It was obvious that he was interested in sex. He asked if it were true that Swedish girls are promiscuous . . . Then he came in two or three times more. He asked me to go out with him, but I refused.'

'Was that when he propositioned you?'

'Propositioned?' The word puzzled her.

'Asked you to pose for photographs?'

'No. That was later.'

'How did he approach the subject – of asking you to sleep with him?'

She hesitated. 'He . . . he asked someone else to ask us.'

'He approached you through a friend.' She nodded. 'And then what?'

'Then . . . then we met him one evening and went back to his house.'

'Did you go anywhere first? Did he take you out to dinner?'

'No, there was food there. And wine.'

'Did he take photographs on that occasion?'

'No.' He could tell she was becoming nervous again. He changed his line of questioning.

'Did he introduce you to any of his friends?'

'No.'

'You went back to his house half a dozen times, but you didn't meet anyone else?'

'No. He met us with his car outside the British Museum and we went back with him.' She said it in a confident way that suggested she was speaking the truth.

'You told me the other day you didn't like him . . .'

'No. We hated him.' Her disgust was obviously genuine.

'Why?'

She wrinkled up her face. 'It is hard to explain. He was

like a child. His development stopped when he was ten years old – you know? His interest in sex was . . . like a dirty-minded schoolboy. He wanted us to lie side by side on the bed while he beat us across the buttocks with a cane. It was all a kind of game . . .'

Saltfleet nodded sympathetically. 'But why did you keep on going there if you disliked him so much?'

She hesitated, looking away. 'We needed the money.'

He sighed. 'What for?'

'For clothes. For going home to Stockholm at week-ends . . .'

'I see. And when did he take the photographs?'

'About . . . four weeks ago. I can't remember exactly.'

'Was that the last time you saw him?'

'Yes.'

'Did you refuse to see him again?'

'No. I think he got tired of us.' She said it objectively, without self-pity. 'He needed a lot of change.'

'But you continued to see him at the shop?'

She thought about this. 'No. He didn't come all that often, you know. Perhaps he was avoiding us. But I don't think so.'

'Have you any idea who could have killed him?'

'None whatever.' She looked him in the eyes and said it firmly.

He said, shrugging: 'Well, that's all. Thank you very much.' She smiled brightly. 'Just one more thing. You said he approached you through a friend. Just for the sake of the record, who was the friend?'

She hesitated, looking in his eyes. She said: 'If you don't mind . . . I don't want to say.' She added quickly: 'It's not important.'

He said soothingly: 'I'm sure it's not important. But you don't seem to understand the situation, my dear. We're looking for a murderer. You told us you didn't know Lytton, and now we find you both knew him . . . well, very intimately. I ought to take you both in to Scotland Yard for questioning . . .' He paused, to let it sink in. He saw that she had suddenly become frightened; she felt trapped. He said: 'I've got to know everything, just for the sake of the record. I've

150

got to put all this in a report.' He repeated gently: 'Who was the friend?'

She said: 'It was . . . Max Engelke . . . the painter.'

He said casually: 'Oh yes, I know him.' He smiled. 'Well, that's all.'

She breathed deeply, nodded, and went quickly out of the room. He pushed the red switch. When Widdup came in, he was staring out of the window. The rain had stopped, but the sky was still cloudy.

'Any luck?'

'A little, I think. She tells me Lytton first came to this shop just before Christmas.'

'Ay. That sounds about right.'

'And it sounds as if Lytton already knew Engelke before that.'

'Did she say so?'

'Not exactly. She said Lytton didn't proposition them direct. He did it through Engelke. Of course, he could have met Engelke in the shop too . . . But it didn't sound like that to me.'

Widdup sat down, sighing. 'I dunno . . . I can't see Maxie killing anybody.' He gave an embarrassed giggle. 'He seems such a nice little chap.'

Saltfleet said: 'I'll tell you one thing. I'd like to bet that one of those two girls finds an excuse to leave the shop this afternoon, to go and warn him.'

'What? Why should they?'

'She'll think back over what she said to me, and realize she practically admitted that Engelke knew Lytton before he came to this shop.'

He asked unbelievingly: 'You think they're involved as well?'

'Not necessarily. Not directly. Have you got Engelke's address, by the way?'

'Somewhere.' He found an address book, and copied it out. Saltfleet glanced at it.

'Isn't this where Madame Galletti lives?'

'That's right.' He laughed. 'You don't think she's involved too?'

'I shouldn't think so. Where do the girls live?'

'Off Bethnal Green Road . . .'

'Not far from that magic shop?' Widdup looked blank. 'On the list you gave me this morning.'

'Oh yes. Did you go there?'

Saltfleet nodded.

'Anything interesting?'

'No. Just a lot of old Indian shawls and folk art . . .' He went to the door.

'By the way, what's Engelke's nationality?'

'I . . . I *think* he's German. Could be Swedish though . . .'

'It's not important.'

Widdup said: 'What do I do if one of the girls *does* want to leave?'

'Let her. It won't make any difference. I'm going to try to call on him now.'

It was raining hard as he climbed the steps to the front door. Most of the doorbell buttons were unlabelled. The address Widdup had written down gave no indication of which flat Engelke was in. He tried ringing the ground-floor bell – Madame Galletti's. There was no reply. He tried the top bell, but this brought no reply either. He heard the sound of someone crossing the hall, and knocked on the door with his knuckles. It opened six inches. A tall, hollow-cheeked man said: 'What is it?' He had a Scottish accent. Even at six feet, his breath smelt of whisky.

'I'm trying to find Max Engelke.'

The man said irritably: 'Top flat,' and started to close the door. Saltfleet put his foot in it.

'I've tried that. There's no reply.'

'I can't help that . . .' The man tried slamming the door hard. Saltfleet pulled out his wallet, and opened it.

'Police.'

'I don't give a fuck who you are. You can't come bursting into people's houses . . .'

Saltfleet suddenly lost his temper; he pushed the door open violently, making the man stagger. He said fiercely: 'Look, if you want trouble, you'll get it.' The man shrank back; Saltfleet closed the door behind him. He said: 'I'll have you for obstructing a policeman in the course of his duty.'

In fact, he had no right to enter a private house except under invitation, but he reckoned the man would not know that. From the way he dropped his eyes, Saltfleet could see he was right. He paid no more attention to him, but went up the stairs. The fishy smell still lingered. After the second floor, the stair became uncarpeted. Loud music was coming from somewhere. The stairs to the top flat were narrow and dark. There was a greasy gas stove on the landing. The music came from behind one of two doors. Saltfleet rapped on it with his knuckles. There was no reply. He tried the handle. The door was locked. He stood there for five more minutes, waiting. The music came to an end, and he knocked again. Something made him turn his head. An eye was looking at him from the centre of the other door. He said:

'I want to talk to you.'

Engelke's voice said loudly: 'You can't. I don't talk to anybody when I'm working.'

Saltfleet said: 'You told me you didn't know Lytton. Now I've found out you knew him quite well.'

The hole in the door closed as a wooden flap slid into place. After a moment, there was the sound of a key turning. The door opened. Engelke was staring at him with suspicion and hostility.

'You'd better come in. But I can't spare you more than five minutes.'

The two doors led into the same large room; it had evidently once been two rooms, but the partition had been removed. There was a smell of turpentine, and of burnt wood. Paintings like the ones he had seen in the gallery leaned against the walls. The furniture was cheap and shabby.

Engelke said: 'Would you mind telling me what you want?'

'Just a routine inquiry. I believe you knew Lytton rather better than you led me to believe.'

Engelke said nothing; he was scratching his chin. The sullen face was expressionless. Saltfleet said: 'Well?'

Engelke said dryly: 'I'm waiting for you to go on.' He went to the table and took up a soldering iron; it was connected to an electric point in the wall. On the easel near the window, there was a square of wood, covered with burnt lines. Engelke touched the iron to it; white smoke hissed from the wood.

Saltfleet took the photographs out of his pocket. He had intended to hold them in reserve; but now he wanted Engelke to look at them.

'Have you seen these before?'

Engelke glanced sideways with indifference. Watching him closely, Saltfleet saw him stiffen. He looked away again, but there was tension in the hand gripping the soldering iron. He said: 'What is that to me?'

Saltfleet said quietly: 'I want to talk to you.'

Engelke laid the iron on a plate on the table. A vein in his forehead was pulsing, and his face was flushed. He looked more closely at the photograph Saltfleet was holding out; it was the one of Lytton and one of the twins against the mantelpiece. He reached out and took the photographs; he almost dropped them, and swore. Saltfleet said:

'You obviously haven't seen them before.'

Engelke glanced at the first two or three, then handed them back. He had a manner of twisting the corner of his mouth, then thrusting out the lips.

'Well, what has that to do with me?'

He was obviously nervous, although an effort of self-control held it in check.

'I've been talking to Sigrid.'

Saltfleet turned away from him, to give him time to recover. He walked over to the gramophone, and glanced at the boxed set of records that lay beside it: Wagner's *Parsifal*. He walked to the mantelpiece, looking at the picture on the wall above it. It seemed to be of Hitler; but he was wearing silver armour, and riding a black horse. Saltfleet picked up the brown medicine bottle from the mantelpiece, removed the stopper, and sniffed; he recognized the sharp pungency of sulphuric acid. He said:

'I was wondering if you had any halothane.'

'What?'

'Halothane. It's an anaesthetic. Used for removing unwanted stains.'

154

Engelke went to the window. He had thrust his hands into his trouser pockets. He said:

'If you have something to say, please say it. I am very busy . . .'

His voice sounded muffled. He was not looking at Saltfleet.

'I've been talking to Sigrid. She tells me that Lytton approached her through you.'

'Yes. Well?'

'You told me you hardly knew Lytton.'

Engelke turned angrily:

'Look, if you think I killed Lytton, you've got to prove it . . .'

Saltfleet said soothingly, but with irony: 'I don't know why you're getting upset. You told me on Saturday that you wanted to kill Lytton.'

Engelke turned around. He was smiling. He had lost the nervousness. He said, as if explaining to a stupid child:

'But I hardly knew Lytton.'

'So you told me. Yet you acted as a go-between.'

'And why not?' He sat on the bed. 'He asked me if I would ask them to sleep with him. He said he would pay them. I passed on his message, that is all.'

'You told me you hardly knew him. You must have known him before he went to the bookshop or he wouldn't have asked you to speak to the girls.'

Engelke said: 'I've told you. I knew him slightly.'

'Before he went to the bookshop?'

'Yes. Slightly.'

'Where did you meet him?'

'I don't know. I can't even remember.'

'Then where did you know him?' Engelke pretended not to understand. 'If you knew him before he went to the bookshop, where did you see him?'

'I don't know. Perhaps a jazz club, or a restaurant. It could have been anywhere.'

Saltfleet said: 'For an innocent man, your attitude's not very helpful.'

Engelke lit a cigarette. His voice was bored.

'But you don't think I am innocent. You think I killed Lytton.'

155

'Did you?'

Engelke shrugged. 'What *reason* had I to kill him?'

'Money.'

'But I don't have money.' Engelke smiled. 'I'm just a poor artist trying to make a living.' He sighed. 'Look, I don't care if you don't believe me. But suppose I confessed that I killed Lytton?' Saltfleet looked at him quickly. 'I didn't say I did. I just said: Suppose I confessed. Would that give you sufficient evidence to charge me?'

After a silence, Saltfleet said: 'No. Not without proof.'

Engelke's voice became cold. 'Quite. And there can be no proof, because the evidence does not exist.' He repeated slowly: 'It does not exist.' He went back to the table, and picked up the soldering iron. 'And now I would like to work.'

Saltfleet said: 'Could I see your passport?'

Engelke shrugged. 'I suppose so.' He went to a drawer, and handed Saltfleet the passport; it was issued in the German Federal Republic.

'You were born in East Berlin?'

'Yes.'

'When did you come to the West?'

'I escaped across the border in 1963.'

'This gives your place of residence as Bonn.'

'Yes.'

'How long were you there?'

'From 1963 until 1970.'

Saltfleet looked in the back of the passport; several pages were franked.

'You travel a great deal for a poor artist – Paris, Amsterdam, Stockholm, Lausanne . . . Lytton has a bank in Lausanne.'

'How interesting.' He said it in a flat, bored voice.

'How does a poor artist manage to travel so much?'

Engelke said, shrugging: 'Travel is cheap nowadays.'

'But not to America. You have an American visa here.'

'I intended to go to America to live.'

'But you changed your mind?'

'Yes.'

'I wonder why?'

156

'I found London more interesting.'

'More profitable?'

Engelke said dryly: 'That is your suggestion.'

Saltfleet handed him back the passport. 'Do you intend to leave the country in the near future?'

'No.'

'Good. I shall probably want to talk to you again.'

Engelke smiled. 'Of course. As often as you like.' He escorted Saltfleet to the door. 'Until you get tired of it.'

A bell on the landing rang. Engelke started, betraying that he was less relaxed than he looked. Saltfleet said:

'So your bell *does* work?'

'As you see . . . Pardon me.' He pushed past Saltfleet, and hurried down the stairs. He went fast, evidently determined to reach the door well ahead of Saltfleet. Saltfleet followed unhurriedly. He was descending to the first floor when he heard the front door open. He heard the sound of a girl's voice, then silence. As he reached the top of the flight leading down to the hall, Engelke was closing the front door.

Saltfleet stopped and smiled at him.

'Poor girl. She's come all that way for nothing.'

Engelke said nothing, but the vein above his right eye was throbbing again. Saltfleet let himself out, and closed the front door behind him. Fifty yards away, hurrying towards the corner, he recognized the Swedish girl, her blonde hair bouncing on her shoulders as she walked.

Nine

He parked outside the new Yard, in George Forrest's space, leaving his keys with the duty constable in case Forrest returned.

'I shouldn't be more than a quarter of an hour. I'll be in with Commander Lamb in case you need me.'

Truscott, Lamb's personal aide, was in the outer office.

'Is the Chief in?'

'Yes. He wants to see you. He's got a reply from Lausanne.'

'That was quick.'

Lamb looked up from his desk as Saltfleet came in.

'Hello, Greg. I'm glad you came. I've got that information from the Credit Lyonnais at Lausanne. There.' He pushed a sheet of paper across the desk top. It contained four dates: 8 December, 2 February, 27 February, 13 April. Each was followed by a figure. He asked Lamb:

'What's the rate of exchange for Swiss francs?'

'About eight to the pound.'

Saltfleet did a calculation. 'Christ, that's over twenty thousand quid.' He took out his own notebook. 'Did you speak to the bank?'

'No, but Meyerstein did.' Edgar Meyerstein was in charge of Interpol Geneva. 'They were quite helpful when he explained their customer had been murdered.'

'Was the money withdrawn in cash?'

'Yes. What have you got there?'

'Some dates I got from Engelke's passport. I managed to get a look at it, and memorized the last three. Engelke was in England on all these dates . . .'

Lamb looked over his shoulder. Saltfleet's entries ran: 19 January, Amsterdam; 15 February, Amsterdam; 2 March, Stockholm.

Lamb said: 'So it looks as if he couldn't have given the cash to Engelke – unless he brought it back into England with him.'

'Or left it somewhere for Engelke to collect – Amsterdam, for example.'

Lamb said: 'Or handed it to a third party.'

'Possible. But Engelke doesn't strike me as the type to work with an accomplice.'

'You've been to see him?'

'Yes. I found out where he came from – Bonn. So now . . .'

'So now you're going to check with Interpol Bonn to see if he's got a criminal record?'

'That's right.'

'Don't bother. I've already done it. He hasn't.'

Saltfleet stared at him. 'How the hell did you . . .'

'Simple. I checked with Traffic Control at the Home Office.'

'Without the date of his entry into England?'

'I thought with a name like Max Engelke it shouldn't be too hard to trace. It wasn't.'

Saltfleet laughed. 'I can see I've been wasting my time.'

'I doubt it. What did you find out?'

'Not much more than that. He had a visa for America, but he hadn't used it.'

'That's interesting. I wonder why not? Did you notice the date?'

'Yes, January last year, a few weeks after he arrived in England.'

Lamb said musingly: 'Bonn's full of Americans. Diplomatic staff . . .'

'That's what I thought. Do you know Bonn?'

'I should. I was there for three months at the time of the Smith and Ziegler business.' Lamb had been head of the Special Branch before his promotion. Smith had been a British Embassy clerk in the pay of the Russians. He and Ziegler – a Russian agent – had murdered a junior embassy official who had caught them photographing secret documents.

'If he got a visa, he must have had an American sponsor.' Lamb picked up the telephone and dialled. 'U.S. Embassy? Could I have the visa section, please?' Saltfleet placed the notepad in front of him, underlining a date with his fingernail. 'Hello, visa section? This is Scotland Yard C.I.D. You issued a visa to a German citizen, Max Engelke, on 10 January 1971.' He spelt the name. 'I want to find out who sponsored him. Could you ring me back here?' He gave the number and extension,

Saltfleet said: 'I must admit, it'd give me real pleasure to put this Engelke inside for the rest of his life.'

'Nasty type, is he?'

'Yes. And conceited. Certain he's covered up all his tracks. He as good as told me that we wouldn't get a conviction even if he confessed, because we couldn't get the evidence to prove it.'

'Any idea why he killed the girl and left her outside?'

Saltfleet shrugged. 'Just to cause confusion, I should think.' He looked at his watch. 'I'd better get back to my own office. I've got some calls to make.'

'Use the phone over there. You may as well wait until the embassy rings back.'

He sat at the other desk and dialled Steinhager's number. Mrs Steinhager's voice answered. Saltfleet said:

'This is Saltfleet, Scotland Yard. Do you think I could have a word with your husband, Mrs Steinhager? If he's still in his lab, it'll do later . . .'

'Just a moment. He's in the kitchen . . .'

Several minutes passed before Steinhager's voice snapped: 'Hello?'

'Sorry to bother you again, Mr Steinhager. I've got a query you might be able to answer. This afternoon I saw a painting of Hitler dressed in silver armour, riding on a black horse. Have you ever come across anything like that?'

'Well . . . yes. What do you want to know?'

'Is there supposed to be any connection between Hitler and magic?'

'A great many people believe that Hitler was a member of a magical group called the Thule Gesellschaft.'

'Can you tell me anything about this Thule group?'

Steinhager said, with a touch of exasperation: 'If I told you everything I knew about it, it would take me all night . . .'

'But briefly . . .'

'Very well. Briefly . . . This Thule group was a magical

society founded around the end of the First World War by a man called Glauer. They were mystical racialists – they hated the Jews and believed in the coming of the Superman. Then when Glauer had to flee from Munich, his place was taken by . . . what's the man's name? . . . Eckart – Dietrich Eckart. And he became one of Hitler's earliest associates when the German Workers' Party was first formed. Ever since then there's been a persistent legend that Hitler was involved in black magic.'

'But what about the silver armour?'

'That would be the armour of a knight of the Grail. Hitler was supposed to be obsessed by the legend of *Parsifal* and the Grail . . .'

The other telephone rang, and, for a moment, Saltfleet was unable to catch what Steinhager was saying. He said: 'I'm sorry. Could you repeat that last bit?'

'I said I shouldn't take it too seriously.'

'Ah. No. Is all this written down anywhere?'

'Yes. There's a book called *Hitler, the Mystic and the Artist*, by Dagmar Johannsen . . .'

'Hold on a moment . . . let me get that down. Hitler . . .'

'It's in German – *Die Mystik und die Kunstler*.'

'Isn't it translated?'

'I don't think so. I'll try and find out. Did you get the name of the author – Dagmar Johannsen?'

'Yes, thank you. That's most helpful. Thanks very much.'

Lamb had already hung up. He said:

'What was all that about?'

'I saw this picture of Hitler dressed in shining armour in Engelke's room. Then I remembered – Lytton's housekeeper said he'd suddenly got interested in books on Hitler in the last few months. And another thing – although this may be coincidence. He was playing music at top volume when I arrived – Wagner's *Parsifal*. Now this man Steinhager tells me Hitler was supposed to be obsessed by *Parsifal* and the Grail legend.'

'Sounds a bit far-fetched.'

'It probably is. But what I've got to find out is how Engelke got Lytton to part with several thousand quid. It must have been something more interesting than a lot of witches dancing in the nude. This might be the answer.'

'Well, I've got an answer from the embassy. They say Engelke was sponsored by Mrs Maxine Feininger. And I'm damn sure I know the name . . . I wonder?' He picked up the phone again and dialled. 'There was a man called Orrin Sternberg who moved from the U.S. Embassy in . . . Hello. Can you tell me if Mr Orrin Sternberg still works there? He does? Could I speak to him, please?' He said to Saltfleet: 'Pick up the extension on the desk over there.'

A girl's voice was saying: 'Who is it calling, please?'

'Commander Lamb of the C.I.D.'

A moment later a man's voice said: 'Is that you, Eric?'

'Hello, Orrin. How are you?'

'Fine. You just caught me as I was leaving the office. What can I do for you?'

'Do you remember a man called Feininger in Bonn?'

'Of course I do. Leopold Feininger – one of our top scientists.'

'Wasn't he the man in the wheelchair?'

'That's right. He had cancer of the hip. He died two years ago. What about him?'

'Was his wife called Maxine?'

'That's right. What has she done?'

'Nothing. But she sponsored a young German for a visa, and he's a suspect in a . . . a crime.'

Sternberg said: 'Good, well I'm glad you don't intend to arrest her, because she's coming to my house for dinner on Friday.'

Lamb said with astonishment: 'She is? Does that mean she's in London at the moment?'

'As far as I know she is.'

'Do you have her address?'

'If I don't, my wife has it . . . can you hold the line?'

Lamb covered over his receiver. He said to Saltfleet: 'Well, luck is with us at last.'

'Hello, Eric. Yes, I've got her address. Got a pencil? It's 5 D'Oyley Mews, Cadogan Place. I don't have the telephone number, but she's in the book . . .'

Saltfleet was already looking in the London phone book. By the time Lamb hung up, he had the number. Lamb said:

'He's a really nice man. He's in security – has to check on people who apply for visas – find out if they're members of the Communist Party or in the Mafia. Got it?'

'Yes.' He was already dialling.

'Better get around and see her. She may be the lead you're looking for.'

'I doubt it. It sounds as if . . . Hello. Is Mrs Feininger there, please?'

A man's voice said he would get her. A moment later, a woman came to the phone.

'Hello. Who is this, please?'

'Chief-Superintendent Saltfleet, Scotland Yard. Are you Mrs Leopold Feininger?'

'Yes.'

'Mrs Feininger, a year ago you acted as sponsor for a German called Max Engelke.'

'That's right. Is he in trouble?'

'In a way. Could I come over and talk to you?'

'When, now?'

'If that's convenient.'

'Well, you'd better make it pretty fast. I'll be going out to a party in half an hour.'

'I'll be over as soon as I can.'

He stood up, putting his hat on. Lamb said:

'You were saying that you didn't think this would lead to anything.'

He said: 'I'll tell you when I get back.'

The small house stood at the end of the mews; parked in front of the door were a Daimler and an open-topped Aston Martin. A man in a grey suit opened the door.

'Oh yes. She *is* expecting you. Do come in.'

He was a mild-looking public school type, handsome in a characterless way, and overweight. Saltfleet followed him to a comfortable room at the back of the house. There was a bar in the corner, and the furniture looked new and expensive. A dachshund began to yap, baring its teeth. A woman's voice called 'Quiet, Poldo!' She came out of the bathroom, a tall woman, unexpectedly good-looking. Saltfleet had expected something less feminine; her voice on the telephone

163

was hard and flat. She snatched up the dog.

'Hi. I'm Maxine Feininger. Hubert, would you get this gentleman a drink? Whisky on the rocks. O.K.?'

'I'd prefer just a beer, if you have it, please.' It was late, and he was tired and thirsty.

'Hubert, what the hell did you do with my martini? Why do you always hide my drinks?'

'I gave it to you.' He was obviously resigned. 'You probably took it into the bathroom.'

'Be a sweetie and see.' He emerged a moment later with a tall glass that seemed to be full of gin and ice. 'What did you say your name was?'

Saltfleet introduced himself again. She said 'Glad to know you,' and told him to sit down. She flung herself on the settee, still holding the dog. 'Now, what's that little pain in the ass done now?'

Saltfleet said: 'I'm investigating the murder of a man called Lytton . . . ah, thank you.' He accepted the glass of lager. 'He withdrew fairly large sums of money from his bank before he died. We're trying to find out what happened to them.'

She gave a snorting laugh. 'That's Max all right.'

'What is?'

'What you just said. It brings him back as clear as if he'd walked in through that door. If there's money around, Max'll grab all he can. The chiselling little bastard.'

'Did he ever . . . swindle you?'

'Not exactly. He two-timed me.' Saltfleet had the feeling that she was more vulnerable than her manner suggested. In spite of the hard, unattractive voice, there was something gentle in her face. Although probably in her early forties, she still had an excellent figure. The teeth protruded slightly, but were so white that they made her smile dazzling. She could have been beautiful; but the voice, and the tense, nervous manner, spoiled the effect. She said:

'Well, I suppose you want to know about my relationship with Max?'

'If . . . you want to talk about it.'

The man slipped quietly out of the room. Saltfleet felt more comfortable. She said:

'I slept with him. Or, as he would have expressed it, he screwed me.'

'Yes . . . I see. Can you tell me how you met him?'

'I don't mind.' She took a long swallow of her drink. 'I met him in Coblenz, in the Castor Church, if you can believe it. He was on a bus excursion. We got talking and I offered him a lift back to Bonn. We talked all the way . . .'

'What about?'

'Architecture, mainly. He knew a lot about it. He'd got some idea about the cathedrals of the Middle Ages being full of secret codes. You know, like the pyramids. He knew so much about the church that I thought he was some kind of religious nut.' She laughed and drained her glass until the ice clinked. 'Would you like another beer?'

'No, thanks.'

She went to the bar. As she talked, he watched her pour a teaspoonful of dry vermouth into her glass, then fill it up with gin and cubes of ice.

'You are probably assuming my intentions were strictly sexual. But they weren't. I just thought he was a nice kid.' She laughed. 'Just shows how stupid you can be.'

'And you became lovers?'

'If you can call it that.' She came and sat down again. She took up the dog and began to caress it; she was obviously fond of the dog. She said : 'I'm telling you all this because I want you to know what sort of a person he is.'

'I understand.'

'O.K., good.' She laughed and took another drink. 'So I'll tell you how we became lovers, as you so delicately put it . . . I went back to his room, because he told me he shared it with two other students. But they weren't in. So he raped me.'

'Literally?'

'I detect scepticism. But yeah, he raped me. No preliminaries, no romance. I've never been so amazed in all my life. Here he'd been telling me about cathedrals and Balthazar Neumann and all that. Then he locked the door and said : "I have a feeling you're a good lay" – just like that. Then he started to undo the zip on my slacks.'

'Didn't you . . . protest?'

'Well, sort of.' She laughed, and its harshness jarred him.

165

'I won't say the idea hadn't crossed my mind. But not just like *that*.' She looked at him over the top of the glass, to see how he was taking it. 'I said: "What are you doing?" and he said "Don't ask stupid questions. I'm going to screw you", only he didn't say screw. I told him no, so he said: "O.K. If you don't want to, you can go." And he unlocked the door.'

He said dryly: 'But you stayed.'

'Well, I mean. Up until that minute I'd liked him. I couldn't understand it. I said: "Why are you acting like this?" and he said: "Ah, I see you *do* want it after all", and locked the door again.' She sighed, and took another swallow. 'Which is how I lost my virginity.'

He said thoughtfully: 'It sounds as if he didn't care whether you stayed or went.'

'You're damn right. He didn't give a screw.'

'Then why did you . . . carry on?'

'I dunno. He could be very sweet. He was intelligent. He had ambition – a *lot* of ambition. And, if you really want to know, he was damn good in bed.'

'Did he ill-treat you physically?'

She sighed, and took another drink. He was wondering how she managed to stay coherent. Her words were unslurred. She said:

'Look, I don't want to shock you . . .'

'Don't worry.'

'All right, then. Well, he's a kind of sex maniac. I mean, he really makes a big thing out of sex. And I don't *just* mean he's promiscuous. I mean he needs to try *everything*. And I mean everything. A friend of mine called him King of the Perverts. He said it gave him magic powers.'

He asked with interest: 'He talked about magic?'

'Oh yeah. All the time. It was his favourite subject. He was always talking about secret traditions . . .'

Saltfleet said: 'Did he really believe in it?' It was the question he had been waiting to ask.

'Oh sure. Completely. He told me he'd made me go to bed with him by magic. He said he saw me there in the church, looking up at the stained glass, and he decided there and

166

then he'd get me into bed before the day was out. So he put a kind of spell on me . . .'

'Did you believe him?'

She frowned. 'I dunno . . . It was strange. It was sometimes like a nightmare. I found myself doing things I just couldn't believe. I used to wonder what my husband'd say if he found out . . . but I don't think he'd've believed a word of it.'

'Were there other people involved?'

'Oh sure.'

'How many?'

'Ten, a dozen. I can't remember.'

'Men and women?'

'Yes. Mostly kids – young girls.'

'And he practised magic?'

'That's what he called it.'

'What would you call it?'

'Screwing.'

'I see . . . Did he ever mention Hitler?'

'Sure, that was his big thing. The Thule Gesellschaft. He said he was the new head of the Thule Gesellschaft.'

'Engelke was?'

'That's right. He was searching for Hitler's secret book – a book of black magic that Hitler was supposed to have written. Called *The Master of the World.* He said Bormann took it to South America. He needed money to go and find it.'

'How much money did you give him?'

'I dunno. Maybe ten thousand dollars.'

'And you intended to take him to America with you?'

'No!' She said it with violence. 'He made me help him get his visa. But I knew I had to get away from him. He was driving me crazy – I mean, really crazy. I was in a mental institution for ten weeks when I got back to the States.'

'So *you* finally left *him*?'

'No.' She shook her head. 'My two brothers came to London and made me go back with them on the next plane. I was sick. I mean, I was really sick. My nails had turned blue . . .'

The man called Hubert had come quietly into the room. She saw him and said: 'Hubert, get me a drink.'

'Do you think you should? We're due at Margot's at seven o'clock.'

'Oh Christ. And I'm already half stoned . . .' She stood up. 'I'm sorry, Inspector, but we're gonna have to leave you.' She frowned at her glass. 'This stuff's stronger than you think.'

'One more question. Has he tried to contact you since you've been back in London?'

'No. I doubt whether he knows I'm back. Anyway, it'd be no good. I couldn't take any more . . .'

'Thank you.' He put his notebook back into his pocket. 'I may need to see you again. There are still several things I'd like to clear up.'

'Any time. I'm curious to know what happens. Hubert, would you show this gentleman out? I've gotta get changed. Goodbye, Inspector.' She went up the stairs, waving vaguely. The man opened the front door. He said:

'Do you think this man committed the murder?'

'It's too early to say. But it's possible.'

'Is she in any danger?'

'No . . .' He added, as he turned away: 'But she may have had a lucky escape.'

The man said: 'I'm not sure she thinks so.' He had closed the door before Saltfleet could ask him what he meant.

It was after seven when he got back to the office. Crisp was still there, his desk surrounded with files.

'What are you doing here, Steve? There was no need for you to stay on.'

'There's a couple of messages for you. And I thought I may as well finish the North London area.'

'What are the messages?'

'Lady Edgton rang up. She's back in England – at the house in Hampstead. She just said she's there if you want to see her. There's the phone number. And that Liverpudlian rang up . . .'

'Widdup?'

'That's right. He just said to tell you he's found the books.'

'What books?'

'He didn't say. He just said to tell you he's found the books.'

Saltfleet sighed. 'I suppose I'd better ring him.'

He dialled Widdup's private number. It rang for several minutes; he was about to hang up when Widdup said: 'Hello.'

'Saltfleet here.'

'Oh, good. Sorry to keep you waiting – I was down in the shop. Listen, I've found the books.'

'What books?'

'The ones Lytton bought – the Crowley *Equinox*.'

'What!' Crisp looked startled at his shout. 'Where?'

'Well, that's the odd thing. I found them by accident. Somebody asked me for a rare book on UFOs, and I thought I'd got one in the store room somewhere. So I went up and poked around and moved some piles of books – and there they were.'

'You say your store room's above your shop. Where, exactly?'

'On the floor above the flat. You have to go through the flat to get into it.'

'And when do you think the books could have been placed there?'

'That's hard to say. Any time since last . . . Oh, last Thursday, I suppose.'

'You've no idea who put them there?'

'No, but your guess is as good as mine. I don't have to name names . . .'

'Quite. Could they have been put there this afternoon – late this afternoon?'

'It's possible. I was out from half past two until nearly six. I found them half an hour ago.'

'Have you mentioned it to anybody?'

'No.'

'Good. Then don't. I'll be over right away to collect them. We'll have to get them checked for fingerprints.'

As he hung up, he said: 'Let's hope that's his first major mistake.'

'What's that?'

'The books Lytton had with him when he was killed –

they've turned up in Widdup's shop. It was good luck that he found them so quickly. They could have been there for months.'

'Any idea how they got there?'

'I think one of the girls put them there – these two Swedish girls. It must have been Engelke's idea. The perfect place to hide books – in a bookshop among thousands of others.'

'Why didn't he just throw them in the river?'

'Because he wanted to go back for them sometime. I think he wanted the books for himself – they were rare first editions. He thought they'd never be missed anyway – it was a hundred-to-one chance that I'd find out about them. So he decided to take the risk and keep them. He may have got one of the girls to plant them in Widdup's store room right after the murder. Or she may have done it late this afternoon, after I'd seen Engelke.'

'Are you certain he's the man who killed Lytton?'

Saltfleet said: 'I am now. I was fairly certain when I found those photographs. Now I've talked to an American woman who got mixed up with him, and I'm absolutely certain. She said she had a friend who called him "King of the Perverts". The one thing I couldn't understand is why anybody should kill Lytton so elaborately. Why didn't he just walk up behind him in the street and shoot him in the back of the head? As I talked to this woman, I suddenly began to understand. He'd enjoy killing somebody by sticking an iron spike in his heart. He must have planned this murder from the time he first met Lytton – otherwise, why did he take so much trouble to make sure there was nothing to link them together? He planned this murder in every detail . . .'

'And what about the girl?'

'I don't know about the girl. She doesn't fit in. I'm inclined to think she was one of the things he hadn't calculated on – like those photographs . . . Get me the murder bag, would you?' It was kept locked in the bottom of the filing cabinet. When Crisp brought it over, he took out the fingerprint powder and a magnifying glass, and slipped them into his jacket pocket. 'You'd better get home.'

'I'll just finish the last dozen files. There's a couple there I'd like you to look at.'

'In the morning.' He dialled Lady Edgton's number. 'Hello. Could I speak to Lady Edgton, please? Chief-Superintendent Saltfleet.' When she came on the line, he said: 'Thank you for letting us know you're back. I'd like to come and talk to you some time.'

'Could you make it this evening?'

'This evening?' He looked at his watch; he'd been hoping to be home by nine. 'Is there any hurry?'

'I'm thinking of leaving London in the morning. To be honest, I have a . . . a rather odd feeling about this house. It may be just my imagination, but I don't like it. I may sell it.'

'I see. Well, I could be up there in about an hour. Would that be convenient?'

'Yes. I look forward to seeing you.'

He said: 'Steve, before you go, would you ring my wife and tell her I shan't be back before half past ten?'

'Has this woman got some information?'

He grunted. 'I doubt it. She's just nervous. Probably wants to hold my hand.'

As he was closing the door behind him, Crisp said: 'Hey, Chief.' He opened it again. 'Come and look at this.' He went over to the desk. Crisp said: 'What about that?'

Saltfleet looked down at the Identikit picture, which Crisp had placed beside the photograph in the file. There was a definite resemblance.

'Could be . . . could be.' He drew up a chair. 'Who is it?'

'Stanley Lewis. Age 23. Three convictions for indecent assault on minors.' His voice became more excited. 'Lives with his parents in Snakes Lane, Redbridge. And, if I remember rightly, that's somewhere near the North Circular.' He pulled a map book out of his drawer. Saltfleet pulled the file over to him.

'Where's the description of the North Circular man . . . ? Let's see . . . fair hair, blue eyes, sensuous mouth, mid-twenties. About six feet tall. This man Lewis is only five foot seven.'

'Kids can never judge height . . . Yes, look.' He pushed the atlas in front of Saltfleet. 'This is the North Circular – at

171

least, an extension of it – Southend Road. Here's Snakes Lane. It could be.'

'That's J Division – Bill Norland. Get on to the Chingford Station and find out whether they've talked to this man. Get the District Collator. If he's gone home, get on to him at home. I'll ring you back in half an hour.'

Driving towards Holborn, he realized his tiredness had gone; he was getting second wind. He had eaten nothing since lunch time, but he had ceased to feel hungry.

He parked outside the bookshop. There was a double yellow line, but the traffic warden had probably gone home.

The place was more crowded than he had seen it. Evidently the evenings were the time it filled up. The shop and the coffee bar were jammed. Both the twins were working behind the bar; but they were so busy that neither noticed him as he went upstairs.

He knocked and went in. Widdup was stretched out on the settee. He said immediately:

'You know, I've been thinking . . .' He opened a cupboard. The three red-bound volumes were in the centre of the shelf. Before Widdup could touch them, Saltfleet said:

'Hold on. Fingerprints.'

'Ay. I thought of that.' He took them out one by one, holding them by the top and bottom of the spine. 'I've been thinking . . . there's nothing very distinctive about this set. They're not even numbered.'

'You're sure they're the books you sold to Lytton.'

'Ay, they must be. I've never seen another copy. But I've checked up with a bloke who knew Crowley pretty well. And he says a lot of 'em were bound like this.'

The binding was red leather, rather worn. They were covered with a design in gold; when Saltfleet looked more closely he saw it was composed of phalluses.

'Hadn't we better lock the door? I suppose one of the girls might walk in.'

'Ay.' Widdup turned the key.

Saltfleet placed the first volume on the desk top, and carefully dusted it with fingerprint powder. He blew away the surplus, then examined it with a magnifying glass. He sighed.

'It's a lousy surface.' The roughened surface of the leather and the intricacy of the design made it difficult to detect a fingerprint, even a smudged one.

He spent the next quarter of an hour painstakingly examining every inch of the surfaces of the three books, including the gold at the top of the pages. He said:

'These have been wiped. Pretty carefully.'

When he had finished examining the covers, he glanced through the pages. It was an expensive paper with a rough surface. He closed the book with a slap and pushed it away.

'No. No joy there.'

Widdup said: 'I expect you could do with a drink. Whisky or vodka?'

'Vodka, please. I've still got another call to make. Just a small one. On its own.'

Widdup handed him the drink, and sat in his armchair. Neither of them spoke. Saltfleet swallowed a mouthful slowly; it made a pleasant burning in his throat. Widdup had given him a large one, but he didn't feel inclined to protest.

Widdup said: 'What do you intend to do with the books?'

'Nothing. I want you to put them back where you found them.'

Widdup shrugged. 'All right.'

'Because, if he thinks he can get away with it, I've got a feeling that Engelke's going to try and get those books back before his girlfriends leave the shop for good. Show me where you found them.'

Widdup led him up an uncarpeted flight of stairs. The room above contained nothing but books: on the shelves, on the window-sills, in piles on the floor, in parcels stacked up to the ceiling.

'They were down here, in the corner of this shelf. If I hadn't knocked this pile over, I wouldn't have seen them for months.' The rest of the shelf contained a dozen or so copies of a book on Cagliostro.

Saltfleet said: 'Well, do you believe me now?'

'About what?'

'About Engelke?'

Widdup nodded. 'Yes. I believe you.' He replaced the books in the corner of the shelf, and pushed another pile of books into position to conceal them. They went back downstairs. Widdup said: 'It suddenly struck me when I found them. The last time I saw them was when Lytton walked out of the shop a week ago. And now they're back. It could only be the girls ... But, you know, somebody must have noticed her carrying three big books like that. Do you want me to make discreet inquiries?'

'No. Don't say anything. Let them think you haven't found them. But try and keep a close check on them. And if they disappear, let me know immediately.'

'All right. But what good would it do? It'd be different if they were numbered copies or something. I *know* they're the books I sold Lytton, but I couldn't prove it.'

'It doesn't matter. We might be able to bluff Engelke into thinking they're traceable ... Mind if I use your phone?'

'Go ahead.'

He rang Crisp.

'What's the news, Steve?'

'Not much. I've talked to the District Collator. He says they checked on Lewis, but his parents said he'd got married and moved to Manchester. So they didn't check any further.'

'Did you talk to Bill Norland?'

'Yes. He says he'll handle it carefully – get a plain-clothes man to check with the neighbours.'

'O.K., Steve, that's about all you can do. Get back home now.'

'Thanks. See you in the morning.'

It was getting dark when he arrived at the Hampstead house. The gate had been closed so he parked the car outside. A group of children, playing across the road, stood and watched him as he went in.

He rang the front doorbell. The house seemed to be in darkness. He yawned, and leaned against the wall. A light came on above his head, startling him. He had leaned against a metal light switch, which turned on a light in the porch. The light also revealed a man's face peering at him through the glass panel beside the front door. The door opened six inches; it was on a chain. An Irish voice said: 'Who is it?'

174

'Chief-Superintendent Saltfleet, Scotland Yard.'

'Ah yes. The missus is expecting you.' The door opened. A short, bald-headed man looked up at him mistrustfully. Saltfleet said:

'Do you normally keep the door chained?'

'Ah no, but we're all a bit nervous . . .' He sighed. 'The missus'll be glad to see you.'

He switched on the hall light. 'This way, please.' He led the way upstairs. 'D'you have any idea who done it yet?'

'We've several suspects. Tell me . . . that light in the porch. Can you turn it off from inside the house?'

'Yes. There's a switch just in the hall there.'

He rapped on the bedroom door, then pushed it open.

'The man from the police is here to see you.'

'Good. Show him in.'

Saltfleet recognized the bedroom. He had seen the mantel-piece in the photographs.

There was a fire burning in the grate. The old lady was sitting up in bed, surrounded by pillows. She was watching the nine o'clock news on a portable colour television.

'Turn that damn thing off, Shaun. Nothing but bad news.' She nodded at Saltfleet. 'How do you do?'

He had formed an idea of her appearance from her voice over the telephone; now he was pleased to see that it was more-or-less accurate. The grey hair was carefully coiffured; the grey eyes were deep set on either side of a nose like a bird of prey. The mouth and chin were firm; he could see that she must have been beautiful when she was young.

Her handclasp was dry and firm. 'Sit down, Superintend-ent. I've had another of my attacks. Damn nearly finished me. Would you like a cup of tea?'

'No, thank you.'

He thought she looked unusually healthy; there was a touch of pink in her cheeks. He could imagine her on horse-back, in hunting uniform.

She said: 'Well, this is a right how d'you do, isn't it? Smoke if you want to.'

'You're sure it wouldn't disturb you?'

'No. Might kill me, I suppose. But that won't be long any-

175

way.' As he hesitated, she said impatiently: 'Go ahead.'

He took out his notebook; before he had time to open it, she said:

'Who killed him?'

Her gaze was so direct that he felt he could be frank.

'This is not for repeating, of course. But I'm pretty certain it was a man called Max Engelke.'

'One of his pansy friends, I suppose?'

'Not exactly . . .'

'What then?'

He said ruminatively, shredding the tobacco:

'A killer. I mean a real killer. A calculator.'

He was surprised when she gave a slight shudder; he was forgetting that, for most people, murder is unreal.

'What did he kill him for?'

'Money. He'd been getting thousands of pounds out of him in the past year.'

She said: 'Poor old devil.'

'You told me on the phone you didn't know much about his private life. But you knew about his pansy friends.'

She said dryly: 'Manfred was a sex maniac, like his poor father. He got one of my maids pregnant when he was fourteen.' There was a knock on the door; a maid came in with a glass and a bottle. 'Excuse me, it's time for my medicine . . .' While she took it, he lit his pipe, and stared at the mantelpiece. He wondered whether there was any significance in Lytton choosing this room for his orgies with the Swedish girls.

The maid went out. The old woman said:

'I feel sorry for Manfred, now you've told me that. I'd been assuming . . . well, that he had only himself to blame.'

He persisted: 'I thought you didn't know much about his private life?'

She said explosively: 'Good heavens, man, you don't expect me to discuss this kind of thing over the phone, with the bloody pantry maid listening in on the extension, do you? She's probably listening at the door now.' A creaking floorboard from outside seemed to confirm her suspicion.

'Er . . . no, I suppose not.' He finished lighting the pipe. 'How rich was your nephew?'

'He had an income of around twelve thousand a year, after tax. A capital of around a quarter of a million, including land.' She shook her head slowly. 'It's a disgusting thought . . . someone killing him for money. Like a spider and a fly.'

'This one's a spider all right.'

'What swindle did he use?'

'I'm not sure of the details. But something to do with magic or witchcraft.'

She shook her head decisively.

'No, no. You must be wrong.'

He asked curiously: 'Why?'

'Manfred was a fool in some ways, but he wasn't gullible. I don't doubt he was interested in magic and that kind of thing – he was rather an intellectual, like his father. But unless his brain had gone soft, he wouldn't let anyone trick him out of hard cash with tales about magic.'

'Well, there were . . . other things.'

'Such as? Don't be afraid to tell me.'

He reached into his side pocket. He had not intended to show Lady Edgton the photographs; but she looked the type who could take it. And he was curious to see her reaction. He selected a photograph showing Lytton in a normal act of intercourse on the bed. Lady Edgton took it. She snapped open a spectacles case, perched her glasses on her nose, and held it at arm's length. She said explosively: 'Good God!' She peered at it more closely. 'How extraordinary.' She glanced at the envelope in Saltfleet's hand. 'What are those?'

He cleared his throat. 'More pictures.'

She held out her hand imperiously. 'Give.' He handed them over, feeling oddly like a schoolboy surrendering contraband to a schoolmistress. She looked through them carefully one by one, in silence. Her only comment was: 'Pretty little bitches.' Suddenly she said: 'Good God! Do you realize where these were taken?'

He nodded. 'In here.'

'Well I'm damned. In this very bed.' She chuckled. A moment later, she looked hard at the mantelpiece, but said nothing. She finally threw the photographs down on the bed, and heaved a deep sigh.

177

'You know, there was something wrong with Manfred. Decadent.' She handed the photographs back to Saltfleet. 'Were the girls anything to do with it?'

'I don't think so.'

'Good. I'm glad of that, anyway. I expect you'll be able to arrest this chap, won't you?'

'That's not certain yet.'

'Why not?'

'Because he took enormous care that no one should ever see him with your nephew. It's going to be *very* difficult to establish that they were more than nodding acquaintances.'

'But you're sure they were?'

'Yes.'

She leaned back into her pillows, making herself comfortable.

'Tell me everything you know. Let's see if I can make any suggestions.'

'All right.' He liked her, and it gave him pleasure to talk to her. 'Three years ago, your nephew joined a magic cult called the Order of the Golden Dawn. Apparently their rituals didn't strike him as exciting enough. He wanted more sex magic. So he broke with them in 1970, and then got mixed up with a strange couple called Dalgleish in Hastings. In February last year, a Sunday newspaper did an article exposing the Dalgleishes. It mentioned your nephew . . .'

She said: 'I know. I saw the damn thing.'

'Quite. It also referred to your nephew as a rich playboy. Well, the Dalgleishes left for America – I think they were encouraged by the local police. And I suspect that this young man, Max Engelke, saw the article and decided to contact your nephew. He'd come from Bonn with a young American widow. She walked out on him at about the time the article appeared. So Engelke looked around for some other source of money. I don't know how he came to meet your nephew, but I'm fairly certain that he used a false name. He called himself Norbert Tinkler.'

'What an odd name.'

'Engelke chose it as a kind of private joke. I don't know what story Engelke told your nephew, but I think I can guess. I think he told him that he was the representative of a German magical society called the Thule Group – Hitler was supposed to have been a member.' She stirred and sat up. 'He probably told him he intended to start a similar group in England. He laid heavy emphasis on the sexual magic. That's where those girls came in. They're both Engelke's mistresses. I also think that Engelke and your nephew had some kind of homosexual relationship. And the chief reason your nephew believed Engelke was that Engelke didn't try to rush things. He met your nephew in February or March, but he didn't try to get any money from him until last November. Then he got him to hand over three thousand pounds in Swiss francs. Since then, he's had another seventeen thousand pounds.'

'My God. He *must* have been a smooth talker.'

'I think there was a point when your nephew suddenly began to have suspicions. He went back to the man who runs the Golden Dawn just before Christmas. But the man refused to speak to him. And then, somehow, Engelke regained his confidence. At one point, your nephew probably found out that Engelke's name wasn't Norbert Tinkler, and that probably started the suspicions . . .'

'Look, excuse me interrupting. A moment ago, you mentioned this idea that Hitler was mixed up with black magic.'

'Yes.'

'This is probably unimportant . . . but the only time Manfred ever mentioned witchcraft to me was when he said he'd met a woman I used to know.'

'When was that?'

'Oh, it must have been a year ago.'

'And what was her name?'

'Dagmar Johannsen.'

'Good God!' He turned back to the previous page of his notebook. 'The author of a book called *Die Mystik und Die Kunstler*? Proving that Hitler was a black magician.'

'Well, she doesn't quite do that. Who told you about her?'

'Steinhager – the man who runs the Golden Dawn.'

'Strange coincidence . . .'

He said: 'You say your nephew met this woman a year ago? Where was that?'

'Er . . . Oh, I'm damned if I can remember. Somewhere in London, I'm pretty sure. He gave me her address, but I lost it.'

'Did he say how he met her?'

'Quite by chance. He bumped into her in the Portobello Road. He'd met her in Zurich in . . . let's see . . . 1948. I introduced him. I'd known her since the twenties, when we were all at the same finishing school in Kitzbuhl.'

'Tell me about this woman. Did she know Hitler?'

'Oh yes. Quite well. She used to edit a magazine called *Astrologische Rundschau*, and she knew a lot of people in the Thule Group. I don't believe she was ever a member herself. Dagmar was a most extraordinary woman. She could call out the correct cards with a bandage round her eyes . . . Look, could you look in that bookcase for me? There should be a book called *Hitler Speaks* – a yellow thing . . . somewhere on the middle shelf, if I remember rightly.' Saltfleet found it after a moment's search, and handed it to her. She turned over the pages, then pointed to a marked passage. 'Listen to this. "One day when Hitler seemed in an unapproachable mood, a far-sighted woman in his circle said to him warningly: 'My leader, don't touch black magic. And yet both black and white are open to you. But once you have embarked on black magic, it will dominate your destiny.'" That woman was Dagmar.' She handed the book back to Saltfleet. He glanced at the title page: *Hitler Speaks*, by Hermann Rauschning. Underneath was written: 'To Connie Edgton, from her old friend, Dagmar Johannsen von Burgdorf, Zurich, 1947.'

Saltfleet said: 'Could you find me that address?'

'Well . . . no. I'm fairly sure I can't. Manfred wrote it on a piece of paper. And I was just on my way back to Ireland. And somehow it got mislaid and I forgot all about it.'

'So you didn't contact her?'

'I'm ashamed to say, I forgot.'

'You realize why I'm asking you all this?'

'Not quite . . .?'

'If it was a year ago, then it was after your nephew met Engelke. If he mentioned this lady to Engelke, he'd almost certainly be anxious to meet her.'

180

'Not necessarily. He might want to avoid her, if he was a fake.'

'I don't think he *was* a fake, in that sense. I think he was fascinated by Hitler and the Thule Group. If he knew that Manfred knew Dagmar Johannsen, he'd almost certainly want to meet her . . .'

She interrupted: 'Good God, of course! Now I see what you're getting at. Dagmar may have seen them together . . .'

'Quite. If they called on her together, we'd have the evidence we need – that your nephew knew Engelke intimately and that they were both involved in magic . . .' He looked around the room. 'Do you have a telephone directory?'

'Yes, under here, but I'm sure Dagmar won't be in it. She's quite obsessed by privacy.'

'Let's check anyway.' She was right; there was no Johannsen in the London phone directory.

'You say your nephew met her in Portobello Road. Do you think she was living in the Notting Hill area?'

'Somewhere in West London, I think . . .'

He dialled Directory Inquiries; it took the operator less than a minute to confirm that Dagmar Johannsen was ex-directory. He said: 'Do you think you could ring her and ask her if she'll take a call from Lady Edgton?' He handed the phone to her. 'Is there an extension where I could listen in?'

'Down in the hall.' As he left the room he heard her saying: 'Dagmar! How are you? It's Connie . . .'

As he lifted the hall phone, he heard her saying: 'I'm afraid he's dead. He was murdered.'

'Good God. But that is terrible.' The voice was so deep that he would have mistaken it for a man's.

'Did you see him after that meeting in Portobello Road?'

'Yes, he came to see me a few days later.'

'Was he alone?'

'No. He had a man with him.' Saltfleet found it hard to repress the desire to interrupt. He could hear the tension in Lady Edgton's voice as she asked.

'What kind of man? Can you remember his name?'

'No . . . But he was a publisher. He wanted me to write a book about magic. I didn't like him. He had bad vibrations. Do you think he had anything to do with Manfred's death?'

'I don't know. How old was he?'

'Perhaps fifty-five. A fat man with a face like a pig . . .'

Saltfleet guessed she meant Bascombe. He sighed and hung up. Back upstairs in her bedroom, he wrote on the edge of a newspaper: 'Ask her if she knows Max Engelke.'

'Have you ever come across a young man called Max Engelke?'

Lady Edgton turned the phone sideways, so that he could hear the reply.

'Oh yes, of course. I know him quite well.'

She made a pantomime of astonishment. 'How did you meet him?'

'He came to see me one day.'

'Did he say how he'd heard about you?'

Saltfleet was unable to hear the reply; in her excitement, Lady Edgton had pressed the receiver against her ear. But he could tell, from her expression, that the answer was negative.

'Did he mention Manfred to you?' She looked at Saltfleet and shook her head. 'You're quite sure of that?'

Saltfleet went and sat in the armchair. He had heard enough to tell him that the result was negative.

She hung up five minutes later.

'You heard that?'

'All I needed to. Did Engelke say how he knew she was in London?'

'He said he'd heard it from "occult contacts", whatever that means. Dagmar says he's a most delightful young man. He keeps on taking her presents. Oh, and she said another thing, Manfred promised to go and see her again, but he never did. That doesn't sound at all like Manfred. He had his faults, but he *was* reliable in things like that . . .'

Saltfleet nodded. 'Yes. I dare say that was Engelke. You see now what I mean? It was a thousand-to-one chance that we'd trace this Dagmar Johannsen, yet he still made sure there was nothing to link him with your nephew.'

She said, with sudden conviction: 'He sounds a thoroughly evil young man.'

He chuckled. 'He's a nasty piece of work. It'd give me real satisfaction to nail him.'

'Do you think you'll be able to?'

'I think so. We'll get him somehow.' He looked at his watch. 'And now I have to leave you. Could I use your phone again?'

'Please do.' He could tell she was disappointed that he had to go. He dialled the C.I.D. number.

'Saltfleet here. Who's that?'

'Sergeant Howarth, sir.'

'Who's on duty tonight?'

'Chief-Inspector Morrison. He's not in yet.'

'That's all right. I've got a little job for you. I'm trying to trace a taxicab that took a girl from the corner of Grafton Way and Tottenham Court Road to a house in Wildwood Road, Hampstead. Have you got that? It was at some time between half past midnight and one o'clock last Friday morning. Get someone from the Tottenham Court Road station to check the regular cabs in the area. They could also try the doormen at the hotels – they often talk to the cab drivers. If that does no good, get the Information Room to put out an all-stations call. And if there's still no result, we'll have to put a note in that cabman's magazine – what's it called?'

'*The Steering Wheel*, sir.'

'Good. Keep trying till you get something.'

As he hung up, she asked: 'Did that poor girl come here by taxi?'

For a moment, he wondered how much to tell her, then decided it could do no harm.

'I think it's possible. If she did, it would explain a great deal.' He sat at the foot of the bed. 'As you probably realize, we've no idea why she was killed. Your nephew had arranged to collect her and bring her here at nine o'clock. He rang up again around midnight, and asked her to meet him at the corner of Tottenham Court Road. But I don't think he *did* meet her . . .'

She noticed his hesitation, and said the words for him.

'He was dead by then?'

'Yes. The medical expert thinks he died between midnight and one o'clock. I don't know whether the murderer realized that she was expected. If he did, he probably assumed

183

she'd wait for half an hour, then go home. What he probably didn't realize is that the girl had been here before . . .'

'Manfred seems to have turned this place into a brothel.'

He nodded. 'I think she waited for a while, then decided to take a taxi.'

She said : 'But he didn't have to let her in.'

'No. He didn't.'

'Perhaps she had a key?'

'Almost certainly not. I don't think your nephew was the sort to hand out keys to his female acquaintances. No. I think she rang the doorbell. She probably rang it several times. And then I think the murderer went down to the hall – perhaps intending to leave by the back door. I think he went close to the front door, hoping to see who it was – it was a moonlit night. And at that moment, the girl remembered there was a light in the porch which could be switched on from outside. I think she turned it on, and saw the man looking at her. And I think it was then that he decided to kill her . . .'

She massaged her eyes with her hand. 'Poor girl . . .'

He stood up. 'After that, he decided to dump the body outside, and make it look like a rape murder. I'm not sure why he did that, but it was probably to make us waste time treating it as a sex murder. Which is exactly what happened. For some reason, he wanted to gain time. Perhaps he got a final cheque out of your nephew.'

'Does the bank know?'

'Oh yes. But I don't think Engelke's stupid enough to be caught as easily as that. I suppose it's possible he may have an accomplice, but I doubt it . . .' He knocked out his pipe in the fireplace. 'I hope all this hasn't upset you?'

She smiled; she had a singularly gentle smile.

'No. I'm glad you told me. I don't know why, but I feel better now I know the details.'

He said, smiling : 'I wish I knew the details.'

Ten

The telephone jerked him out of a heavy sleep. For a moment, he thought he had overslept, and sat up violently. Then he saw that it was only a quarter to seven.

'Is that you, Greg?'

'Yes.'

'It's Sid Morrison.' That was Chief-Inspector Morrison, who had been on night duty at the Yard. 'There's been a big bank job in Baker Street – they've got away with a quarter of a million quid. The Chief wants you to get in as soon as you can.'

'O.K. I should be there in an hour.'

Miranda sat up. 'What is it?'

'Big bank robbery in the night. Can you get me a sandwich?'

He ate as he drove in. He was feeling fresher than he had expected; he had stayed up until 1.30 watching a late-night movie. He was still unshaven; but he kept a spare electric razor in his office drawer for these occasions.

Eric Lamb's office was full of cigarette smoke. Eight men sat around the two desks, which had been pushed together: Lamb and his two aides, Chief-Inspector Morrison, George Forrest of the Flying Squad and his personal assistant, Detective-Sergeant Brewer, and two C.I.D. men who worked in Criminal Records. There was a huge coffee percolator on the table – a gift from B.O.A.C. when the C.I.D. had foiled a half-million-pound bullion robbery at Heathrow.

Lamb said: 'Help yourself to coffee and grab a chair.'

Saltfleet knew why he was there. This was no ordinary bank job. In the past eighteen months, there had been nine big bank robberies in London, the home counties and southern England, and the C.I.D. was fairly certain that they had all been committed by one gang, consisting of at least eight men and two women. They were also fairly certain of the names of five of the gang, and that one of them was Chris Gallagher, the East End gangster who had escaped from

Strangeways in 1969, and had been at liberty ever since. Everything indicated that the gang was one of the best organized since the Great Train Robbers; for nine months now, the Yard had been working slowly to draw all its members into the net.

He sat down next to George Forrest.

'How's it going?'

Forrest grunted. 'Lousy.' Then he said: 'No, I don't mean it. I was up till four this morning. We thought we'd got this bloke Carossa. But I think he got wind of us.'

'What happened?' Saltfleet tasted the coffee; it was hot and strong, and he was glad of it.

'Little charter airline near Rayleigh got suspicious of a bloke who wanted to go to Mulhouse. That's France. He claimed he had some business to finish, and he wasn't sure when he'd want to fly. But he wanted to be able to leave at a couple of hours' notice. They thought he seemed nervous, so they contacted the local police. They checked with us. Had he got a beard or moustache when you saw him?'

'No.'

'This bloke has. Otherwise he sounds like Carossa. He's got a scar running from behind his left ear, and he's over six feet tall. Speaks with a French accent, and has papers in the name of Duval. We've had a stake-out round the airfield since yesterday afternoon, but he hasn't showed up yet . . .'

Another detective came into the room; he was Tom Cresswell, Saltfleet's local man at Marylebone Lane. He mumbled his apologies and sat down. Lamb said:

'Good, I think we're ready to start. What's the news, Tom?'

'The watchman's all right. He's had four stitches, but he'll be out later today.'

Saltfleet said: 'The bank had a watchman?'

'No. The jewellers next door. They've had four robberies in two years.'

Cresswell summarized what had happened. The boldness of the method sounded typical of the gang led by Big Foot Gallagher. The bank should have been doubly safe, with a watchman on the premises next door – a young man supplied by a security firm. But the watchman had broken a basic

186

safety rule: he had allowed a girl into the shop. He had met her in a Baker Street pub a week before and gone back to her room. Since then, he had let her into the shop on three occasions when he was on duty, and they had made love. On the previous evening he had fallen asleep after lovemaking, and been wakened by a noise; then someone had hit him on the back of the head. The girl had admitted several men to the shop. They had gone to the top floor, by-passing the jeweller's burglar alarms, and made their way into the house next door along a parapet. An old couple in a bedroom had been tied up. Three hours later, the raiders left with the contents of the safe. The old couple said there were at least six men involved.

Detective-Inspector Tony Boulton, of Criminal Records, continued the story. He had noticed the number of cases in which doors and safes had been opened without any sign of forcible entry; he and his colleagues had been responsible for tracing the firm of safe manufacturers where the bank safes – and duplicate keys – had originated. Someone there had been taking copies of safe keys, and then making a note of the destination of the safes. An informer declared that at least two gangs were involved in the robberies.

George Forrest's assistant had also come into possession of information that one of the gangs – it was not clear which – was using a farmhouse in Wales as a hide-out. The crime squad in the area had already been alerted, and was watching the farm, but with orders to await further instructions. George Forrest's men were keeping watch on three houses in East London where the gang might take the loot.

The question that had to be decided – quickly – was whether to make arrests now, with a chance of recovering the stolen money, or to wait until they had enough evidence to make a swoop on both gangs.

Lamb said: 'What do you think, Greg?'

Saltfleet said: 'I'd like to give it a while longer. I've got a tip that there'll be a raid on the central post office in Guildford next Saturday. George's man, Parker, was going to lead a Squad team to set a trap.'

Forrest said: 'Yes, but Parker's been on that kind of caper before. Three times in the past few months. His blokes spent six nights sitting in mail bags in Beckenham, and nothing happened . . .'

Saltfleet admitted that this attempt to set a trap might be a failure. It would probably be best to pick up as many members of the Big Foot Gang as possible, and try to recover the money. On the other hand, another week's patience might give them the whole gang. His informant had been reliable on two previous occasions, and they had recovered thirty thousand pounds.

They were still discussing the merits of various informers half an hour later, when Truscott handed Saltfleet a note. It was in Crisp's handwriting: 'Cab driver Bert Matthews, No. 83441, picked up young blonde girl near Goodge Street station at 12.45 a.m. last Friday, and dropped her at the corner of Wildwood Road, Hampstead, twenty minutes later. The girl was carrying some kind of bag or overnight case.' The man's address, and the address of the cab company, were given.

Lamb said: 'Greg, I'd like a word with you.' They went into the outer office, which was empty.

'What's happening to your schoolgirl case?'

'Some new developments.' He waved the note. 'But I've still got no connection between Engelke and Lytton. I'm thinking of putting a team to work on all Lytton's friends and acquaintances.'

'So it could be weeks?'

Saltfleet knew what was coming. 'It could be months.'

'I want you and George Forrest to concentrate on this Gallagher case until we pick them up. What do you think?'

'All right. I'd been thinking of pulling Engelke in for questioning this morning . . .'

'Did you find anything from his American lady friend?'

'A lot. She called him King of the Perverts. I think it explains why he killed Lytton in the way he did – and the girl . . .'

The phone in the outer office rang; Lamb took it. He called : 'George, it's for you.' Forrest came in. 'Hello, Bert. What news? . . . Good! Excellent! Was he any trouble? . . . He did . . . Good. Bring him back here. To my office . . . Good work, lad.' He hung up. He told Saltfleet: 'We've got

188

Carossa. It's him all right. They've had a hell of a fight – had to knock him cold.'

Lamb said: 'Have you got the extradition papers?'

'Not yet. Van Looy said he'd bring them with him. I'll ring him now.'

'You know the rules – no arrests without extradition papers.'

Forrest said, grinning: 'He's not under arrest yet. We're just bringing him in for questioning. Anyway, we owe Van Looy a favour – he stretched a point for us on the Swieten case . . .'

Lamb didn't press the point. He was not one to interfere with these matters of practical routine.

Boulton came out of the inner room. He asked Saltfleet: 'When can I come and see you?'

Saltfleet said: 'Give me a couple of hours . . . Make it after lunch.'

'Right.'

Back in his office, Saltfleet said: 'This is a right fuckup.' He didn't usually swear; but now he was on edge. He glanced through the papers in his 'In' tray. Crisp said: 'Nothing important. I've dealt with most of it.'

'What about the North Circular bloke?'

'Haven't heard yet. The parents are on holiday in Blackpool. They'll ring us back.'

Saltfleet said: 'I'm going to pull in Engelke for questioning. Would you go and get him?'

'Now?'

'Yes. No point in delaying. Lamb wants everybody to go flat out on this Gallagher mob.'

'What was the message about the taxi driver?'

'I think I know why he killed the girl. She took a taxi up there and rang the doorbell. She didn't want to lose her hundred quid for a night's work. Damn . . .' The telephone rang. The switchboard said it was the Commander of the Birmingham Crime Squad. 'Put him on.' He said to Crisp: 'Get up there – here's the address – and bring Engelke back here.'

'Squad car or taxi? My car's out of commission.'

'Squad car. It'll impress him more . . . Hello?'

It was a query about a gang who were hi-jacking lorries on the motorways. Saltfleet had been responsible for putting the leader inside ten years ago. By the time he'd dealt with it, it was already past ten o'clock. He rang Widdup.

'Those books. I've changed my mind about them. I'm coming over for them now. Is that all right?'

'All right by me. Funny you should ring – I've just been talking about you.'

'Anyone I know?'

'Juanita – Madame Galletti.'

He asked quickly: 'Is she still there?'

'She was five minutes ago. Drinking a coffee downstairs.'

'See if you can keep her there. I'd like to talk to her. I'll be along in ten minutes . . .'

He was still a hundred yards from the shop when he saw Madame Galletti. She was walking quickly toward Holborn. He stopped suddenly. A car behind him blew its horn angrily. He waited until she drew abreast, then called to her. She looked startled and guilty. The car behind him hooted again. As she hesitated, he said: 'Come and get in for a moment.'

She came and climbed in. She avoided his eyes.

'I am sorry. I have to go. I am in a hurry . . .'

'I shan't keep you a moment.' He drove on, and turned into Red Lion Square, so the car could pass him. He pulled on to a double yellow line and turned off the engine. She was still avoiding his eyes. He said gently:

'You know what I want to ask you.'

She made a movement as if to go. He took her hand. She allowed it to lie in his without protest. He said:

'Listen, I already know that it was Max Engelke.' As she looked up at him quickly, he said: 'No, I don't want you to confirm it. I know you're not mixed up in this.'

She looked at him for the first time. He noticed it again: there was a definite link between them, as if they had known each other a long time, or had been lovers. She said:

'Then you know there is nothing I can tell you.'

He released her hand. 'I don't want any help from you. I

190

just want to know one thing, to satisfy my own curiosity. Why do you want to protect him?'

Her eyes became angry. 'I don't want to protect him. I don't want to protect anybody . . .' She added, in an under-tone: 'I wish he would leave my house.'

'Your house?'

'Yes. It belongs to me.'

'I see.'

Her face reddened. She said quietly: 'I know what you are going to ask me.' He waited for her to go on, but she said nothing.

He said: 'No, I'm not.' Out of the corner of his eye he saw the traffic warden approaching. He started the engine. 'Where do you want to go?'

'Anywhere . . . To Holborn . . .'

As they drove down Dane Street, she said: 'Will you ar-rest him?'

He said shortly: 'I can't arrest him. I've no evidence to connect him to Lytton. None at all.'

He stopped at the corner. She said: 'Thank you.'

He said curiously: 'Look, I know I said I wouldn't ask you questions. But tell me one thing.'

'Yes?'

'You knew it was Engelke when I gave you that glove?'

She shook her head immediately.

'No. But I knew afterwards.'

'But not at the time?'

'No. Sometimes it is like that. The mind clears slowly . . .'

She got out of the car. He said:

'Thanks for your help.'

She stood hesitating, the door open.

'I will tell you another impression . . . I am not sure . . . But I think there were two of them.'

'What!' He stared at her. 'You mean . . . Engelke and someone else?'

'I cannot be certain. But I think so.' She slammed the door suddenly, and hurried away. He stared after her for a mo-ment, then turned into Holborn.

The bookshop was almost empty. One of the twins was

191

sitting by the cash register, looking bored. He ignored her, and went through the shop, and up the stairs. He knocked on Widdup's door.

'Come in.'

He went in. Widdup pointed to the books on the desk. 'There they are. I picked them up with gloves on, so there shouldn't be any extra fingermarks . . .'

'Thanks.' He took out the plastic shopping bag he had brought with him. Widdup said:

'What's happening, then?'

'I'm going to pull him in for questioning. Have you seen him today?'

'No. He usually sleeps all morning. He's a night bird.'

'Good. Do you know if he's got any friends – male friends?'

Widdup said promptly: 'Not as far as I know. Why don't you ask Juanita Galletti? She's his landlady.'

'She's gone.'

Widdup said dryly: 'I thought she might. She didn't look too keen when I said you were on your way.'

The sergeant on duty said: 'Sergeant Crisp came in ten minutes ago.'

'Did he have someone with him?'

'Yes, a young chap.'

His office was empty. He sat down and lit his pipe. A few minutes later, Crisp came in.

'I've got him next door.' There was an empty office that they used as a waiting-room. 'He's an awkward young bastard.'

'Why?'

'Refused to come at first. He said he wanted to talk to his consul. So I let him ring. The consulate advised him to come along . . .'

'Has he eaten?'

'No. He was in bed when I got there. With a nice young bird.'

'A girl! A blonde?'

'No. A plump, dark-haired little piece. Talked like a Londoner.'

192

'Did you get her name?'

'No. I asked her, and he told her not to tell me. Said it was none of my business. He's a right little bastard.'

'One of his pick-ups, I suppose . . .' He took the books out of the bag, and placed them in the centre of the desk.

'Shall I bring him in?'

'Not yet. Is there someone in there with him?'

'Redburn.'

'He can wait for a bit.' He smoked in silence for a moment. Crisp lit a cigarette. 'I'm wondering if I was wise to bring him in . . .'

'Why?'

'There's a new development. I've got a tip that he may have had an accomplice.'

'Reliable?'

'I'm damned if I know. Remember the woman I told you about, Madame Galletti?'

'The witch?'

'That's right. She turns out to be his landlady.'

'Think he sleeps with her?'

'Not now. I think he probably has, at some time.'

'So she's probably lying.'

'I don't know . . .' He looked at his watch. 'Better bring him in.'

Engelke was dressed in jeans and a blue shirt. He had not had time to shave; his chin was covered with a golden stubble. He was scowling as he came in. He said immediately:

'I hope you realize you are wasting my time.' He saw the books in the middle of the desk, and stopped.

Saltfleet said: 'You've seen them before?'

Engelke looked at them more closely. He said casually:

'Yes, I think so.'

'Where?'

'In the bookshop. One of the girls showed them to me. That must have been . . . oh, last Monday or Tuesday . . .'

Saltfleet said: 'That's why your fingerprints are on them?'

'Possibly.' Engelke smiled. He was no longer annoyed. Now he was playing the game.

Saltfleet said: 'Sit down.'

'Thank you. May I smoke? Or am I under arrest?'

Saltfleet said: 'You know you're not under arrest.'

Engelke took a packet of American cigarettes out of his shirt pocket, and lit up.

Saltfleet watched him without speaking for several minutes. Engelke finally said:

'I enjoy sitting here, but I'm sure you have other things to do.'

Saltfleet said: 'You still say that you hardly knew Lytton?'

Engelke nodded. When Saltfleet repeated the question he said sullenly: 'Yes.'

'Lytton left the bookshop with these books last Wednesday. On the day he was killed, he took them out with him. I've got proof that he had them with him that day. On Thursday night he was killed, and the books disappeared. They reappeared in the bookshop.'

Engelke smiled. 'Amazing.'

Saltfleet leaned forward. 'Your friend Ingrid was seen taking them upstairs.'

Engelke reached inside his shirt to scratch his chest. 'I see.' He looked bored.

Saltfleet said: 'I have a witness who saw her.'

Engelke allowed his lips to twitch. He said deliberately: 'Yes, I am sure you have.'

Saltfleet said: 'You gave her those books to look after. You told her to hide them in the shop. The books have her fingerprints on. And yours.'

There was a long silence. Engelke said finally:

'That proves she is innocent. All the efficient criminals nowadays wear gloves.'

'If she's innocent, what was she doing with the books?'

Engelke shrugged, smiling. 'How do I know? Perhaps she's not innocent. Perhaps *she* killed Lytton. Is that what you mean?'

Saltfleet said quietly: 'No. You killed Lytton. But not alone. You had an accomplice.' He knew as soon as he said it that he was right. Engelke dropped his eyes. He took a long draw on his cigarette.

Saltfleet said: 'As you rightly point out, most criminals wear gloves nowadays. You wore gloves when you killed

Lytton. Yet you wiped the rooms clean of all fingerprints. Why? Because somebody else left fingerprints.'

He allowed the silence to lengthen. Engelke said finally: 'Am I supposed to say something?'

Saltfleet shook his head. 'No. You don't have to. We know who the other man was.'

He was staring into Engelke's eyes as he said it. He wanted to know if the accomplice was a man. If it was a woman, Engelke's face would show it; there would be a smile, a flicker of relief. Engelke's expression remained unchanged. Saltfleet stood up. He was experiencing a sense of lightness, a certainty. He said:

'I'm going to leave you to think it over for a few minutes.' Engelke said nothing. Saltfleet went to the door. He beckoned to Crisp, who followed him. Outside the door, Crisp said:

'Shall I get Redburn to keep an eye on him?'

Saltfleet shook his head. 'If he tried to escape now, it'd be an admission of guilt. He wants to find out how much we know. Come on in here.' He led the way into the office next door. He picked up the telephone, dialled for an outside line, then dialled the Flying Squad number. Sergeant Brewer's voice answered.

'Is George there? Saltfleet here.'

'He's interrogating this French bloke. Is it urgent, sir?'

'Yes.'

Crisp was hanging around by the door; he was still convinced that Engelke would try to escape.

'Hello, Greg. What do you want?'

'George. Have you managed to get anything out of Taupin?'

'You mean Carossa? That's his real name. No, nothing yet. He just told me to go and get stuffed.'

'Listen, George. I want you to do something for me. I want you to bring Carossa over to the old Yard building. What's the time by your watch? I make it five past twelve. Bring him over in exactly ten minutes, and come to my office.'

'What's it all about?'

'I'll tell you when you get here. When I hear the lift arrive, I'll be standing there with a man called Engelke. I want

195

Carossa and Engelke to see one another. Right? Then go on to my office.'

'O.K. See you in ten minutes . . .'

Crisp said: 'Carossa's this French pimp, isn't he? Does he know Engelke?'

'That's what I want to find out. It suddenly struck me just now – when I was talking to Engelke about wiping the fingerprints. Suppose he killed that girl because she *recognized* him? She went to the house by taxi. She rang the doorbell. Engelke came downstairs to see who it was, and while he was looking through the window, trying to see her face, she remembered the light in the porch. She'd been there before. She knew the light can be turned on from the outside. And when she switched it on, she saw Engelke's face looking out at her. Now what would you do if you switched on a light and saw a face looking at you?''

Crisp gave a throaty chuckle. 'Jump two feet in the air.'

'Quite. And a girl would be terrified. Or at least very suspicious. Yet she went into the house, and didn't even demand to see Lytton. I think she knew Engelke. But how would she know him? Not through Lytton – he was too careful for that . . .'

'Through Carossa?'

'I think it's possible. Anyway, we've got them both here. There's no harm in letting them see one another. Get Redburn . . .'

He went back into the office next door; Engelke was standing by the window, looking out. He said casually:

'Do you think I could go now? I didn't have anything to eat before I came out.'

'Not yet. I'll send out for a sandwich. Let's move downstairs. Someone else has to use this office.'

Engelke yawned as he turned from the window; but his indifference seemed overdone. He seemed to be intent on examining the end of his cigarette.

'You know you can't keep me here against my will.'

'Unless we charge you.'

'With what?'

Saltfleet said: 'Come on. Let's go.'

Crisp and Redburn were already standing by the lift. Saltfleet looked at his watch: it was a minute to a quarter past. As he reached out to press the button, the lift door opened. Forrest stepped out. Behind him, Taupin was handcuffed between a sergeant and a constable; his right eye was almost closed, and the cheek was swollen. When he saw Engelke, he stared, then glanced down at his hands. Engelke glanced at him, stiffened for a moment, then looked away. They brushed against one another as Taupin stepped out of the lift. Taupin's face and neck had reddened. Saltfleet ushered Engelke into the lift, and Crisp pressed the button. As they descended, Saltfleet looked down at Engelke; a vein in the side of his neck was throbbing, and his face had flushed. His eyes met Crisp's over Engelke's head; Crisp nodded imperceptibly.

When the lift stopped at the third floor, Saltfleet said: 'Take him to the governor's old office. I'll be along soon.' He caught Crisp's eye, and jerked his head towards the lift. When Crisp came back he said quickly: 'Listen. If I ring you and tell you to bring him down, *ignore me*. Got that? Don't bring him unless I ring twice.' Crisp nodded. Saltfleet pushed the button for the second floor.

Forrest was waiting outside his office. Saltfleet beckoned him into the next-door office. He closed the door quietly.

Forrest said: 'What's the score?'

'Do you think they knew one another?'

'Definitely. He's turned green.'

'Carossa was involved in that Hampstead schoolgirl murder. The man I took upstairs did the actual killing. His name's Engelke.'

'Have you got a confession?'

'No. And I doubt whether we shall. But I'm hoping to get something out of Carossa.'

'You'll be lucky. He knows all the tricks.'

'Give me a quick rundown on him. What's this Moberg murder about?'

'They've got shares in a brothel in Amsterdam. It caters mainly for kinks.'

'What's the evidence against Carossa?'

'They found the gun. Moberg was shot in the back of the head. The police got a tip that a fishing boat had a load of

197

heroin. They went on board and arrested the owner – the heroin was strapped under the boat in a watertight tin. And they also found the gun – a Luger. When they checked it, they found it was the gun that killed Moberg. When they told the owner they were charging him with murder, he said Carossa had given him the gun to get rid of. And he admitted dumping the oil drum with Moberg's body in the harbour.'

'Why didn't he get rid of the gun?'

'I think he probably intended to blackmail Carossa.'

'Who were the drugs for?'

'Carossa.'

Saltfleet whistled. 'So he's in the drugs trade too. Very interesting . . .'

'Carossa's in everything.'

'We'd better get back in there. Let me do the questioning.'

Taupin was handcuffed to Saltfleet's armchair behind the desk. The books were on the table in front of him. He was staring sullenly at the floor; the half-closed eye was bloodshot.

Saltfleet took a chair and placed it by the desk. He pointed to the books.

'We found your fingerprints on them. They were in Engelke's room.'

Taupin glanced at him, then looked away. He said nothing.

Saltfleet turned to Forrest. 'Is there time to catch Van Looy before he leaves Amsterdam?'

'Plenty. He's leaving on the three o'clock plane. Why?'

'Tell him not to come. We're charging Taupin with the murder of Mary Threlwall and conspiracy to murder Manfred Lytton.'

Forrest said: 'Who the hell's he?'

'He knows.' He looked at Taupin. 'We also found one of your fingerprints in the house. Engelke missed the one on the stair rail. What made you decide to go there? It was pretty stupid, wasn't it?'

Taupin said; 'If you want to know, I wanted to save her life.'

'Then why did you kill her?'

198

'If he says I killed her, he's a liar. She was already dead when I arrived.'

'Are you willing to say that in front of Engelke?'

Taupin shrugged. Saltfleet picked up the phone. Taupin said quickly: 'I don't want to see the little bastard.'

'Don't you want to hear what he's accusing you of?'

Taupin breathed deeply, but said nothing. Saltfleet dialled the extension number. When Crisp came on the line he said:

'Steve, bring Engelke down here, would you?'

He hung up, then sat back in his chair. He took out his pipe, and began to clean it. A minute passed by without anyone speaking. Taupin said:

'May I have a cigarette?'

Forrest gave him one, placing it in his mouth. Saltfleet lit it. Taupin could reach it by leaning his head forward. Saltfleet said, as if making conversation:

'What I don't understand is how a professional like you could get mixed up with an amateur like Engelke. Why didn't you tell him to leave the books where they were, or get rid of them?'

Taupin said savagely: 'You can't tell him anything. He thinks he knows it all.'

'Why did you decide to kill Lytton? Why not just take his money and disappear. He wouldn't have dared to make trouble.'

'*I* didn't want to kill Lytton.'

'Engelke says you planned the murder.'

Taupin said angrily: 'Listen, why should I want him to die? It is like you say – I am a professional. Professionals don't murder for the pleasure – for the fun of it. But *him* – he kills for pleasure. He's mad.'

'If he's mad, why did you get mixed up with him?'

He shrugged. 'Huh. Because I didn't know . . .' He smoked broodingly, staring at the floor.

'Did you introduce him to Lytton?'

'They met at my place.'

'At the brothel you run in Amsterdam?' Taupin shrugged but said nothing. 'And then Engelke got the idea of going into partnership with you? Right? With the money he could get from Lytton?'

'No. At that stage he had a rich American woman. But she left him. I think he killed her too. Then he started to get money from Lytton.'

'But why did Engelke need you? With twenty thousand pounds, he could start up in business on his own.'

Taupin shook his head. 'Never. He didn't know enough about the business.'

'I still don't understand why you got mixed up with an amateur. Did he talk you into it?'

'At first I thought he was crazy. Then later I thought maybe he wasn't so crazy. We tried his idea, and it worked.'

'What was his idea?'

'He said there are thousands of people all over Europe who are involved in magic and witchcraft. He said there are young girls who let themselves be whipped and possessed by men dressed as priests. But they don't get paid for it. And there are plenty of people who want to join these groups . . .'

'So the idea was to combine the brothel business with black magic? You say it worked?'

Taupin grimaced. 'It was beginning to work.'

Saltfleet nodded, with mock sympathy. 'That's hard luck . . . Well, if you can prove you didn't kill the girl, you might get off with a few years as an accessory.'

Forrest grunted: 'And a few years more for killing Moberg.'

Taupin said sullenly: 'I didn't kill him. I found him dead with the gun beside him.'

Saltfleet said: 'How did you get to the house in Hampstead? Car? Taxi?'

'Taxi.'

'Well, we can trace the driver. We know the girl was killed at a quarter to one. If you arrived after that, it lets you out.'

'I arrived at a quarter past.'

'Why as late as that? Sheila must have told you she set out at midnight.'

'I didn't get there until a quarter to one. I tried to ring, but the phone wire had been cut. I thought she might still be alive. So I went there right away . . .'

'And if she *had* been alive, what then?'

Taupin waved his hands expressively. 'Then I would have

sent her to stay with friends . . . in the Lebanon.'

'You mean to a brothel in the Lebanon?'

Taupin shrugged. 'Well? Is it not better than dying?'

Saltfleet stood up. He said: 'I'm going to see what's happened to Engelke.' He said to Taupin: 'Why don't you make a statement now? Say the girl was already dead when you arrived. It can't do any harm.'

'O.K.'

Saltfleet said: 'I'll send Miss Larkhill. Shall I ring Van Looy?'

Forrest said: 'Yes, do that.'

Engelke was staring out of the window. There was a paper plate with crumbs, and an empty coffee cup, beside him. Crisp and Redburn sat on either side of the door.

Saltfleet said: 'Sit down.' He indicated the chair opposite the desk. He picked up the telephone and dialled. 'Miss Larkhill. Saltfleet. I want you to go down to my office. You'll find Mr Forrest there, and a man called Carossa. I want you to take down a statement.' He hung up.

He swivelled round to look at Engelke.

'Do you feel like making a statement now?'

Engelke said: 'No.' But the coolness had gone; under the rigid self-control he was tense and jumpy.

Saltfleet said: 'I'm charging you with the murder of Manfred Lytton and Mary Threlwall. Anything you say now can be used in evidence against you.'

Engelke started to speak, but had to clear his throat. He said:

'I never met any girl of that name. And I hardly knew Lytton.'

Saltfleet said: 'Perhaps you'll change your mind when you've read Carossa's statement.'

'I don't know anyone called Carossa. If he says I do, he's a liar.'

The telephone rang. The switchboard operator said:

'Chief-Superintendent Saltfleet. There's a man called Skipper who says he has to speak to you.'

'All right. Put him on.' Skipper was one of Saltfleet's best informers.

'Hello guv.' It was a hoarse cockney voice. 'Skip 'ere. I've got something to tell you about this Baker Street bank job. A couple of names.'

'Where did you get them?'

'Can't talk over the phone. Can you meet me in the usual place in half an hour?'

'All right. I'll be there.' He hung up. The 'usual place' was on the seats overlooking the river near the Festival Hall. It would take him ten minutes to get there. That gave him another twenty minutes.

Engelke was leaning back in his chair, his left foot on his right knee; he was studying his finger nails. But Saltfleet could sense the tension under the apparent unconcern. He leaned forward, and said quietly, and not unkindly:

'Listen, let me give you a word of advice. You're caught and there's no way out. Your first reaction is to say nothing and leave us to prove everything. Am I right?' Engelke shrugged slightly, but said nothing. 'You think there's no point in confessing, because you're confessing to double murder, and that means life imprisonment whatever happens.' Engelke was avoiding his eyes. 'And if you were in this alone, you'd probably be right. But you're in it with Carossa, and that makes a difference. Shall I tell you why? Because if you don't make a statement, the jury's going to believe everything Carossa says. He says you planned the murder of Manfred Lytton, and he didn't know about it until after you'd done it. He says he'd have tried to stop you if he'd known. They'll believe him, because a real professional tries hard to avoid murder. He says he rushed up to the house to try to stop you killing Mary Threlwall, but she was already dead when he got there. They'll believe him, because they'll see he had no reason to go to the house except to try and stop you killing her. And his girlfriend will testify that he rushed out as soon as she told him where Mary had gone. He'll say it was your idea to dump her body outside, just to confuse the police. His defence counsel is going to tell the jury that you're a completely cold, calculating killer who worked this whole thing out a year in advance. And they're going to believe him. And the result is that you're going to find yourself inside for twenty-five years, and he'll get off with five years or less.' Engelke blanched, but said nothing. 'If you've got a defence, you'd better start thinking about it now. Because . . .' The phone started to ring. 'Because it'll soon be too late.' He picked it up and snapped 'Hello?'

'George here, Greg.' It was Forrest. 'The governor's just been on. He wants to see us both right away. That O.K.?'

'I think so. I've about finished here.' He looked at Engelke. The interruptions were making him tense. 'What is it, the bank job?'

'Sounds like it. News from Wales, I should think.'

'I've got to see a snout in ten minutes, but I'll come down. What's happening there?'

'Carossa's making a statement in your office. I'm next door. Oh, by the way. He says he didn't kill Hedberg, or Moberg, or whatever his name is. He says your bloke did it – the bloke you've got there.'

'O.K. I'll see you in two minutes.'

'You still there? Bill Norland rang. Wants you to ring him back.'

'All right. I'll do that now.'

He looked up Norland's number in his pocket book. While he waited for a reply, he told Crisp: 'Sounds as if it could be news on the North Circular . . . Hello. Chief-Superintendent Norland please. Saltfleet, Scotland Yard . . . Hello, Bill, Greg here.'

'Ah Greg. I just wanted to tell you we've picked up this Lewis character. At his aunt's place in Haringey. He put up a hell of a fight. But they tell me he's just admitted to raping that girl yesterday. At least, he says she accosted him and submitted willingly. He's a real moron . . .'

He put his hand over the mouthpiece and told Crisp: 'Sounds as if they've got him.'

'You there? . . . We're setting up the identity parade this afternoon, around five. If your bloke Crisp's free, why not let him come over? I'm told he spotted this one.'

'Thanks, Bill. I'll send him over. Chingford, is it? Thanks for ringing.'

He looked at his watch. 'Bill Norland wants you to go over there for the identity parade at five this afternoon. He thought you'd like to be there.'

'Can you spare me?'

'Of course.' He indicated Engelke, who was staring sullenly out of the window. 'Lock this one up.' He turned to Engelke. 'It will give you time to think. And I'll give you something else to think about.' He went to the door. 'Carossa says you shot Moberg.'

Engelke looked up sharply. 'He is mad.'

'Oh no. Not mad. He just knows he can blame you for everything. And the jury'll probably believe him. Unless you decide to give your own side of the story.'

Engelke said: 'Wait. I will make a statement.'

'I can't wait now. Steve, take it down, will you? I'll be back in half an hour.' He nodded to Engelke. 'I'm glad you've got some sense.'

The look he got was completely cold and malevolent. Suddenly, with a shock, he knew how easily this man could kill.

Forrest got into the lift at the second floor. He slapped Saltfleet on the shoulder.

'Well, Greg, I think that's a bloody good morning's work.' He added, as an afterthought: 'Thanks entirely to you.'

'Yes. Not bad.' Saltfleet never felt comfortable with compliments.

They walked out into the sunlight. Saltfleet said:

'Tell me, George . . . Do you ever feel sorry when you've got somebody into a corner?'

'Oh yes. Sometimes. I mean, for instance, that bloke Goodwin who killed his mistress and two kids. When I saw the bodies, I thought I could have strangled him with my bare hands. But when we got him . . . you know what I mean? He was . . . pathetic. You couldn't really hate him. Mind, this Carossa's a different matter. He's a real professional. Drugs, white slavery, murder, anything to make money. I can't feel sorry for a bastard like that. Could you?'

'Well, not sorry exactly . . .' The roar of traffic drowned his voice as they waited at the Parliament Street lights. 'I know this Engelke's a murderous little bastard. But that's not what I mean . . . *Why* is he a murderous little bastard?'

'That's not part of your job.'

'I know. And I'm damn glad I've got him. Yet suddenly,

204

when I knew I'd got him in a corner, and he knew it, I felt a kind . . . a kind of sympathy . . .'

'What, for a man who . . .'

'Yes, I know. He's a killer, and I reckon that twenty thousand quid he got out of Lytton went into buying drugs. He'll get what he deserves. All I'm saying is . . . some people kill because they've no sense of reality. Now if Carossa killed somebody, he'd know exactly what he was doing. But with Engelke . . . I've got a feeling he kills in a kind of dream. He's born in East Berlin, he reads about people being shot as they try to escape to the West, finally he manages to escape himself . . . He thinks it's that kind of world. But it's not. He's living in a dream.'

'A nightmare.'

'Yes. A nightmare. And he'll spend the next twenty years in prison waking up. I suppose he deserves it. But I can't help feeling a kind of pity. It's lousy for his victims and it's lousy for him . . .'

'I know. It's a lousy world. Don't you agree?'

Saltfleet pushed open the glass door of New Scotland Yard. 'Well, no. That's what puzzles me, I suppose. I *don't* think so.'

Forrest patted him on the shoulder. 'You should have been a clergyman. You're wasted in the police force.'

Bestselling European Fiction in Panther Books

QUERELLE OF BREST	Jean Genet	60p	☐
OUR LADY OF THE FLOWERS	Jean Genet	50p	☐
FUNERAL RITES	Jean Genet	50p	☐
DEMIAN	Hermann Hesse	40p	☐
THE JOURNEY TO THE EAST	Hermann Hesse	40p	☐
LA BATARDE	Violette Leduc	60p	☐
RAVAGES	Violette Leduc	50p	☐
MAD IN PURSUIT	Violette Leduc	40p	☐
IN THE PRISON OF HER SKIN	Violette Leduc	35p	☐
THE TWO OF US	Alberto Moravia	50p	☐
THE LIE	Alberto Moravia	50p	☐
PARADISE	Alberto Moravia	35p	☐
COMMAND AND I WILL OBEY YOU			
	Alberto Moravia	30p	☐
LASSO ROUND THE MOON	Agnar Mykle	50p	☐
THE SONG OF THE RED RUBY	Agnar Mykle	40p	☐
THE HOTEL ROOM	Agnar Mykle	40p	☐
RUBICON	Agnar Mykle	50p	☐
THE DEFENCE	Vladimir Nabokov	40p	☐
THE GIFT	Vladimir Nabokov	50p	☐
THE EYE	Vladimir Nabokov	30p	☐
DESPAIR	Vladimir Nabokov	30p	☐
NABOKOV'S QUARTET	Vladimir Nabokov	30p	☐
A VIOLENT LIFE	Pier Paolo Pasolini	40p	☐
INTIMACY	Jean-Paul Sartre	40p	☐
THE AIR CAGE	Per Wästberg	60p	☐

The Children of Violence series

MARTHA QUEST	Doris Lessing	60p ☐
A PROPER MARRIAGE	Doris Lessing	75p ☐
A RIPPLE FROM THE STORM	Doris Lessing	50p ☐
LANDLOCKED	Doris Lessing	50p ☐
THE FOUR-GATED CITY	Doris Lessing	90p ☐
ALFIE	Bill Naughton	40p ☐
ALFIE DARLING	Bill Naughton	60p ☐
HEAD TO TOE	Joe Orton	40p ☐
FRIENDS IN LOW PLACES	Simon Raven	35p ☐
THE RICH PAY LATE	Simon Raven	35p ☐
THE SABRE SQUADRON	Simon Raven	35p ☐
FIELDING GRAY	Simon Raven	30p ☐
THE JUDAS BOY	Simon Raven	35p ☐
PLACES WHERE THEY SING	Simon Raven	35p ☐
SOUND THE RETREAT	Simon Raven	50p ☐
BROTHER CAIN	Simon Raven	35p ☐
CLOSE OF PLAY	Simon Raven	35p ☐
DOCTORS WEAR SCARLET	Simon Raven	30p ☐
THE FEATHERS OF DEATH	Simon Raven	35p ☐
COME LIKE SHADOWS	Simon Raven	65p ☐
THE QUICK AND THE DEAD	Thomas Wiseman	45p ☐
THE ROMANTIC ENGLISHWOMAN		
	Thomas Wiseman	40p ☐

All these books are available at your local bookshop or newsagent; or can be ordered direct from the publisher. Just tick the titles you want and fill in the form below.

Name _____

Address _____

_____

Write to Panther Cash Sales, PO Box 11, Falmouth, Cornwall TR10 9EN
Please enclose remittance to the value of the cover price plus 15p postage and packing for one book plus 5p for each additional copy. Overseas customers please send 20p for first book and 10p for each additional book.
Granada Publishing reserve the right to show new retail prices on covers, which may differ from those previously advertised in the text or elsewhere.